**JACKIE
MANTHORNE**

FINAL TAKE

gynergy
books

To Mona, my life partner, with love

Cover illustration by:
Karen Gallant

Edited by:
Jennifer Glossop

Printed and bound in Canada by:
Marc Veilleux Inc.

gynergy books acknowledges the generous support of the Canada Council.

Published by:
gynergy books
P.O. Box 2023
Charlottetown, PEI
Canada, C1A 7N7

Canadian Cataloguing in Publication Data
Manthorne, Jackie, 1946-

Final take

"A Harriet Hubbley mystery"
ISBN 0-921881-41-X

I. Title.

PS8576.A568F56 1996   C813'.54   C96-950122-6
PR9199.3.M3495F56 1996

Contents

"California, here we come!" Richie Matthews sang, tapping his fingers on the steering wheel. The three passengers in his late-model car were startled by his rich baritone, which was so unlike his rather high-pitched speaking voice. "We should drive down to San Francisco more often," he mused. "I mean, it's not all that far from Vancouver."

"It helps that your older sister owns a gorgeous house right in the middle of the gay district," teased his lover, Buck Thomas. Buck stuck the unlit cigarette he'd been sucking on back in his mouth.

"How can you stand that thing?" asked Celia Roberts. The svelte, blonde, long-legged Celia, who was in her mid-fifties and looked it, was a vehement adversary of tobacco unless its use was related to First Nations' rituals.

"Would you rather I light it?" Buck retorted dryly.

"Stop bickering, you two," said Richie. "We're supposed to be cheering Harry up, not giving each other a hard time."

Harriet Hubbley, known to many of her friends as Harry and to the teenagers in her physical-education classes as "The Hub," although they would rather have died than admit it to her face, stifled a sigh and wished she was anywhere but sitting beside Celia Roberts in the back seat of Richie's car. She wasn't opposed to good intentions, having succumbed to them fairly often herself. But not only was she too depressed to enjoy her visit to San Francisco, she was also smothering under the weight of her friends' concern about her state of mind.

"Think of all those horny lesbians," Celia said, placing her hand on Harry's knee. "And for the boys among us, way up there in the front seat of this blessed conveyance, all those horny men."

Harry stifled a sigh and closed her eyes.

"I'm sure Buck's been fantasizing about nothing else," Richie commented with a curt laugh. Both men were in their early forties, but the tall, thin, olive-skinned and dark-haired Buck seemed to get better looking as he aged, while Richie had been battling premature wrinkles, cellulite and an unwanted beer belly for years. Richie's graying sandy hair was thinning at the temples, and his pale, freckled skin reddened after five minutes' exposure to the sun. Even though he jogged nearly every day and cross-trained regularly in a trendy, primarily gay Vancouver health club in English Bay, he still seemed pudgy. He was pleasant-looking in a middle-aged, innocent, and even guileless way, but he fretted about losing Buck. Harry sympathized; looks weren't everything, but in the gay male community, they certainly counted for a lot.

Buck opened the window and discarded his soggy cigarette. "I'm not interested in other men."

Richie glanced at his lover but didn't say anything.

"Litterer," Celia muttered.

"It's biodegradable."

"Not the filter."

"Stop it, you two," Richie scolded, "and admit that you're excited about going to San Francisco. You can't have forgotten that it's *the* gay mecca of the known universe."

"Of course not," Buck said. "But I've no intention of cruising some nebulous fag I've never met. Perhaps you should speak for yourself in that regard."

"Don't be arch," Richie said. "It doesn't become you."

"Don't quarrel," Harry interjected.

"So you *are* awake!" Celia exclaimed.

Harry shut her eyes again.

"I know you're in there," Celia warned, giving Harry's knee a squeeze.

Harry had never been able to fall asleep on demand or she would have curled up and retreated from her travelling companions the moment they had left Vancouver. If she had been strong enough to resist her friends' badgering, she would be home in her apartment in Montreal now. Still, she wasn't sure which was more depressing — the thought of returning to Montreal or spending ten days in San Francisco in her current dismal state of mind.

Six weeks ago, in mid-May, when the first heat wave of spring settled over Montreal and buds sprouted on the trees and tulips blossomed overnight, Harry's lover of twelve years had left her. Judy Johnson had taken her belongings from their centre-city apartment and set up housekeeping in her sister's spare room in a split-level bungalow in the Montreal suburb of Longueuil. Harry suspected that Judy was in transition and would soon move into the West Island townhouse belonging to Sarah Reid, the woman with whom she had been having an affair for the past two years. So much for Judy's claim that she was capable of managing two relationships at the same time. Harry had always suspected that no one could love two people equally, which was why she had never believed Judy's assertion to the contrary. Now Harry both loved and hated Judy with a hopelessness that astounded and enraged her. She supposed those feelings would fade, but feared it would take as many years to fall out of love as it had to fall in love.

Harry had turned fifty scant days before Judy left her. To celebrate her birthday, Judy had taken her to Chez Pierre, one of the most exclusive French restaurants in Montreal. Dinner had not been a great success, although the food had been flawless *cuisine minceur*; a perfectly cooked rack of lamb placed artfully on a plate decorated with half a dozen baby carrots, several crisp spears of asparagus and three round, roasted, garlic potatoes. But once she demolished a slice of chocolate cheesecake and finished a cappuccino and cognac, there was an aftertaste of imminent disaster, of things left unsaid. Harry had believed that their conversation at dinner that night was low-key because she was still mourning for her first lover and close friend, Barbara Fenton, who had been attacked in March, during spring break. Barb had succumbed to her injuries without regaining consciousness and Harry had inherited Isadora's Hideaway, Barb's guesthouse in Key West, as well as investments worth more than three-hundred-thousand dollars. Pearl Vernon, a displaced Brit who had lived in New York for many years, was managing Isadora's Hideaway. It was only after Judy had left her that Harry realized Judy had been slowly distancing herself from their relationship, and she felt chagrined that she hadn't noticed it earlier.

At the beginning of June, Harry had taken a leave of absence from her job and flown to British Columbia to visit her parents. They had relocated from a fishing village on the South Shore of Nova Scotia to a small town on the outskirts of Vancouver when they had retired several years earlier.

Her mother recognized an anguished child when she saw one, and provided a supportive atmosphere while leaving Harry to lick her wounds in private. She served Harry's favourite childhood meals and left presents in Harry's bedroom, whimsical things like women's magazines, which Harry normally wouldn't be caught dead reading but which she now leafed through, obsessively poring over articles about divorce and other sundry family tragedies like the death of a child or random accidents and unpreventable disasters that separated people from those they loved. She cursed fate and munched on potato chips, sucked the succulent centres from cherry chocolates and sipped warm cognac while tears streamed down her face until she couldn't eat another thing or cry a minute more or keep her eyes open a second longer. Falling asleep alone in a strange bed wasn't as difficult as she thought it would be, although she woke up every time she reached out and found there was no one beside her. But she knew that reclaiming the bed she had shared with Judy back in Montreal would be a much more troublesome matter and wished she could dispose of her memories, distance her emotions and dispel her anguish as easily as she could redecorate her bedroom and get rid of the offending bed. She despised being alone and wondered how long it would take before she felt ready to date again. Unfortunately, she was so out of practice that just thinking about it terrified her.

As usual, her father didn't realize that anything was wrong. But he was glad to have her home for a while, for whatever reason. Harry helped him hoe the vegetable garden, feed the chickens and split firewood into kindling. In the late afternoons, she put on a rain slicker and a pair of her father's rubber boots and took long walks in the woods skirting the town. The forest was sodden and the weather was chilly, but she didn't mind; the dripping trees and bone-chilling damp suited her mood.

When she was a child, Harry couldn't wait until she was grown up so that she could be her own person and run her own life. Like most teenagers, she had erroneously believed that, when she became an adult, all her insecurities would disappear and her uncertainties would be resolved. It hadn't been true, of course. And now, at the age of fifty, she was baffled that she was alone, bemused by her new wealth, astounded that her life had radically changed. Being a single, middle-aged lesbian was not a prospect she enjoyed contemplating for extended periods of time. She was starting over again, but she would give back her riches if only Barb were still alive. She would swap her unwanted independence for Judy. And she would relinquish both to stop caring about either.

When she had arrived on the West Coast, Harry had contacted a few friends to let them know she was there, including Richie, Buck and Celia. Buck had been active in one of the gay liberation groups Harry had joined back in the eighties, and he and Richie had met while Richie was in Montreal to act in a movie being filmed there. Since Richie had been based in Toronto at the time, they had initially conducted a long-distance affair. Five years ago, they had both relocated to Vancouver and they had lived together ever since. As for Celia, Harry had known her for years. They had become friends in university and kept in touch when Celia had moved to Vancouver over two decades ago and built a small but thriving public relations firm. So when Celia had called toward the end of her visit to her parents to propose that Harry accompany her, Richie and Buck to San Francisco to attend the International Gay and Lesbian Film Festival and participate in Gay Pride celebrations the last weekend in June, Harry had reluctantly agreed. Celia had just broken up with Mandy Perkins, her most recent and overly possessive lover, and she wanted another woman to travel with. Harry hadn't really wanted to spend a lot of time with other people, even friends, but she could tell from the way her parents were acting that it was time to move on.

Harry's thoughts returned to the present when the tips of Celia's fingers gouged her thigh.

"She's not asleep," Celia insisted. "Her muscles are rigid."

Friendship had limitations, Harry reflected wearily, and Celia had just reached them.

"Leave her alone," Richie said. "She's taking a nap."

"Nap, snap," Celia said scornfully, although her fingers relaxed, much to Harry's relief. "She playing possum."

"So let her," Buck said. "She's been through a lot. And anyway, maybe she really is asleep."

Celia gave a theatrical sigh and her hand left Harry's knee.

"You're mean, do you know that?" Richie opined.

"I am not. It's not good for her to feel sorry for herself," insisted Celia.

"Says who?"

"Says me. I'm a *woman*, I know about these things."

"Well, damn it," Buck muttered.

Harry stifled a grin, and as her three companions discussed her state of mind and their ability to diagnose it, she sagged farther into the corner of the back seat, her head resting on the soft upholstery. At least somebody cared about her, she thought as she finally fell asleep.

"Rise and shine," Richie called.

"Yes, enough is enough," Celia pestered. "Wake up, will you?"

"Jeez, Celia, what's biting you?" Harry muttered, grimacing as she stretched her stiff muscles.

"We've driven miles out of our way through rush-hour traffic just so you could see this, and you won't even open your eyes," Celia complained. "Besides, I have to pee."

"So, my eyes are open." It was dusk. The Golden Gate Bridge, which linked San Francisco to Marin County, was incandescent. The view was so stunning that Harry's eyes filled with tears. The last time she had seen the Golden Gate Bridge had been with Judy, when they had celebrated their fifth anniversary together in San Francisco. How in love they had been, Harry thought. Where had it gone?

"We certainly didn't intend to make you cry," Richie muttered, turning the key in the ignition.

"I'm all right," Harry said, impatiently wiping her cheeks. "Seeing the Golden Gate Bridge brings back memories, that's all."

"Perhaps you'd have been happier if we had stopped in Seattle," said Buck.

"No, I'm glad we came," Harry said. "I can't leave my memories behind no matter where I go, and I can't hide from the past forever."

"No wonder you're upset — it hasn't been that long since Judy walked out on you," Celia commented.

"It's not Judy's fault. It just happened, that's all." Harry glanced over her shoulder and took one last look at the Golden Gate Bridge. As Richie turned the car, its interior momentarily glimmered with burnished gold and the sun bathed the bridge in radiant light. Harry let the sight of the luminous, orange sky burn into her memory.

"Stop defending Judy. She doesn't deserve it," Celia scolded, although her voice was kind. "You don't always have to be charitable, you know."

They drove from the bridge to the Castro District in silence. Harry lowered the window, and the smell of the city and the salty tang of the Pacific Ocean blew into the car. There was a lot of traffic and Richie had to ride the brake most of the way. They went up and down and along the sides of San Francisco's ubiquitous hills, passing through neighbourhoods and shopping districts. Cars lined up for parking spaces, which Celia claimed were harder to find than faithful lovers.

"Fran will be wondering where we are," Richie commented.

"Are you sure she doesn't mind us staying with her?" asked Harry.

"No more than she minds anything else," Richie responded, his voice filled with irony.

Harry wasn't sure what he meant, although it didn't sound promising. But she kept her mouth shut. They were in the Castro now, driving slowly along Market Street and then turning onto Castro Street itself. The Castro District of San Francisco was one of the gayest neighbourhoods in the world. The sidewalks were filled with lesbians and gay men, some dressed flamboyantly, although most were not, others holding hands, still others rushing about on business. Harry was distracted momentarily by a group of butch-looking women gathered in a knot on the sidewalk outside a café. It was a refreshing scene, but Harry was nervous about navigating this very appealing — not to mention seductive — world alone.

"Fran is quite the tyrant, you see," Buck remarked. "And a particularly dictatorial one at that." He had a cigarette between his lips and a lighter in his hand, and not for the first time Harry wished he would stop smoking. She knew that smoking was an occupational hazard for nurses, but Buck must have witnessed innumerable cases of lung disease, cancer and other smoking-related illnesses and deaths in his work at the Vancouver General Hospital. But he never talked about his job. In fact, he rarely talked about personal matters at all. Although he was friendly and had a sense of humour Harry could relate to, she had always found him a hard man to get to know. Unlike Richie, who didn't know the meaning of the word "secret," Buck kept his thoughts and feelings under wraps.

"You and Fran are friends, aren't you?" Buck asked Celia.

"Not really," Celia responded. "The only time I met her was when she was up for the Vancouver Gay Games, and that was quite a few years ago."

Harry wondered whether Celia and Fran had been lovers, but there was no point in asking. What Celia wanted them to know, she would tell them. Otherwise, she could be as close-mouthed as a clam.

"Well, Fran's alone now," Richie announced, taking advantage of a lull in traffic to change lanes and turn onto a side street. "She and her girlfriend, Moira Chelso, broke up. They weren't together long, actually. Apparently Moira was a handful."

"Really? You didn't tell me that," Celia said.

"What difference does it make?" Buck asked absently.

"None, I suppose," answered Celia. "Look at that dyke, Harry."

Harry joined Celia in staring at an androgynous woman walking down the street.

"Would I ever like to meet her," Celia whispered. "Do you know what I mean?"

Harry frowned.

"You don't, do you? Judy's still got you spellbound," Celia grumbled. "So when did Fran and Moira's relationship end?"

"I don't know, exactly," Richie admitted. "Four or five months ago, maybe. Fran and I talk on a regular basis, but she doesn't tell me everything. In fact, sometimes she doesn't tell me anything." He flicked his turn signal and pulled into a parking spot in front of a row of renovated Victorian houses. Mature eucalyptus trees lined the street, their silver leaves shimmering in the light breeze.

Buck opened the door, stepped out, lit the cigarette dangling between his lips and took a deep drag. Harry got out of the car and slipped her arm through Buck's. As they moved aside to let several pedestrians pass, Harry gave his arm a squeeze. "It's good to spend some time with you."

"Like the old days," Buck said with a grin.

"I wish it felt that way," mused Harry. "Do you ever wonder if you were more content back then?"

Buck looked at her for a moment and then said, "I've never really thought about it."

"Richie doesn't seem very happy about staying with Fran," Harry commented.

Buck shrugged. "Richie isn't very happy in general at the moment."

"He does seem upset. And, if you don't mind my saying so, surprisingly insecure. I don't understand how someone who has the confidence to get up and perform in front of an audience or act in front of a camera could be so vulnerable," remarked Harry.

"But don't you see, he's playing a role when he's on stage," Buck said, flicking his half-smoked cigarette into the gutter. "It's when he's off-stage that he doubts himself. Unfortunately, he's been off-stage a lot lately. He's had mostly boy-next-door parts during his career, and most of those roles have dried up as Richie has aged. How many Hollywood boys-next-door are over forty, after all? And the problem is that, with his looks and portfolio, it's hard for him to change his image. No one wants him for the heavy in a TV crime series or a regular on a situation comedy or the host of a talk show. He doesn't look the part."

"I see what you mean," Harry said.

"Add to that the fact that the boy-next-door never ended up with the girl. Not that he cared about girls, but on some level it made a difference. You know what I mean. If he couldn't get the girl, he most certainly wouldn't get the boy. Of course, he never realized how tall-dark-and-handsome types like me are attracted to cute, blond, boy-next-door types like him. But I digress. Let's get the trunk unpacked. I don't know about you, but I'm starving."

Celia had brought enough luggage for a month instead of the ten days they would be in San Francisco. When Richie threatened to drop his pants to show her the hernia he claimed to be developing from lifting her suitcases, she retorted, "But I need a different outfit for the Dyke Parade and Pink Saturday, not to mention each movie."

"That won't be easy, considering there are at least five hundred screenings," Buck said. "What have you got in here, a few thousand tubes of lipstick? The *Encyclopaedia Britannica*? A gross or two of dental dams?"

"Don't be smart," Celia retorted, hoisting one of her lighter suitcases from the trunk.

Harry retrieved her one and only suitcase from the bottom of the pile and stared in admiration at the three-storey Victorian house to which Richie was leading them.

"Does Fran really live here? In *this*?" Celia asked, looking up at the house. It was painted peach with white trim and had bay windows on the first two floors and a balcony on the third.

"Yes. It's quite a prime piece of real estate, isn't it?" Richie put down his suitcase and punched the doorbell. "Not to mention a marvellous place to live."

Celia seemed impressed. "It certainly is. Fran really must have come up in the world."

"She bought it years ago, when the Castro was just another SoMo neighbourhood," Richie explained.

"He means 'South of Market,'" Celia clarified.

Harry vaguely knew that downtown San Francisco and the business district were north of Market, but the city's topography remained largely elusive in her mind since she hadn't had the time to do her usual exhaustive search through travel guides before she left Vancouver. There were a lot of hills, the city was nearly surrounded by water and its streetcars were world famous, but that was all she remembered. She stood on Fran's porch and stared at the cleverly designed stained-glass rainbow flag hanging on the inside of the bevelled-glass window in the front door and recalled that Gilbert Baker, known as the gay Betsy Ross because he had designed the original rainbow flag, lived in San Francisco.

"Harry knows what I mean by 'SoMo,'" Richie said.

"Stop it," Harry said. She was tired of Celia's penchant for needling the two men, especially Richie. Just because he responded in such a satisfactory manner was no reason to bait him. Why were things always so complicated? People in relationships didn't trust each other, and people who were single constantly fretted because they were alone. It seemed there was no happy medium, which didn't bear thinking about, somehow. She put down her suitcase even though it wasn't heavy, shifted from one foot to another and wished she was somewhere else. She felt homesick for a time in her life that no longer existed.

"Don't worry, I know she's home," Richie said. "It's a big house." He pressed on the doorbell again.

Moments later, a tall, stout woman in faded black leggings and a loose, white tee-shirt that ended halfway between her hips and her knees opened the door. She ran fingers through her frizzy gray hair, but since it already resembled a fright wig, her ministrations made it look worse rather than better.

"It's about time you came for another visit, little brother," Fran grumbled, giving Richie a brusque hug. "How long has it been since you were here? The turn of the century?"

"Now, Fran," Richie said with an irritated laugh. "It wasn't that we didn't want to come, we just couldn't get away. You know how it is."

"Oh, I know all right, but we'll leave that conversation for another time." Fran turned her affections on Buck, gave Celia a warm embrace and then looked at Harry. "Who's this?"

"Our good friend from Montreal, Harriet Hubbley," Richie said.

"Nice to meet you," Harry said automatically.

"Yes, yes," Fran said with an off-putting grin. She grasped Harry's hand and gave it a firm shake. "I'll show you to your rooms so you can get settled, and then we'll go out to dinner. I'm famished."

"A woman after my own heart," joked Buck.

"You'll want to unpack and freshen up a bit, so just follow me." Fran grasped one of Celia's suitcases, swept past Richie and led them up the narrow staircase. "This is your room," she said to Richie and Buck. "The bathroom is right next door."

"Thanks," Buck said as Richie disappeared into the bedroom.

"And, girls, I didn't know quite what to do with you, since Richie told me you weren't an item," Fran said. "There's another guest room, but it contains only one bed. It's on the other side of the bathroom."

Harry didn't mind sharing a room with Celia, but sharing a *bed* with her would be intolerable.

Fran smiled and opened the door. "I'm sure you'll be quite comfortable here."

At least the room was large, and it was a queen-sized bed, Harry mused. But still.

"On the other hand, one of you could take this room and the other could bunk down in my study just down the hall. It's a bit messy — I have a strict rule about doing my filing twice a year and no more often than that — but it has a sofa bed with a real mattress."

"I'll take the study," Harry said swiftly. Celia looked relieved.

"Fine." Fran helped Celia move her suitcases into the bedroom and ushered Harry to her study. "I'll leave you to get settled."

"Thanks." Harry looked around. Fran hadn't been exaggerating when she had said that her study was untidy. A total mess would be more like it. The shelves, which covered two walls from floor to ceiling, were crammed with books, magazines, yellowed newspapers, several telephone directories and stacks of thick manila files, and there wasn't a clear spot on the large, wooden desk. It was piled high with bills, correspondence and more old newspapers and files. Well, it was a place to sleep, and Harry much preferred having some privacy to sharing with Celia. She tossed her suitcase onto the sofa and returned to Celia's room. The door was closed, so she knocked.

"Come in."

Harry went in and sat down on the bed beside one of Celia's open suitcases.

"Thanks for taking the study," Celia said. "I prefer to do my sleeping in private. Unless I'm with a lover, of course."

"Me, too."

"So where's the closet? There must be a closet," Celia muttered, examining the walls. "I can't possibly survive for ten days without a closet. Ah! Here it is, hidden behind all this hideous wallpaper. There aren't many coat hangers, though. Are you unpacked already?"

"No."

"But you'll want to change for dinner, won't you?"

"No."

"You're depressed, aren't you?" Celia sat down beside Harry and began stroking her shoulder.

"Not really. And I'm not into flings," Harry added primly when Celia's hand strayed quite far down her back.

Celia recoiled as if she had been slapped. "And who said I was?" She stood up and strode to the door.

Perhaps she had misinterpreted Celia's intentions, Harry ruminated as the door slammed behind Celia's stiff back. Although she thought not. How depressing. She fell back on the bed, tugged a plump pillow from under the covers and wrapped an arm around it.

Celia breezed back into the room a couple minutes later. "I'm going to pretend you didn't say that."

Harry sat up. "Fine." She knew she wasn't going to get off that easily, but she could dissemble as well as the next woman.

"Girls!" came Fran's voice. "We're leaving!"

Harry got up. Celia was pouting into the dresser mirror, putting bright red lipstick on her lips.

"We'll be down in a minute!" Harry shouted. She went back into the study, unzipped her suitcase and changed into a black tee-shirt, a pair of faded blue jeans and a matching denim jacket. She went into the bathroom, where she freshened up, ignoring the dark circles under her eyes. The bathroom fixtures were antique. There was a claw-footed bathtub, an old-fashioned porcelain sink and a toilet with an overhead tank and a pull chain. But the shade of rose paint on the walls was a bit too modern to maintain the illusion.

"Girls!"

"Coming," Harry yelled. She dried her hands on a towel, left the bathroom and knocked on Celia's door again. "Aren't you ready yet?" she poked her head through the door frame to ask.

Celia stared at her in the mirror. "I'll be down soon."

"Celia —"

"I said I'll be down soon."

Great, Harry thought, just great. She turned away before Celia could see the look on her face, closing the door so quietly that she might as well have slammed it.

"So where's the princess?" Fran asked, turning toward the stairs as Harry rushed down to the first floor. She hated making people wait.

"Repairing her façade," Harry replied.

Richie looked amused. "Do I feel the turbulence of a tiff in the air?"

"Whatever gave you that idea?" Celia replied as she marched stately down the steps. "Just because Harry doesn't want to make out with me doesn't mean we're not friends."

"Leave me out of this," said Buck, raising his hands in front of him, palms outward. "It's enough that Richie isn't talking to me."

"Never mind," Richie growled.

Fran arched her eyebrows and turned to leave, twirling a bunch of keys with her right hand. It was a silent but very effective put-down and it seemed to Harry that the only place the evening could go from there was downhill.

But once she drank half of the Long Island Iced Tea Fran had insisted on ordering at the trendy gay and lesbian restaurant to which they'd walked, she was too mellow to care. She sipped from her glass, felt her lips grow numb and put her unfinished drink on the table. She'd had enough; alcohol had a depressing effect on her, and she didn't want to exacerbate her already despondent state of mind. She forked a piece of moist grilled chicken into her mouth, wondering when the waiter had served dinner. She had missed it entirely. But never mind. It didn't matter. She was depressed by the effect San Francisco was having on her friends. Richie and Buck had obviously quarrelled, and the normally affable Richie was in a royal funk, slurping his drink as if it was real tea instead of unadulterated alcohol. Celia sat between a pensive-looking Buck and Fran, flirting with Fran in a fundamentally uncaring manner, although that didn't seem to bother Fran.

"Drink with me, Harriet," Richie muttered, his speech slurred.

"I've had enough, thanks," Harry replied.

"No one ever has enough in San Francisco," he responded. "It's against the law."

Harry laughed, ordered a decaf coffee and ate the rest of her grilled chicken salad. Sometimes being in an exclusively gay and lesbian environment brought out the worst in everyone, herself included. Certainly bars were that way; lesbians with butch tendencies turned into wolves, and femmes responded to them like lambs on the way to slaughter. Maybe it was mindless parody. Harry didn't know. She herself had lived through those experiences in her pre-Judy days, although she had never quite been able to decide whether she was butch or femme. She supposed she wasn't the only lesbian with a split personality.

She wasn't enjoying the single life. All she wanted was to escape to somewhere safe, wherever that was. Perhaps she should resettle in Key West and run the guesthouse herself rather than let Pearl Vernon do it for her. Or resign from her teaching position, leave the high school in which she had taught for nearly three decades, and move away from Quebec. Not only did she hate the thought of constantly running into Judy in Montreal's shrinking English-speaking community, she was also wary of the fragile political situation in that province and tired of the machinations of the separatist movement. Maybe the best thing would be to relocate to her home town in Nova Scotia, although it would be difficult to meet other gay women in such a small community. Or she could settle in another urban centre in Canada, like Toronto, Vancouver or Ottawa. She had friends in all three cities. Somehow, though, Harry knew that, at least temporarily, she would return to Montreal and wallow in misery like a pig in slops. It didn't much endear her to herself.

"Are you ready to pack it in for the night?" Fran asked, raising her voice to be heard over the din. "We've got quite a busy day tomorrow."

Harry wanted another cup of coffee, but she surrendered her empty plate to the waiter and dropped her credit card on the table. It was immediately covered by three others, and the waiter pounced, obviously eager to repossess their table.

"Why didn't someone remind me that Long Island Iced Tea is lethal?" Richie muttered, grasping his head between his hands.

"Come," Harry said, helping Richie to his feet. She looked around for Buck, annoyed that he wasn't taking responsibility for his inebriated lover, but she couldn't see him anywhere. Perhaps he was in the men's room or he'd already left the restaurant.

"Do we really have to go home now?" Celia said. "The night's still young."

"It's entirely up to you," Fran said with a shrug. "I just thought you'd be tired from your drive from Vancouver."

"Of course I'm tired, but I'd rather go dancing," insisted Celia. "I can sleep when I get home."

"Ditto," said Richie. Harry led him from the restaurant, hoping that some fresh air would sober him up. Fran and Celia went on ahead.

"I've been poisoned," Richie muttered.

"You've been drinking," Harry said affectionately. "No more booze for you tonight."

"You sound like my mother," Richie complained.

"You could do worse," Harry quipped.

"My mother *was* worse," Richie insisted. "I'd have traded her for someone like you without a second thought, and I bet Fran would have, too. Although come to think of it, Fran is a lot like our mother."

Richie sounded so sorry for himself that Harry couldn't help but grin. "You're not young enough to be my son, but I've no doubt that you should be more respectful to your elders, including Fran. But seriously, why don't you try to patch things up with Buck?"

Richie screwed up his face like a little boy. "I'm fed up with him."

"Don't say that," admonished Harry. She was sure it was just the liquor speaking, but still. "Never tempt fate."

"Who's tempting fate?" asked Buck as he caught up with them. "And, Richie, why didn't you pay your bill? The waiter grabbed me before I could leave and told me he was missing a signature on one of our credit-card slips. It turned out to be yours, so I tore it up and used mine again," he added, putting his arm around Richie's shoulder.

"Leave me alone." Richie's tone was petulant, but Buck ignored it.

"Come on, Richie, loosen up," Buck urged. He grasped Richie's hand, raised it to his lips and kissed the back of it.

Harry decided to give them some privacy. She increased her pace until she caught up with Celia and Fran.

"Fed up with the boys?" Celia asked.

"Not at all," Harry replied.

"I wouldn't blame you if you were," Fran added.

"I just wondered where we were going," Harry said.

"I thought you might enjoy the Café Bar on Market and Castro. It's mostly for women, and it's one of the only dance bars in the neighbourhood," said Fran.

Celia linked her arms through Fran and Harry's. "Wonderful."

Actually, it sounded pretty good to Harry, too.

Although they didn't have to wait in line, the bar was crowded, mainly with women.

"You see if you can find a table and I'll get us something to drink," Fran shouted over the music. "You can try the outdoor balcony, although it's probably packed."

Celia led them through the bar, dancing in time to the music as if she was head of a conga line. Harry followed directly behind her, a silly grin on her face, and tried not to look like a three-footed dolt.

"Aren't we lucky," Buck commented, pushing past the two women to claim a balcony table being vacated by several punk-looking lipstick lesbians.

"On second thought, maybe we should stick around," said one of the lipstick lesbians. She approached Harry and fingered a metal stud on Harry's jean jacket.

Only Harry's inability to believe what was happening stopped her from backing all the way to the front door. She looked at the hand touching her; it was thin with finely tapered fingers. The long fingernails were painted blood red. Perhaps it was the lingering effect of the Long Island Iced Tea, but Harry didn't flinch, much less pull away, when the woman slid her hand inside Harry's jean jacket and lightly touched her breast.

"It looks to me like you've got a real fan," Richie exclaimed as he appeared on the balcony.

That broke the spell, and the lipstick lesbian's hand fell away. She smiled and attempted to slip past Harry, who moved to block her way.

"You're not playing fair," protested Harry. A fine sweat had broken out on her upper lip and her legs were trembling, but she wasn't about to let fear totally paralyze her.

The lipstick lesbian gave Harry a long, speculative look, which Harry forced herself to return. She appeared to be in her mid-twenties and she was extremely attractive.

"You're right, I'm not," the young woman said finally. "Normally, that wouldn't matter, but this is different, isn't it?"

Harry nodded dumbly.

"Here, take this, then," the young woman said, sliding a card into Harry's hand and fleeing after her friends.

Harry flopped into a chair and turned the card over, ignoring Buck and Celia's suggestive comments. The card had a full-colour rainbow background and printed on it was "Raven," followed by an address and phone number.

Raven?

Oh no, Harry decided, crushing the card in her fist and dropping it to the floor.

"Another litterer," Celia commented as Fran deposited a pot of coffee and five mugs on the table.

"It's biodegradable."

Celia looked amused. "I suppose it is, but I never thought about sex in quite that way."

She was right. Harry bent down, picked up Raven's card and stuffed it in the breast pocket of her jean jacket.

"How wise."

"Never mind," Harry muttered.

"Couldn't you have brought some water?" Celia complained as Fran filled their mugs with coffee. "I won't sleep a wink tonight if I drink this."

"I didn't know you wanted water. You can always get some yourself, you know," replied Fran.

Celia made a face but didn't respond.

The feel of a stranger's hand on her breast and the knowledge that she had the woman's phone number on a card in her pocket had thoroughly sobered Harry. She sipped the strong coffee and stared out over Market Street. The sidewalk was congested with people. There were queens dressed to the nines, gay men in leather or lace or plain ordinary duds, and lesbians in drag or jeans or polyester. Many of them seemed to know each other. They waved, stopped to kiss on the cheek, to chat.

"She sure had the hots for you," Celia said across the table.

"I guess." The question was, did Harry have the hots for her?

Lipstick lesbians were another generation, outside Harry's realm of understanding. They embraced the butch and femme identities which many of the members of Harry's generation had attempted to eradicate from their lives. She wouldn't have changed into denim if she had realized she would be sending a specific — and obviously butch — message. Imagine what would have happened if she had thoughtlessly donned her suede vest or her leather jacket. Raven might have thrown her to the floor and ravished her right then and there. Harry finished her coffee and held out her mug for Fran to refill.

"A penny for your thoughts," Richie said, shaking his head as if to dislodge the effect of the Long Island Iced Tea he had imbibed earlier.

"You don't want to know."

"Oh, but I do," Richie insisted.

Harry sighed. "I was just thinking that I don't understand women."

"How depressing for you."

"Tell me about it."

"Was that why Judy left you? Oh hell, I'm sorry," he hastened to say when Harry flinched. "I've had too much to drink. I mean, I don't want to pry into something that isn't any of my business. I've always been a bit of a nosy parker, but I didn't intend to hurt your feelings."

Harry felt weary. "That's all right."

"Buck and I are having a major difference of opinion about where to spend the rest of our lives. That's not the only thing, but it's the most contentious issue at the moment. I'm in dire need of answers, Harry. Nuggets of wisdom, so to speak."

"Wisdom has never been my forte. And I find myself completely out of answers. But if you want to discuss it, we can talk."

"I'd appreciate it," Richie said as Buck approached the table with two bottles of beer in his hands. "But not right now."

"Later, then," Harry said. The frenetic cadence of a popular song enveloped her senses. "I'm going to dance." She rushed from the balcony to the bar and squeezed onto the crowded dance floor. "The Rhythm of the Night" fugued into "What is Love." The beat throbbed inside her body. Sweat collected on her brow, along her hairline, under her breasts, between her thighs. When Enigma's "Return to Innocence" blasted from the speakers, she finally slowed down and took a deep breath. Catharsis was one thing, a heart attack another. She hadn't worked out in her health club for quite some time now.

"Do you know who Raven is?" Harry yelled to Fran, who had joined her on the dance floor and was hopping and shaking like a grizzly bear in heat.

"I know her quite well," Fran shouted back. "She's pretty neat, isn't she?"

Was a woman who touched the breast of a stranger a neat person? Harry danced on.

"Do you want a drink?" Fran asked.

"Sure."

Fran led Harry to the bar and ordered two glasses of mineral water. "I'm kind of worried about my little brother. I don't like the way Buck is treating him."

"I wouldn't know anything about that," Harry said.

Fran downed her glass of water in one gulp and gestured to the bartender for another. "How could you not notice? Buck is behaving like a real asshole."

Harry remained silent, although she was taken aback by Fran's peevish manner. Was Fran involved in the dispute Richie and Buck were having? Perhaps it would all become clear to her when she and Richie discussed what was bothering him. But one thing was certain, she wasn't about to tell Fran what Richie had recently confided in her.

"Hello, you two," Celia said, materializing from the crowd clustered around the bar.

"Hello yourself." Fran leaned an elbow on the bar and looked at Celia.

The attraction between Celia and Fran was so strong that Harry retrieved her half-empty glass of mineral water and wandered off to the other end of the bar, not wanting to witness their mating rituals. She fumbled in her jeans' pocket for some cash, leaned over the bar and ordered a soft drink. Just as the bartender set a diet cola on the bar, Richie squatted on the stool next to hers.

"I'm thinking of going to a sex club," he said, staring into his empty beer stein.

"I hope you don't." Not that she was a prude. Oh, all right, she *was* a prude. But Richie was too drunk to go anywhere near a San Francisco sex club.

"You're not me."

How right he was. Harry thought about asking if he wanted to talk, and then decided that he was also too intoxicated for that.

Richie leaned on the bar and ordered another beer.

"You need to sleep, not — well, you know," Harry said. "Besides, getting drunk and going to a sex club isn't going to solve your problems with Buck. Where is Buck, anyway?"

"Around somewhere."

The bartender served Richie a beer and Harry another diet cola, for which she paid even though she hadn't ordered it.

"Did you know that there are sex clubs for women?" Richie claimed. "They move around from place to place, but I bet Fran knows how to find them. She wouldn't be my sister if she didn't."

"Why are you telling me this?"

"Aren't you interested in going to one?"

"No."

"You're such a wimp."

"And you're changing the subject."

"Oh, come on."

Who was Richie to accuse her of cowardice? So San Francisco had women's sex clubs. Did she care? Actually, yes and no. Yes because she was curious, and no because she wasn't interested in public sex or sex with someone she didn't know.

"Richie! I'm so glad I've found you!" exclaimed a slim woman with medium-length, dark brown hair.

"Mandy?"

"I thought Celia might have convinced the rest of you to go dancing — I've been searching for you in half the bars on Castro Street," said Mandy Perkins. "Where's Celia?"

"Over there. With my sister, Fran."

Mandy Perkins exposed her teeth in a feral grin and stalked off.

"I can't believe that she followed Celia all the way down from Vancouver," Richie remarked.

"I suppose they'll work it out between them." Harry picked up her drink and left the bar. She returned to the balcony, but their table had been occupied by a large group of women who had borrowed chairs from neighbouring tables. She walked to the edge of the balcony and stared into the street. It was nearly midnight, but the sidewalk was still crowded. She finished her cola and was suddenly tired.

"I'm sorry I've been hassling you," Richie said, approaching her from behind.

"It's all right," Harry replied. "I know you're under a lot of stress."

"That's no excuse, not really. You and me, we're the sheep in the lion's den," Richie said.

"Not me." Harry pulled away. She didn't want to play this game, whatever it was. Perhaps once he sobered up, they could have a conversation without Richie going up and down like a yo-yo.

Harry sighed and opened her eyes. Even a single Long Island Iced Tea was one too many. She should know better at her age, she thought sternly. Her bladder was about to burst, so she rose slowly and put one foot on the floor. Just because she was suddenly single, just because she was newly rich, just because a strange woman had cruised her didn't mean she had to throw caution to the wind and end up with a hangover, mild though it was.

She got up, rummaged through her suitcase until she found her toiletries kit, and slowly opened the door, looking from left to right to make sure the coast was clear. Then she hurried into the bathroom and locked the door. She desperately needed a shower after the long drive from Vancouver to San Francisco and dancing in the Café Bar the night before. She deciphered the workings of the tub's antique fixtures and unfurled the lavender shower curtain that hung from a circular metal hoop.

The hot water washed away not only her sweat, but also her headache. She lingered after she had shampooed and rinsed her neatly cropped, blonde but graying hair, letting the water cascade over her body. She didn't like the pads of flesh that had suddenly sprouted on her hips and buttocks while she was going through menopause, but there wasn't much she could do about them except try to keep in shape. At least her belly was still firm, but if she missed her regular workouts at her health club for more than a week, her tummy muscles started to grow flaccid. Still, no matter how much she exercised, nothing would stop her breasts from drooping or her pubic hair from turning gray, which took more than a little getting used to.

Turning forty had been traumatic, but at least it had been possible to think about being alive in another forty years. Reaching eighty was not an impossibility, especially for a female born at the leading edge of the baby boom. But turning fifty was another matter. It was unlikely that she would live to be a hundred, and she wasn't sure if she wanted to. She had no desire to end life as an old woman whose friends had gone before. But she didn't want to die, either. Sometimes she wondered if it would eventually come down to which was more distasteful, life or death.

She towel-dried her hair, rubbed moisturizing cream on her skin and returned to her room, where she changed into a pair of black jeans, a white tee-shirt decorated with a multicoloured rainbow, and a black denim jacket cut short at the waist.

It was nearly noon and Harry was starving. She decided to leave her purse behind, so she stuffed her driver's licence into her wallet and hid it in the inside pocket of her jacket. After a moment's dithering, she retrieved Raven's card from her jean jacket and put it in her pants' pocket. She wasn't intending to use it, but she felt better knowing it was there. She glanced at her watch and realized that, if she didn't get a move on, she would miss the beginning of her first film.

Harry's Film Festival pass and schedule were where Fran had said they would be — on the coffee table in the living room. She stuffed them into her pocket and hurried from the house, disappointed that no one else was around. Perhaps everyone had risen bright and early. On the other hand, perhaps not. Maybe most of them were still in bed.

Her first film was in the Castro Theater, a historical building constructed in 1922 and since modernized. The Castro was one of San Francisco's most illustrious repertoire theatres and a natural gathering place for the gay community. It was also the headquarters for the Film Festival. Other screenings were held in the Roxie, located in the Mission District, with spillover in several smaller theatres in the area.

Harry walked along Castro Street, her tummy growling from hunger. Her mouth tasted like a clogged septic tank, and her stomach was running on empty, but she didn't have time to stop at one of the many cafés and restaurants on Castro for something to eat. She rushed into the theatre minutes before the film began, its wonderful atmosphere barely registering on her consciousness as she lined up at the concession counter. She purchased a medium popcorn, a supersize box of Rosebuds and a large diet cola and dashed to her seat just as the credits flashed across the screen.

Once she had momentarily sated her hunger and quenched her thirst, she turned her attention to the screen and swiftly realized that the movie was awful. It was a pretentious art film that had something to do with gay people, but it was so postmodern that it had no logical meaning. She loathed deliberate randomness, whether it was in music, film or life. But since she was there anyway, she decided to give the film the benefit of the doubt.

"Outstanding," muttered the young man to her left when the screen went blank and the lights came up.

Outstanding crap, Harry thought testily, embarrassed that the film had been directed by a Canadian. She turned sideways to let the others in her row file past her and then slowly followed them out. As she hesitated on the sidewalk outside the theatre, Richie approached her.

"What a yawn," he said plaintively.

"Quite." Harry grinned. "But I'm sure things will get better. After all, there are hundreds of movies. What are you going to see next?"

Richie consulted his schedule, which was already tattered. Then he sighed, refolded it and put it back in his pocket. "I don't know why I bothered to look at it. I've heard of some of the filmmakers, but I'm embarrassed to say that I don't know much about their films. There are a couple I thought I might go to, but I haven't quite made up my mind."

"What about Buck?"

"He isn't much of a movie-goer, and he made it clear that he doesn't want to attend anything the least bit arty. So we decided to split up, at least for today. Listen, I missed lunch. Why don't we have something to eat? We've got time."

"Sounds good to me."

They went to a nearby restaurant, where Richie ordered a burger and fries, and Harry had a spinach salad. After all the junk food she had consumed during the movie, that was all she wanted. Besides, it made her feel virtuous.

"Fran can be damn unreasonable at times," Richie said once he had demolished the burger, wiped his hands on a napkin and tossed it on his empty plate. "In fact, she's unreasonable most of the time. She's been after me for years to move down here and live with her. She thinks I'm wasting my time trying to make it big in Canada, that

I should use her house as a base and spend some time down in Los Angeles. Do some tests, try to get some parts on television or in the movies. She says she knows some people who might be able to help me."

"And you don't want to?"

"I'm open to the idea, but Buck won't hear of it." Richie looked cautious, as if he was choosing his words carefully. Harry got the impression that he wasn't sure he should be discussing it with her, but she persevered.

"Why on earth not? Wouldn't he be able to get a better job?" Harry asked. "From what I've heard, nurses can earn incredible amounts in the States."

"I know, but he still doesn't want to move."

"Why not?"

"Because he loves Vancouver," Richie replied, looking troubled.

Harry had often heard that sentiment expressed. No one ever felt neutral about Vancouver; it was a city that people either loved or hated. Very few had no opinion. Celia vowed she would never live anywhere else, while another ex-Montrealer Harry knew detested the rainy winters and the laid-back pace of life. Still, no matter how Buck felt about leaving Vancouver, moving to San Francisco would have given both Richie's and Buck's careers a jump-start. So why was Buck reluctant to take Fran up on her offer?

"Is there something you're not telling me?"

"Undoubtedly." Richie's tone was dry and Harry wondered whether it was because he had no intention of revealing everything he knew or if he simply didn't know what Buck's reasoning was. Buck was so closed-mouthed that it would be difficult to find out what he really thought. Not that she had a reason to pry. Other than friendship, she reflected.

Richie rose from his chair and tossed a ten-dollar bill and a couple of ones on the table. "I'd better be going or I'll miss my next movie. I'll see you later."

"Right," Harry nodded. Richie left and she finished her glass of water.

"Anything else?" the waitress asked.

"No, thanks." Harry took out her wallet and added a ten-dollar bill to Richie's pile of cash. She was procrastinating because she didn't feel like going to another movie, especially by herself, not even if it was the best lesbian film ever made. Maybe Celia was at the house. Or even Fran, although Harry hadn't been impressed by Richie's sister. She was definitely lacking in the tact-and-charm department. Harry wondered what Celia saw in Fran and then gave it up. After all, who knew what one woman saw in another. She returned her wallet to the inner pocket of her jacket and left the restaurant.

At first the house seemed empty, so Harry ran upstairs and knocked on Celia's door.

"Come in," called Celia, her tone wary.

Harry opened the door and went in. Celia was sitting stiff-backed on the bed and Fran was standing behind her, one hand on Celia's shoulder, the other on her hip. While Celia seemed apprehensive, Fran looked cocky. From the expression on Celia's face, they had apparently been expecting Mandy, and Fran was clearly showing off.

"Gawd! What a letdown. I was sure it was the Vicious Viper from Vancouver," chortled Fran, dropping her hand from Celia's shoulder.

"Stop it," Celia chided her, although it was clear that she was enjoying Fran's maliciousness.

Harry decided to ignore the whole thing. "Are you two planning to take in a movie tonight?"

Celia glanced at Fran and then said, "Why don't we go dancing instead?"

"But we came to San Francisco to attend the Film Festival," Harry objected.

"I like movies as much as the next person, but I don't intend to sit in a theatre and watch films from early morning until late at night," Celia said.

Harry had the feeling that Celia and Fran hadn't yet been to a movie, but she didn't say so.

"And I wouldn't mind going dancing again," Celia said.

"Why don't you give Raven a call and see if she wants to meet us there?" asked Fran. There was a shrewd look on her face.

"Yes, Harry, do," Celia gushed. "We could double-date."

What a thrill, Harry thought sourly.

"Come on," implored Celia.

In the end, Harry let herself be persuaded to call Raven, who seemed not at all surprised to hear from her. Harry arranged to meet her at the Café Bar in half an hour and then went back to the study and dithered about what to wear. Before she had even undressed, there was a loud rapping on the door and Celia rushed in.

"Aren't you ready yet?"

Harry stared at the rumpled clothes in her suitcase.

"Never mind about changing. You look fine." Celia grasped her hand and led her from her room and down the stairs.

Compared to whom? Harry wondered. Celia was dressed in a tunic and wide-legged pants made of raw silk. Rhinestone earrings dangled to her shoulders. Harry was wearing denim.

It was a short walk from Fran's house to the Café Bar. They found Raven sitting at the bar, nursing a bottle of beer.

Fran bent down and gave Raven a casual peck on the cheek. She straightened up, gestured to the bartender and ordered two glasses of white wine. "Celia and I will see if we can find a table out on the balcony. Join us when you're ready."

Raven continued staring at the bar. "Fine."

Fran scooped up their glasses of wine and led Celia through the throngs of women surrounding the bar.

"Hello," Harry said to Raven, hoping that the pounding dance music hid the shyness in her voice. She felt fat, frumpy and, most of all, emotionally overextended. What was she doing, approaching this young, thin, trendy woman?

"Hello yourself," Raven said, smiling at Harry. She reached out and drew Harry down beside her. "Have some beer."

Harry sipped from Raven's bottle, but she didn't like beer, not even when it was mild-tasting and frosty. Unfortunately, what she was drinking was lukewarm and tasted like ale. She handed the bottle back to Raven. "I'm not really thirsty."

"Beer isn't always about thirst," Raven remarked.

Harry knew Raven wasn't talking only about beer, but she had never been good at dealing with hidden meanings. She gestured to the bartender and ordered a cola. Once it came, she realized that what she really wanted was a glass of water. The salad she had eaten earlier had been quite salty.

Raven finally cut through her dithering. "Why don't we dance?"

Perhaps there would be safety in numbers, Harry thought, as she rose from the bar stool. Raven's hand touched her shoulder, slid over her back, caressed her waist. The music was hot: "This is the Night," "Total Eclipse of the Heart," the house version of "The

Power of Love." As a Céline Dion ballad began to play, Raven moved toward her. There was no pretence of keeping a discreet distance between them; their bodies came together swiftly, almost forcefully. Harry felt winded. She clung to Raven in near-panic. It was too soon for such intimacy. She didn't know what to do with it. She and Raven were so different, their clothes, their hairstyles, their ages ...

"You feel so good," Raven murmured in her ear.

Harry suddenly became aware of the smell of Raven's soap, the motion of Raven's hips against her belly, the rotating of Raven's hand on her lower back and the hypnotic swaying of their bodies. Her fear dropped away and she laughed rather breathlessly, hugging Raven to her.

"I'm rather overwhelmed."

"There's no rush," Raven assured her. The ballad ended and they moved apart, their hands touching, joining, their eyes locking. Sexual heat flowed through Harry's body.

They were so engrossed in each other, so oblivious to the other women on the dance floor, that Fran's voice startled them.

"Come on, Raven, have a dance with me, for old time's sake. We'll change partners — Harry can take a turn with Celia."

"I'm rather busy at the moment," replied Raven, giving Harry's hand a squeeze.

Fran cackled and put her arm around Raven's shoulder. "I don't doubt it. We go back a long way, you know," she said to Harry and Celia, who was leaning against the wall, her hands shoved deep in the pockets of her silk pants.

Harry felt irritated. Couldn't Fran see that they didn't want to be interrupted? She attempted to look detached, but failed.

"Mind you, she doesn't always listen to her elders," Fran added.

A look of annoyance passed over Raven's face, but she didn't respond to Fran's taunt.

"Harriet, let's retrieve our drinks from the bar," she said.

Fran removed her arm from Raven's shoulder. "Don't be such a bitch," she hissed.

"Fran," Celia protested. She moved closer to Fran and tentatively placed her hand on her arm, but Fran shook her off.

"Stop acting like this," Raven retorted.

"Come on, honey, let's go back to our table before somebody else takes it," Celia cajoled. "I'm all danced out, anyway."

Fran glowered for a few seconds longer and then the spell broke. Her facial muscles relaxed and her lips curled in a cynical grin. "How can I resist an appeal from such a beautiful woman?" she asked rhetorically, putting her arms around Celia and giving her a wet kiss. "Listen, forget this ever happened. It didn't mean anything, anyway. Why don't you two get your drinks and join us on the balcony? It's not so smoky out there, or so hot."

Harry smiled weakly, nodded and gripped Raven's hand and led her back to the bar. Their drinks were still there, but the stools they had been sitting on were taken. Harry retrieved her half-full glass of cola and Raven's nearly empty bottle of beer. She finished her cola and then asked, "What the hell was that all about?"

"Did no one tell you what Fran was like?" Raven asked, draining the rest of the beer from her bottle.

Richie had mentioned how unreasonable Fran could be, but Harry had assumed that was only about family matters. "Not really."

"Fran's a control freak," Raven explained. "She likes to have a say in everything. She has a fierce temper, and she can also be quite mean and vindictive."

"So I see. But why is she picking on you?" Harry glanced at Raven, startled when she saw how uncomfortable she looked. Was it possible, she wondered? "Were you and Fran involved with each other?"

Raven nodded. "We never lived together, but we were lovers for over two years. Our relationship ended a year ago. Fran said she didn't want to see me any more, that I was too young for her. I think the difference in our ages made her feel uncomfortable. She was fifty when we became lovers, and she had a hard time getting past the fact that she was old enough to be my mother. But I like older women," Raven said, leaning against Harry. "I don't know why, but I do."

Harry felt shocked that she had somehow become an older woman, but she wasn't going to say that to Raven. She was also the same age Fran had been when she and Raven had become lovers, which was not something she wanted to think about. At least Raven was three years older now. "Why did you get involved with someone who was so — er — complex?"

"You know, for the longest time, I don't think I realized just how difficult she could be," Raven said with a crooked smile. "I thought she was super intelligent, incredibly sophisticated, and that she had an acid wit. It took me quite a while to realize that she was neurotic and mean-spirited as well, but by then I had really fallen for her. But it's been over for a year."

"Is she still jealous?"

"She hates to let anyone go because then she loses control over them," responded Raven. "What you saw just now was a prime example of Fran doing a number on someone. I used to think that I could avoid getting into an argument with her by giving in, but I soon learned that not standing my ground made things worse. If I had danced with her just then, she would have come on to me in a major way even though she wasn't really interested."

"She would have risked alienating Celia just to make me jealous?"

"Yes, although her main aim would have been to upset me."

"I don't understand people like that."

"Just as long as you realize that they exist," Raven said, her tone grim. "One thing I've leaned is never to underestimate Fran."

"What does she do?" Harry asked. "I mean, it can't be cheap to live where she does or to keep that house in a state of good repair."

"She's a professor of philosophy at Cal," Raven replied. "The University of California at Berkeley. A *full* professor."

"That's amazing," said Harry. "That she's a philosopher, I mean."

"Quite. Listen, why don't we gird our loins with something cold and wet and join those two lovebirds out on the balcony?"

Harry groaned. "Really?"

Raven gave her such a warm smile that Harry wanted to kiss her. "We have been invited. Twice."

"Celia asked us to go on a double date, and I suppose we do have to be sociable," said Harry.

Raven nodded. "Fran is your host, after all."

They looked at each other, then joined hands and rushed from the Café Bar, laughing all the while.

Harry rolled over and opened her eyes. She reached out and plucked her travel alarm clock from the corner of Fran's desk, smiling softly to herself when she saw that it was after noon. She turned over on her back and thought about the previous evening. After she and Raven left the Café Bar, they had strolled hand-in-hand through the streets of the Castro, pausing to window-shop, stopping now and then for an ice cream or a coffee. It was a balmy night and the streets were crowded with Film Festival patrons and gay men and lesbians out on the town. When Harry had started to tire, Raven offered to walk her home. As they had sauntered toward Fran's house, Harry began to get nervous. Did Raven expect to be invited in? And, even more important, did Harry want to invite her in? They had arrived at the stairs to Fran's house before Harry could answer that question. But nothing had happened, and Harry still wasn't certain whether she was relieved or disappointed. She replayed their parting outside Fran's.

"It's been a nice evening," Raven had said, releasing Harry's hand and turning to face her.

"Yes, it has," Harry had replied. She had unconsciously held her breath, waiting for Raven to insist on pushing their attraction to its logical conclusion, but Raven hadn't. She had cupped Harry's chin in her hand, given her a soft kiss, whispered "Goodnight" and swiftly disappeared into the shadows.

Harry rolled over and got up. The restlessness she felt was sexual and it was clear to her that, whether she was ready or not, she was interested in Raven. She stood up and reached for her jeans just as the door to the study burst open and Mandy rushed in.

"Where is she?"

Harry hugged her jeans against her naked body and sat back down on the sofa bed.

"And don't ask who!"

No wonder Celia had broken up with her.

"Who?"

Even the resounding slam of the door didn't wipe the grin off Harry's face. She hurried through her morning routine and dressed in yesterday's castoffs with the exception of clean undies and a new tee-shirt. Then she went downstairs, searching for the kitchen. She wanted a glass of juice and a bowl of cereal instead of yet another restaurant meal.

"Ah! The Mystery Lady from Montreal!" exclaimed Fran. "Where did you and Raven get to last night, or should I bother to ask? I was incredibly offended that you ignored my invitation to join us; however, I'll forgive you this one time. The two of you were so hot that it would have been a shame not to get it on the second you had the chance. I haven't opened that sofa in a donkey's age, but I'm sure you didn't notice whether the mattress was lumpy, at least not last night. So where's Raven?"

"I slept just fine," Harry responded. Under the circumstances, she decided not to mention the cookie crumbs, spare change and piles of lint she had uncovered when she had removed the cushions from the sofa the night before last. She considered telling Fran that she hadn't spent the night with Raven, then decided that it was none of her business.

"Raven's not here."

"So she left without saying good morning, did she? I thought I'd taught her better manners than that," Fran grumbled. She was dressed in a floral dressing gown and was hovering over a large, cast-iron frying pan, scraping at what looked like scrambled eggs with a wooden spoon. "My eggs are burning. Do you suppose the heat's too high?"

Harry approached the stove. The element under the frying pan was bright red. "I think it might be."

Fran cursed and turned off the burner. "I love food, but I've never been able to cook. Not that philosophers should know how to prepare food. Being able to think is far more important, although in this society you'd never know it. Why I'm not up to three hundred pounds from all the junk food I eat, I'll never know. My ex-husband used to claim I was poisoning him, and he wasn't half joking. I'm certain that's one of the reasons he left me."

"You were married?"

"Yes. Isn't that a lark? It's so out of character for me. I don't usually make mistakes of that magnitude, if at all. I suppose that at this point it doesn't matter. It was so many years ago that it seems like another lifetime. And I haven't seen the bugger for more than twenty years. Would you like to join me? There's enough for two." Fran upended the frying pan over a dinner plate. Half the charred eggs fell into it and the rest stuck to the bottom of the pan.

"Thanks, but I never bother much with breakfast," Harry lied. In reality, it was the most important meal of Harry's day. Raven had understated the situation; Fran was a truly awful person. Harry began to plot how she could escape from her clutches.

"You could show how much you appreciate my hospitality by pretending to eat some of my scrambled eggs. Or you could demonstrate some enthusiasm about sharing my breakfast to express how grateful you are that I've decided not to hold a grudge against you for screwing Raven. But never mind," Fran said, prying the burnt eggs from the pan. "I'm in a good mood this morning and it'll take a lot more than your lousy attitude to make me lose my temper." She flashed Harry a spiteful smile and carried her plate to the table in the breakfast nook. It was made of mottled yellow Formica with metal legs, and the chairs were padded with matching yellow Naugahyde. The set dated from the fifties, was in perfect condition and was probably worth thousands.

"Sit down," Fran ordered, wagging her fork at Harry. Bits of singed egg stuck to its tines.

Harry perched on the edge of a chair despite her desire to flee.

Fran put her fork down, set her elbows on the table and clasped her hands together. For a moment, Harry thought she was going to lead them in prayer, perhaps to ask for divine deliverance from the indigestion those rubbery eggs were bound to cause. "I want you to understand something, Harriet Hubbley, Mystery Lady from Montreal. In contrast to both of us, Raven is quite young. She needs a mother figure in her life, and frankly, you're not up to it. She's as horny as hell and ready to screw every older woman she meets, and, at the moment, that's you. Unfortunately, you don't know how to walk on water, so you're going to let her down. Badly."

What a load of bull, Harry thought irritably, although she said nothing. Fran picked up her fork and shovelled more eggs into her mouth. Harry decided that she must not have much of a sense of taste. Menopause did that to some women. It served Fran right.

"I take it that you and Celia spent the night together."

"It's really none of your business, but yes, Celia joined me in bed," Fran couldn't help but brag. "I don't think she could resist my charms. Actually, I didn't get much rest. She's quite an energetic girl, isn't she? Not that you would know. She told me the two of you had never got it on, poor dope that you are. You don't know what you've been missing. Or maybe you're afraid of bedding a woman your own age."

Harry stared fixedly at the swirls in the Formica table top, wishing one of them would turn into a snake and coil itself around Fran's neck.

"Cat got your tongue? I'm not surprised. It's pretty hard to refute the truth, isn't it? Anyway, I suppose I should get dressed and let the day begin."

Harry watched her get up and leave the room. When she was sure she was alone, she picked up a piece of egg and stuffed it into her mouth. It was cold, had the consistency of rubber and tasted as burnt as it looked. She swallowed it anyway, certain that it was going to sit undigested in her stomach all day long. She hoped it would do the same in Fran's.

"What's that you're eating? Eggs?" Celia asked.

"They're burnt," Harry said.

Celia sat down and glanced distastefully at Fran's abandoned plate. "How'd you manage that?"

"Fran cooked them, not me," Harry responded.

"Oh."

"Did Mandy ever find you?"

"She busted in on Fran and me this morning, and you should have heard what she said."

"No, thanks."

"I don't blame you," Celia remarked. "Why don't we see if there are more eggs in the fridge and scramble up a real breakfast? Once we've eaten something, we can poke around the Castro a little before we go to the Film Festival. I hear that there are a lot of great boutiques and I wouldn't mind doing a little shopping. How about it? Let's do the girlfriend thing for a while. We haven't done that for a really long time. It'll be fun."

"I've already had breakfast," Harry lied again. Actually, she had lost her appetite watching Fran eat those lousy scrambled eggs and listening to her pompous blather. And she felt annoyed with Celia, irritated by her show of bad taste in choosing to have an affair with a woman like Fran. "Another time, though. Definitely."

"Fine, then. I'll see you later."

Harry left the house and walked to Castro Street. She paused on the corner and consulted her Film Festival schedule to see what was next. Unfortunately, she had missed the beginning of most of the afternoon screenings and had no desire to see the last half of any of the films listed. The next movie which looked interesting was entitled *Blueberries*. It was being screened at six in one of the smaller theatres. She searched for a description of *Blueberries* in her program, but all it said was "a lesbian potpourri that will stimulate every woman's imagination."

Fine, she thought. She was ready to be stimulated, but only after she had been fed. It was early, so she would have time to eat a decent meal before the movie began. She stuffed her program into her pocket and walked along Castro, squinting in the bright sunshine. It was marvellous to encounter throngs of gay men and lesbians parading on the sidewalk, but once she joined them, she felt lonely. She regretted having spurned Celia's offer to go shopping. In this gayest of all cities, it didn't feel right to be alone. Perhaps she should call Raven; maybe they could see *Blueberries* together and go on from there. Harry side-stepped a group of leathermen and entered a restaurant, wiping a tear from her cheek.

"Would you like a window seat?" a nose-ringed waitress asked. Her head was shaved except for a ponytail of thick brown hair.

"No," Harry snuffled.

The waitress inspected her and frowned.

"Some of those movies are too sad for words," Harry said.

"Oh, yeah. Okay." The waitress nodded and led her to a narrow booth at the back of the restaurant. It was off the kitchen, and the prevailing odour was of grease. "Do you know what you want?"

Harry glanced at the menu and ordered a double burger with the works, french fries and coffee. She should have unearthed a vegetarian restaurant and had salad or quiche or a veggie burger with celery, carrot and red- and green-pepper strips with low-cal dip on the side and a mango shake. Funny how misery loves fat and carbohydrates, she thought.

"Have you got a phone?"

"Back by the washrooms."

Harry got up and retrieved Raven's card from her pocket. She fed a quarter into the pay phone and dialled, her heart sinking when it rang five times. When Raven finally picked up the receiver and said "Hello," Harry had to take a deep breath before she could reply.

"Hi," she said, annoyed when her voice squeaked. She cleared her throat and continued. "It's Harriet Hubbley. I'm going to *Blueberries* tonight. Want to join me?"

"I'd love to, but I hear it's sold out."

"Oh."

"Never mind, though," Raven said. "I'll see what I can do."

Harry replaced the receiver and returned to her booth. The waitress carelessly plopped a cup of coffee down on the table and coffee slopped over the side. Harry mopped it up with a napkin, added two-percent milk and artificial sugar and took a sip. It was delicious. By the time her burger and chips came, she had finished it.

"Want a refill?" the waitress asked.

"Yes, thanks."

Harry was so ravenous that she would have eaten it anyway, but luckily the burger was juicy, the bun was crisply toasted, and the fries were thin, crunchy and lightly sprinkled with salt, just how she liked them. She cleaned off her plate and washed down the last mouthful of her burger with her third cup of coffee. Now *that* was delicious, she thought, tossing her napkin on her plate. And she still had twenty minutes to get to the theatre.

"Going to *Blueberries*?" The waitress finished writing up Harry's bill, tore it from her book and placed it on the table.

"Yes. How'd you know?"

The waitress snorted. "Hon, who *isn't* going to *Blueberries*? I'd sure be there if I didn't have to work. Look, if you ask me, they should've put it in the Castro or the Roxie and not in that excuse for a theatre a couple blocks over. It's sold out, and a lot of people are royally pissed that they couldn't get tickets."

"Is that so?" Harry paid the bill and left, worried that Raven wouldn't be able to purchase a ticket. The theatre wasn't far, but there was a line-up. She got in line and stuffed her hands in her pockets, stifling a greasy burp as she perused the crowd without seeing anyone she knew. There were far more women than men, and most of them were young.

Just as Harry reached the entrance, Raven rushed up and kissed her on the cheek. "I was hoping to see you before the movie started," Raven said. She was dressed in black tights, a leather mini-skirt and a crocheted singlet which exposed her black bra and her remarkably trim midriff. "What a circus! I had to buy a ticket from a scalper, so we probably won't be able to sit together," Raven said, following Harry inside. "Tickets are assigned by seat number, and I'm in the back of beyond."

The usher gave Harry's ticket a cursory glance. "Upstairs to your right. First row. And you, you're on the same side but in the last row," he added, pointing at Raven.

"I told you." Raven sighed. "Lucky you; I hear that this is one hot movie."

Hot? That was news to Harry.

The lights dimmed as they climbed the only staircase to the balcony. It was in the centre of the theatre and was surprisingly narrow. Raven's hand touched Harry's waist, impeding her progress.

"We haven't even had time to say hello," Raven whispered.

Suddenly Harry was in Raven's arms, breathing in her perfume. It was sweet and sultry at the same time, like heavy incense. Young women were so thin, she thought absently, running her hands down Raven's sides. Their open-mouthed kiss was like an electric shock, and the taste of her lipstick made Harry tremble.

"You're blocking the way," someone complained.

Harry jumped back.

"I'll see you later," Raven whispered, rushing past her.

Harry shrank against the wall as several people went by. She climbed the stairs, felt for the railing and blundered into the first row, tripping over feet until she found an empty seat.

"Pst! PST!"

Harry craned her neck and saw Celia waving at her from the other end of the row. She was sitting next to Fran and Richie. Harry waved back.

"Your seat's next to mine, but somebody took it," Celia called.

Since she had somewhere to sit, Harry gave Celia a shrug and turned her attention to the screen. The movie was just starting. It was in black and white and the track was grainy. Another bloody art film, she thought disparagingly. She closed her eyes and licked her lips. When she tasted Raven's lipstick, she began shivering again. The feeling was different, without remorse, because she wasn't in a relationship any more. Whenever she had strayed from Judy, she had felt guilty, even when she wasn't doing anything her lover wasn't already doing. Monogamy was supposed to be just that, she thought, and two wrongs hadn't made it right.

But while her body ached for Raven, she couldn't stop her heart from yearning for Judy. She didn't think she would ever understand how things had fallen apart after twelve years. That was something that happened to other couples, not to them. She and Judy had built their relationship on trust and mutual respect, love and sexual attraction, and it was supposed to last a lifetime. When had it all come undone? Perhaps it wouldn't have ended had Harry been able to accept Judy's desire for an open relationship. But it didn't matter now; it was over.

But wait, what was that up there on the screen? A vulva? And a dildo? And in living colour, yet. Harry blushed in the dark and looked around, but everyone's attention was riveted to the screen. The dildo and vulva came together, and Harry's mouth dropped open. She was watching an erotic lesbian video in public. The dildo seemed to grow and fingers intruded. Harry remembered to breathe but was afraid to move.

"What the hell?" the stranger to her left muttered, standing up. "Did you see that?"

"What?" Harry tore her eyes away from the screen.

"I think somebody fell over the railing," she replied.

A woman screamed. The screen went blank and the lights suddenly came on, blinding everyone.

6

"**W**hat do you mean, do I know Fran Matthews?" Harry asked. She retrieved her driver's licence from the uniformed police officer and returned it to her wallet.

"I mean, did you know her?" he insisted.

"Actually, I'm staying at her house," Harry replied, wondering why she was being questioned in this manner. Had the stranger sitting next to her been right? Had someone really fallen over the railing?

The police officer turned to a middle-aged man in a nondescript suit. "She knew Matthews. She's staying at her house."

"Do you live in the San Francisco area?" the plain-clothes cop asked.

"No. I drove down from Vancouver with some friends, but I'm actually from Montreal."

"You're a Canadian, then."

"That's right."

"Where were you sitting?"

"In the balcony."

"Which row?"

"The first."

"Near Ms. Matthews?"

"No, at other end of the row, nearly. Look, what's wrong?"

"I'm sorry to have to tell you this, but Fran Matthews is dead," the detective said, even though he didn't look the least bit sorry.

"What?" Harry's breath caught in her throat.

"She's dead, ma'am. She went over the railing and landed hard. Look, I'd appreciate it if you'd wait with the others. I want to have a word with everyone who was sitting in the balcony."

"Where's the family?" Harry asked.

"Her brother, you mean? In the office."

"Can I see him?"

"Certainly."

The uniformed police officer led her through the crowded lobby and ushered her into a room. The smell of stale popcorn and the sharp odour of roach spray couldn't disguise the musty reek emanating from the carpet and the tatty sofa.

"Harry!" Richie exclaimed, rushing toward her.

"Richie — I'm so sorry," Harry said, grasping his hands.

"They said that she fell over the railing," Richie said. He looked confused, apprehensive.

"How could she do something like that?" Celia groaned.

"I don't know," Harry said. She wanted to sit down, but the sofa looked filthy, possibly infested with vermin. Richie was flushed; Buck's hand rested lightly on his shoulder as if to steady him. Celia grimaced and plucked at Harry's jacket. She seemed excited, as if she was exhilarated by sudden death. Mandy sulked in a corner, but to Harry's relief, she and Celia were ignoring each other.

"She must have been standing up and leaning over the railing," Harry said, putting her arm around Richie. He was trembling.

"Come on, Rich, let's sit down," Buck said.

Harry watched Buck lead his distraught lover to the grimy sofa, sit on it and pull Richie down after him. She thought about the movie and the torrid sex scene which had unfolded, larger than life, on the screen. Why would Fran stand up at that particular moment?

The door opened and Raven walked in. Harry was about to approach her when several police officers entered the room. They were followed by a silent, subdued-looking group of young people, mainly women, who, for the most part, slumped against the dingy walls. Every single one of them looked as if she wanted to be anywhere but there.

"I wonder who they are?" Celia asked in a low voice.

"Probably the other people who were sitting in the balcony," suggested Harry. "Those the police could round up, that is."

"We should have been smart and taken off before the cops arrived," Celia said.

"But we were there," Harry protested. "And we knew Fran."

"Oh, Harry, sometimes you're so naïve."

"Excuse me, ladies and gentlemen," the plain-clothes police officer interrupted. "I'm Detective Manley from the San Francisco Police Department and I'd like to thank you for being so patient. As you likely know by now, Ms. Fran Matthews fell to her death from the balcony about a half an hour into the screening of a film named *Blueberries*. We've asked everyone who was seated in the balcony to remain behind. Now, did anyone see anything that could help us determine what happened?" The detective flipped open a tattered notebook, his pen poised over an empty page.

No one said a word.

"Come, now, someone must have seen something," the detective encouraged them. "Who was sitting directly beside her?"

"Well, I suppose I was," Celia said reluctantly. "She wanted the aisle seat so she could stretch her legs. But I wasn't there when it happened. We'd had a few drinks before the movie. I was just coming back from the ladies room when the lights went on."

"Where were you, precisely?"

"On the stairs to the balcony."

"Near the first row?"

"More or less."

"So you weren't that far from her."

"I suppose not."

The detective waited expectantly, but Celia didn't say anything else.

"Do you mean that you saw nothing?"

"It was dark and I was in a hurry. I didn't want to miss much, because the film was so — er — interesting."

Celia's choice of words provoked subdued laughter, although it did nothing to decrease the tension in the room.

"Pornographic, you mean?" The detective's tone was cool.

"*Blueberries* is a prime example of lesbian erotica, about which there is nothing unnatural," Raven said, enunciating slowly and precisely so that the detective would know she was throwing her words in his face and that she didn't care whether he chose to eat them or spit them back at her.

There was a moment of strained silence. Then a woman slouched against the back wall snickered and everyone relaxed.

"Didn't anyone notice anything?" the detective asked. "Who was sitting behind Ms. Matthews?"

"I was in the aisle seat in the second row." A middle-aged butch came forward. She was wearing blue jeans and a white tee-shirt and she had an arm around the shoulders of a younger woman with sallow skin and faded blonde hair. "But we didn't see a thing. We were kind of busy at that particular moment."

"Were they *doing* it right there in the theatre?" Celia whispered. "Imagine, if I'd been in my seat and happened to look over my shoulder, I would have seen them in action."

"It couldn't have been any more explicit than what was on the screen," Harry said.

"Spoilsport," Celia griped.

"Anyway, I looked up when somebody screamed, but she was gone by then," the butch said with a shrug of her shoulders.

"This is pointless," Celia protested. "It was an accident. Fran slipped or lost her balance and fell off the balcony, so why are you holding us here as if we'd committed a crime? This is very painful for her brother and the rest of us who knew her well. I can't imagine how you can be so insensitive."

There was a stirring and a rumbling, to which the detective responded by saying, "Of course you can go, all of you, but if anyone thinks of anything important, please give me a call."

Harry watched Raven leave the room. She was considering going after her when Buck and Richie rose from the sofa and walked over.

"Let's get out of here," Buck said. He stuck a cigarette between his lips and lit it in contravention of a multitude of *No Smoking* signs. Celia grasped Harry's arm as they crossed the carpeted lobby and left the theatre. It was dark outside, but the sidewalk was teeming with people.

"It's good to breathe fresh air again," Harry commented.

"I feel contaminated, somehow," Celia said. "That room was so grungy."

"Maybe we should go back to the house and change," Harry suggested. "Good lord, has anyone got a key to Fran's house?"

"I've got one," Richie said.

"Me too," added Celia.

"But I don't want to go back right away," Richie said.

"Then why don't we go somewhere for coffee?" Buck suggested.

"That sounds good," agreed Celia.

"I still can't believe she's dead," Richie said.

Harry reached out and squeezed his arm. "It's going to take a while for it to sink in. Let's walk over to Castro."

Poor Fran, dying in such a meaningless way, Harry thought as they made their way through the crowded streets. She felt as if she was reliving Barb's death all over again, although Barb had been murdered rather than falling victim to an accident.

"Let's go in here," Buck said, stopping at the first restaurant they came to.

"But it's so packed," Celia said plaintively.

"They're *all* crowded," Harry said. "It's that time of night."

"Don't argue," Richie snapped. "Let's just go in."

"Sorry," Harry muttered.

Celia looked chagrined, although her expression soon turned to exasperation when Mandy Perkins emerged from the crowd.

"Celia, can I talk to you? In private?"

"I suppose so," Celia responded rather gracelessly.

"Why don't we get a table and you can join us when you're ready?" Buck suggested.

"Fine."

Harry watched Buck and Richie enter the restaurant. "I think I'll join them," she said, not the least bit interested in Celia and Mandy's on-again, off-again relationship. She went into the restaurant, the smell of good food assaulting her nostrils.

An effeminate waiter led them to a table which a busboy was still clearing. The tables were tiny and close together, but at least theirs was near an open window.

"We'll just have coffee," Buck said once they were seated.

The waiter nodded and left.

Poor Richie, Harry mused. Fran had been a good ten years older than him and they hadn't lived in the same country since Richie was an adolescent. But losing *anyone* you loved was devastating, especially a family member. Tears welled up in Harry's eyes. She bit her upper lip and perused the crowded room until the waiter returned with their coffee.

"I keep expecting Fran to walk in, order a jug of sangria, put a straw in it and suck it up like it was Coke," Richie said. "Then she'd spend the rest of the evening claiming that the sangria had been watered down, that it contained far too much sugar and that the fruit in the bottom of the jug was stale. She'd work herself into a frenzy and drive the waiter nuts trying to satisfy her demands. When he finally had the nerve to put the bill on the table, she'd tell him in no uncertain terms that the paucity of the service had been matched only by the tastelessness of the food and that, not only wasn't she going to pay for the sangria, she was also not intending to leave him a tip."

Buck gave a curt laugh of recognition.

Richie slumped in his chair. "It's so absurd. How could she die like that? She was always so in control of everything."

"Did either of you see what happened?" Harry added milk and sugar to her coffee and took a sip. It was strong but good.

"No. I was sitting a couple of seats over from Fran, next to Celia, actually, but I was looking straight ahead at the screen, not sideways," Richie said.

"I must have climbed over Fran, Celia and you on my way to my seat, but it was dark when I came in. The movie was just about to begin and I was looking down, trying not to trip over anyone's feet." Harry didn't mention how flustered she had been from Raven's kiss, how the taste of lipstick had intoxicated her and made her oblivious to her surroundings. That seemed irrelevant now.

"The balcony rail wasn't all that high, was it?" Richie commented.

"People in the first row have to be able to see over it," Buck reminded him.

"That's true. But I didn't notice what happened to Fran until the lights came on." Richie sighed. "Isn't that dumb?"

"Not really," Harry said. "Not if you were watching the movie."

"Yeah. I guess," Richie said. He sounded doubtful, guilty, as if he might have been able to save his sister had he been monitoring her movements.

"I didn't see anything either," Buck added, lighting a cigarette. "I was in the second row, next to those two women who were making out. It wasn't all that bad, you know. As far as I could tell, they were just necking."

"You didn't see Fran get up?" Harry asked.

"No. Do you really want to know the truth? I wasn't really watching the movie," Buck confessed. "I'm not a film buff, not like Richie. And the first part of that movie was as boring as hell. I had just closed my eyes and drifted off when someone downstairs screamed and the lights came on."

The waiter hurried over. "More coffee?"

"Yes, thanks," Buck replied.

"He sure earns his pay," Harry mused after he had refilled their cups and rushed off.

"I hope Celia isn't going to be annoyed that we ordered," Richie said.

"I wouldn't worry about that. She and Mandy probably went off somewhere quiet to talk," Harry said. "I don't suppose it's going to be easy for them to work things out."

"I think you're right," agreed Buck. "Mandy is too timid. Celia means well, but she's a smart woman, and she needs a little intellectual stimulation in her life. She needs the challenge that a woman with a strong personality would provide. Sometimes I think Mandy brings out the worst in her. If she would just show a little spunk, Celia might stay interested in her for more than five minutes at a time instead of hopping into bed whenever an attractive woman comes along. Mandy sure gets jealous, though. She might act like a wimp, but she's got a formidable temper. Unfortunately, Celia ignores her, even when she's throwing a temper tantrum, because she knows that Mandy's bark is worse than her bite."

"People are who they are," Harry said, thinking of herself and Judy.

"Don't be so fatalistic," Buck admonished her. "People can change."

"Unfortunately, that's true," Harry nodded. But they generally changed for the worse and then walked out, disappeared or died. "So nobody saw Fran fall," she said, changing the subject.

"It appears not," replied Buck. "Maybe she got up to go to the bathroom and lost her balance. She was a heavy woman, after all, and you heard Celia say that they'd had a couple of drinks before the movie."

"I wonder how often people fall off balconies?" Harry mused.

"It does occur, at least once in a while," Buck said. "I've read stories in the newspapers about people tumbling over the railing at rock concerts in stadiums and arenas. But I don't remember that happening to anyone in a movie theatre."

What if it hadn't been an accident? Harry looked at Buck, who was sipping his coffee, and then at Richie, who was staring out the window, a vacant expression on his face. That such a stupid mishap had occurred was appalling. But it would be even more dreadful if Fran had received a little assistance in her fatal journey over the railing.

Harry was in a theatre watching an art film. The butch who had been sitting behind Fran was kissing her girlfriend. Harry was sitting beside Fran, who suddenly sighed, rolled her eyes and said, "It's boring, isn't it? They're not even particularly good-looking or skilled kissers, and I don't think they're ever going to take off their clothes. If this is what passes for lesbian erotica these days, count me out. I was doing better than that before I turned fourteen. Why don't we create a little excitement? Come on, follow me."

"What are you doing?" Harry protested as Fran climbed up on the railing.

"I've always wanted to walk the tightrope." Fran laughed.

"Hey — I can't see — get down off there," Celia shouted.

"I thought you were in the bathroom," Harry said.

"I am, stupid," Celia retorted.

"We'd better get her down before she falls," Buck said.

"My big sister won't fall — she's too stubborn to die, ever," Richie said.

Harry stood up and reached for Fran. Her fingers brushed the rough denim of Fran's jeans just as Fran tilted forward. When she swayed back toward Harry for a moment, Harry's hand clutched Fran's thigh, but her jeans were too tight to get a good hold on them.

"Get her! She's going over!" Richie shouted.

Empty hands circled the air as Fran slowly fell forward and executed a perfect swan dive. Harry stared over the railing at the body splayed on the floor below. Fran's head was resting at an unnatural angle and one of her legs was twisted under her. As Harry stared at her lifeless body, Fran suddenly sat up and pointed toward the balcony.

"You!" she shouted. "It was you!"

Harry turned around to see whom Fran was pointing at, but no one was there.

When a woman screamed and the lights came on, Harry woke up to discover that someone was climbing into bed with her.

"You're soaked with sweat," Raven whispered.

"I was dreaming about Fran. It was a nightmare." Harry had fallen asleep with the desk lamp on. She glanced at her travel clock and saw that it was just after one. She sat up, smoothed out the dishevelled covers, and then reached out and turned off the lamp. "What are you doing here?"

"I didn't feel like being alone," Raven whispered. "And I want you."

That much was evident, Harry thought as Raven's fingertips brushed her nipples. She reached up and grasped Raven's bare shoulders to steady herself, even though she was lying down. The touch of Raven's skin ignited a flashfire that turned Harry's flesh to burning cinders and emptied her mind of both questions and misgivings.

"Just a minute," she gasped.

"What?" Raven moaned.

"I have to find my gloves."

"You're right. I've got a couple of dental dams somewhere here."

Moments later, they were in each other's arms again. Their arousal was swift, their lovemaking rapid. Harry felt herself floating; the intensity of her passion surprised her.

"Stay with me, Harriet," Raven whispered in her ear.

Harry came moments later, and Raven rolled off her body. "That felt good."

"It *was* good," Harry said, her voice husky. She pulled the covers up over her, chilled by the damp night air.

"The fog came in while I was on my way over," Raven said, cuddling against her side.

"It feels damp."

"I find fog incredibly romantic," Raven added.

"Mysterious."

"Slippery."

"What are you doing?" Harry laughed, moving away.

"Can't you tell?"

Indeed. This time Harry took the lead, rising over Raven, slowly bringing the younger woman close to orgasm and then taking her back until it was impossible for either of them to retreat one more time. It was a game she and Judy had played, although Judy was the last person she wanted to think about right now. She let herself come, her powerful orgasm surging in tandem with Raven's. When she slumped on Raven's body, her muscles were trembling.

"How many times in a row do you think we can do it?" Raven asked.

"It's quality, not quantity, that counts."

"Both is better," Raven asserted, her hands going on the offensive.

Harry laughed, chagrined to hear how breathless she sounded. A thought like that hadn't passed through her mind since she was in her twenties.

Gawd.

"Harriet?"

"Mmm?"

"I saw someone push Fran."

Harry sat up. "You're joking."

"I wouldn't joke about something like that."

"Tell me what happened." Harry got up and turned on the desk lamp. A pile of papers perched precariously on the edge of the desk fell off. She left them on the floor and returned to bed.

"Everyone in my crowd was going to *Blueberries*, but I hadn't bothered to buy a ticket. So, when you called, I had to purchase one from a scalper," Raven said. "Actually, from a sexual point of view, I found the movie rather tame. And from a critical point of view, the attempt to superimpose realistic sex on an art-film format didn't work. It's been done quite a few times, although not the way they tried it. Unfortunately, their technique was too amateurish. The switch from black and white to colour during the erotic scenes was hackneyed, too."

Harry was impressed. "You were able to tell all that during the half-hour the film was showing?"

Raven shrugged. "I go to a lot of films, and I know what I like. I've also read a lot of books on film. Anyway, I was relegated to the back row of the balcony, but I didn't care, especially after you kissed me on the stairs."

What kind of revisionism was this? And so early in their relationship. Raven had kissed her, not the other way around.

"Once I realized that the movie wasn't going to live up to its top billing, I watched the crowd instead. Besides, observing sex on the screen is never as interesting as actually doing it. Sometimes I think that people who like to watch porn aren't getting any sex in their own lives," Raven said.

"Uh-huh."

"You don't agree with me," Raven said, cupping Harry's cheek in her hand.

"I didn't say that." But it was true; Harry thought that Raven's comment was naïve. People, including lesbians, watched porn for a variety of reasons, not just because they were experiencing a sexual drought.

"Don't coddle me, Harriet. I'm not a child."

Damn. That was precisely what she'd been doing.

"I know I'm a lot younger than you," Raven went on. "Or, to put it another way, you're a lot older than me. I'm twenty-five, in case you're wondering, although most people don't think I look that old. But from past experience, I've come to realize that age doesn't mean much. Just because someone's older doesn't mean that they're any better at relationships."

Harry had never spent much time thinking about it, although she had the feeling that this state of affairs was about to change. Raven was a surprisingly articulate young woman. "So what makes you think that someone pushed Fran?"

Raven put a pillow behind her, leaned back and pulled the covers over her breasts. "You don't smoke, do you?"

"No."

"I didn't think so," Raven said. "Neither do I. At least not often. Sometimes I just feel like it, though. But it doesn't matter. Anyway, I was thinking of you and watching people come and go. Then Fran got up and just seemed to stand there. I guess that was why I noticed her. Other people were on the move, but not Fran. I was surprised that no one told her to sit down, actually. She was pretty close to the steps, but she didn't go downstairs."

"Was she waiting for someone?"

"I thought so at the time."

"Did anybody come along?"

"See, that's the problem," Raven said. "Right about then a whole group of people went by. Some of them were coming up the stairs; others were going down. No one stopped, or even slowed down, when they passed Fran, but suddenly, someone seemed to be standing beside her. Then Fran went over the railing."

"What happened to the other person?"

"You might think this is strange, but the person just seemed to disappear," Raven replied.

"Was it a man or a woman?"

"I couldn't tell. The person was shorter than Fran, but most people were."

"I wonder if he or she simply sat down," Harry mused.

"But where? All the seats were taken," Raven objected.

"Not really," Harry said. "Celia was seated next to Fran, and she was on her way up the stairs when Fran fell. Or was pushed. So both Celia's and Fran's seats were empty. And there were likely other unoccupied seats nearby. And the person could have turned around and gone right back down the stairs."

"That would take a lot of nerve," Raven commented. "But I guess murder does."

"You're certain that you saw someone push her?"

"As sure as I could be from where I was sitting."

Harry didn't want to believe it. She'd had enough murder in her life lately, thank you very much. She plumped up her pillow with her fist, propped it against the wall and leaned back. "Are you going to tell the police what you saw?"

"Are you kidding? I don't want to talk to the police," Raven said. "I don't trust them. And if you tell them what I said, I'll deny everything."

"Don't you realize that you might be helping Fran's murderer to escape?"

"But she's dead, isn't she? So what difference does it make?"

Was this a new generation speaking, or just Raven? Harry didn't want to know. "But it does make a difference. People shouldn't get away with murder."

"I won't talk to the police."

Raven looked so stubborn that Harry gave up. For the moment, anyway. "I'm sorry you feel like that." She felt sorry for herself, too. If Raven was opposed to telling the police what she had seen, and if Fran's death hadn't been an accident, then Harry knew that she would have to take it upon herself to discover who had given Fran a helping hand from this world into the next.

"I hate depressing discussions in the middle of the night," Raven said.

So did Harry. Especially when they revolved around murder. Raven reached under the covers to touch her, and even though she was well aware that Raven was changing the subject, she soon found it impossible to concentrate on anything other than her growing arousal.

"I want you," Raven whispered.

Harry set about proving that she felt the same way.

"**H**arriet Hubbley!"

Harry sat up and stared bleary-eyed at Celia, who was standing over her bed with a disgruntled look on her face.

"Hi, Celia." Harry yawned, raising her arms over her head in a prolonged stretch. Then she realized that she was naked and inadvertently exposing her dubious charms to Celia, and that Raven was still in bed beside her. She lowered her arms, and, with as much dignity as she could muster, gathered the sheet around her.

"I'm totally shocked!"

"I don't see why," Harry remarked. "This isn't the first time you've seen me without any clothes on, and I've been known to have lovers."

"But she must be half your age."

"That's my business," Harry retorted, although she was cut to the quick. It was undeniably true that she was much older than Raven, and Harry had certainly thought about it between bouts of lovemaking. But it was another thing entirely to hear it uttered out loud by someone else. "And anyway, what are you doing, barging into my room so early without knocking?"

"I knocked, but there wasn't any answer. Besides, I didn't think you'd be here like this, with *her*," Celia retorted.

"It's my business who I choose to spend my nights with, not yours."

"Girls, girls," Raven mumbled, lifting her head. Her short hair was mussed, making her look younger than she was.

"I am not a *girl*. I am a *woman*," Celia hissed.

"Well, excuse me," Raven said with a snort. "I didn t realize who I was dealing with here."

Since Celia obviously wasn't amused, Harry suppressed a smile. She was about to intervene when Raven rose from the bed and padded across the floor. This in itself would have meant nothing, except for the fact that she was stark naked.

"I'm going to take a shower."

"Fine," Harry said, her mouth suddenly dry. Both she and Celia tracked Raven's progress until she disappeared behind the closed door.

"I hate to admit it, especially to you, but I'm definitely impressed," Celia said.

"I'm kind of impressed myself, actually," Harry admitted.

The two friends looked at each other and burst out laughing.

"Did you spend the night with Mandy?" Harry asked.

Celia nodded. "Actually, yes, but against my better judgment."

"Perhaps it'll work out this time."

"I wish I could be even a little optimistic, but frankly I don't think so," Celia said. "She's the most passive-aggressive person I've ever met, and she's too possessive. Maybe I'm not the world's most generous person — on an emotional level, I mean — but I give what I can. But Mandy always wants more. I know it's impossible to reassure someone who has absolutely no self-confidence, and I always get sucked into these dramatic scenes with her."

"You could choose not to see her," Harry suggested.

"That's easier said than done, since she persists in following me everywhere. She calls my office and says that she's a client with an urgent question, so they tell her where I am. Look how she tracked me here."

"I *was* rather surprised to see her," Harry said.

"Well, I wasn't. It's just par for the course," Celia said. "And it's always the same. She hangs around and begs until I give in. Then she talks and talks and talks. When she sees that I'm not about to change my mind about our relationship, she begins crying. I start feeling guilty, so I give her a hug, and the next thing you know we're in bed together and the cycle starts all over again. Honestly, Harry, she's so jealous that she just sucks the life out of me."

"That's hard," Harry sympathized. "But if you don't want to be with her, you have to put your foot down."

"I wish it was that easy." Celia sighed. "But that's my problem, not yours."

"Listen, why did you leave during that erotic scene in *Blueberries*?" asked Harry, deciding that there was no time like the present to start interrogating people who were there when Fran died.

"Like I said, I had to pee," Celia answered, looking puzzled. "What difference does it make, anyway?"

"Oh, you know me — always curious. And it occurred to me that maybe you were meeting someone in the lobby."

"Who on earth would I be meeting? Everyone was riveted to that damn screen."

But from what Harry had learned, hardly anyone had watched the movie. Buck was taking an early-evening siesta, Raven was bored and scrutinizing the crowd rather than the screen, and Celia was responding to a call of nature. And if Raven's description of the crucial moments before Fran's death were correct, Fran had been waiting for someone. Of their immediate entourage, Richie and Harry were the only ones actually paying attention to the movie.

"Did Mandy enjoy the film?"

"What? Why are you so intent on making conversation?"

"I'm just curious."

"Look, Harry, I'm not sure what you're up to, but there's something I have to say to you. Be careful. Don't be a fool about Raven. She's from a whole other world, and she's young. Enjoy yourself, but don't get serious. You always did have a tendency toward puritanism, but you don't have to fall in love with every woman who gives you an orgasm," Celia pontificated.

"I know that, Celia. Now, what aren't you telling me?"

Celia blinked. "How do you manage to make me feel so darn guilty when I lie to you? Oh, never mind. I really did have to go to the bathroom, so that part of it is true. But Fran was supposed to meet me in the lobby. I waited for a while and then started up the stairs to see where she was. That was when someone screamed and the lights came on."

"So you were planning to skip out early."

"Yes. I didn't want Mandy to make a scene or follow us."

No wonder Mandy didn't trust her, Harry mused. It was a shame that their relationship had come to that.

"I know it seems devious," Celia said.

"It *is* devious. Why bother to keep stringing her along while you date other women? How do you think Mandy feels when she finds out you're seeing someone else? Or when she walks in on you when you're in bed with another lover?"

"It's not my fault that she won't leave me alone," Celia said stubbornly. "Look, I don't want to spend the rest of my life explaining myself to her."

"If you'd stop sleeping with her, perhaps she'd finally believe that you aren't interested in her any more," Harry remarked dryly.

"I'm a bloody coward, that's all. Look, Fran and I had the hots for each other. You of all people should understand what I'm talking about, what with that young thing spending last night in your bed."

"My name is Raven Stone," the young thing said. She was standing inside the doorway with a tattered bath towel wrapped around the essentials. Raven walked toward them, casually removing the towel and draping it over the steno chair that was pushed into the desk. The beauty of her body took Harry's breath away. "My clothes must be here somewhere. I've got to get to work. I've got a short shift this morning."

"What do you do?" Harry asked as Raven stepped into her briefs and then her black tights.

"I'm a waitress at this place near Union Square," Raven replied. "Square crowd, but heavy tippers. Mostly businessmen who work in the area and straight tourists with money to burn." She bent over and kissed Harry, a short but open-mouthed kiss that made Harry tingle inside. "I'll call you," Raven said abruptly. Then she left.

"A *waitress*?"

"At least she's got a job. So many of her generation don't. And don't start with your sarcastic comments," Harry warned Celia.

"Fine. Date who you like."

"Whom."

"And be a bitch about it. I'm going out," Celia announced, hoisting the purse over her shoulder.

"Where?"

"To a movie."

Harry had completely forgotten about the Film Festival. "Aren't you just a little upset about Fran's death?"

"Of course I'm upset, what do you think? That's why I'm going to the movie, to keep myself busy. I was attracted to Fran, after all, or I wouldn't have gone to bed with her. But it wasn't as though she was the love of my life, so I don't see why I should pretend that I'm distraught," Celia said, sounding defensive. "The truth is, we hardly knew each other."

"You were lovers, though."

"I've had a lot of lovers, Harry. Maybe you think I'm being insensitive, but I'm no longer inclined to collapse every time a relationship breaks up. And Fran's not the first women I've known who died. Face it, we're all getting older, and some of our former lovers are going to die. I feel sorry she's dead — I would never wish it on anybody — but life goes on. *My* life goes on. Anyway, what do you want me to do? Stop everything and go into mourning?"

Harry knew that she would. She had when Barb died, just as she had when Judy broke up with her.

"Ta-ta. Don't wait up. And, Harry, *carpe diem*, for god's sake," Celia said as she left.

Carpe diem yourself, Harry thought with a yawn. She slid into bed, pulled the covers up to her chin and closed her eyes. She drifted off into sleep thinking of Raven. When she woke up, it was nearly noon.

If she was not only going to seize the day but also track down a killer, then she'd better get out of bed, Harry reflected. The study looked as if a cyclone had passed through on its way to the Pacific Ocean, but she ignored the papers scattered on the floor and the clothes strewn over every surface and went into the bathroom. The lack of a hostess was already evident, for there were no clean towels and she couldn't find a roll of toilet paper anywhere. She used tissue instead, and then retrieved Raven's soggy towel from the steno chair.

Harry washed the sweat of a night of lovemaking from her body and mused about the task ahead of her. It wasn't going to be easy to find out whether Fran had been murdered and, if so, who had killed her. The dead woman had lived in San Francisco for a long time, and she probably had a large number of friends and acquaintances. The killer could be someone Harry didn't know, like one of Fran's former lovers or an offended friend or one of the enemies she had doubtlessly made in her fifty-three years of life. There were bound to be a lot of them, especially with her attitude. Or her murder could have been motivated by homophobia, although it was unclear to Harry why a rabid heterosexual would attend a gay and lesbian film festival. If it had been a random act of violence, an impetuous shove by a stranger walking past, then neither Harry nor the police would be likely to discover who did it.

Harry found it hard to seize the day when it involved suspecting a woman who had kindled the kind of passion she hadn't felt in years. But Fran and Raven had been lovers and Raven had been in the theatre when Fran was killed, so Harry had to face it: Raven was a suspect. Maybe she had been angry that Fran had ended their relationship. Perhaps she was jealous about Fran's relationships with Moira, and now Celia. And, knowing Fran, there had likely been other women in between. But if she had killed Fran, why had Raven mentioned having seen someone push her over the railing, especially since everyone, including the police, thought it was an accident? Harry sighed and turned off the shower. Distrusting her lovers tied her in knots. But life was like that, especially hers. If there was a case of suspicious death in the neighbourhood, chances were that she was either a suspect or had recent carnal knowledge of one or more of the suspects. At least she had resisted Celia's advances, although that hadn't been difficult. Some women were never meant to be lovers, possibly because they knew each other too well. A case of familiarity breeding contempt.

Still, her old pal Celia was a suspect. Perhaps Celia had done something quite out of character and had fallen in love with Fran. But why, then, would Celia kill her? Because she was jealous of Fran's other lovers? But that didn't make sense; Celia's lovers often had other lovers, as did Celia. Perhaps her feelings about Fran were different. Maybe she wanted Fran all to herself. Or perhaps Celia had confessed how she felt and Fran hadn't taken her seriously. What if Fran had laughed at her? Could Celia have been spiteful enough to push Fran over the railing?

And what about Richie and Buck? Perhaps Fran had discovered something one of them wanted kept secret and had threatened them with disclosure. Richie might also have an additional motive, depending on whether he thought he was going to inherit Fran's estate. A house in the Castro District would likely be worth a small fortune.

Or had Mandy, who was extremely possessive of Celia, reacted to Celia's affair with Fran by committing murder? And then there was Moira, Fran's ex-lover, and even Fran's ex-husband. What part had they played in this equation? There was so much she didn't know, Harry reflected as she stepped out of the tub. She wrapped Raven's damp towel around her and bent down to turn off the shower.

Just at that moment there was a knock on the bathroom door.

"Harry," Celia called. "That damn cop is here, and he's asking all sorts of foolish questions. He's waiting for you downstairs."

"I'll be there in a minute." As Harry combed her wet hair, she could hear the snick of Celia's heels on the hardwood floor. She darted from the bathroom to the study and dressed swiftly in her black jeans, a white tee-shirt and her black jacket. Her heart was thumping rapidly as she rushed down the stairs. Were the police merely fishing or had they found another witness to Fran's murder?

"I'm in here," Detective Manley said. "And you're Ms. ... uh ..."

"Hubbley," Harry replied. She had never been in Fran's living room, and she was surprised to see that it was furnished in a more formal style than the rest of the house. She was about to sit on the sofa but didn't when she realized the detective intended to stay on his feet.

"That's right. Ms. Hubbley, from Montreal."

"How can I help you?" Harry leaned against the arm of an upholstered chair and crossed her arms.

"By telling me the truth," the detective replied.

Harry raised her eyebrows. "What makes you think I won't?"

"Everyone has something to hide, especially in this town," he said. "But that's neither here nor there."

Harry would hate to go through life with his attitude. But that was neither here nor there, either.

"Tell me what you know about Fran Matthews," he said when she didn't respond.

"I just met her four days ago," Harry answered.

"You weren't lovers?"

"Certainly not!"

He looked put out. "Celia Roberts was, and the two of you drove down together."

Harry couldn't see what the connection was, but she was beginning to believe that was par for the course with Manley. "How did you find about Celia and Fran?"

"Ms. Roberts told me all about it. In excruciating detail." He sounded tired. Knowing Celia, Harry thought she knew why. Celia took great pleasure in giving straight people blow-by-blow descriptions of her sexual escapades, and the more outrageous they were, the better. "Anyway, tell me what you know about Fran Matthews," he persisted, writing in his notebook.

"She was difficult," Harry said.

He stopped writing and looked at her. "In what way?"

"She was temperamental. And nasty."

The detective frowned and flipped through the pages of his notebook. "Would you say that she was depressed?"

"Who, Fran?" Harry said. "No, just the contrary."

"Then, in your opinion, she was too cheerful?"

What was he implying? Harry was tired of standing, so she perched on the edge of the chair and immediately tumbled backwards, her behind sinking into the soft cushion. So that was why the detective had remained on his feet. She struggled to get up but stopped when she realized how undignified she must look.

"I don't know what you mean," she said. "She seemed to be in a good mood whenever I was with her."

Manley closed his notebook. "Look, either Ms. Matthews fell off the balcony accidentally or she went over it on purpose."

"What?"

"Perhaps she intended to kill herself."

"You think Fran committed suicide?"

"Sometimes people act cheerful after they've made up their minds to end it all."

"And sometimes people act cheerful because they are." But Harry's acerbic wit was evidently lost on the detective. "Besides, vaulting off the balcony in a movie theatre doesn't seem the most dependable way to kill yourself. How could Fran have been certain that she'd die and not just break a few bones or end up with a concussion?"

"There is that," he admitted. "And people who want to jump usually take a flying leap off the Golden Gate Bridge. It's a spectacular way to go, over two hundred and fifty feet down, but, even then, some jumpers survive."

Harry shivered. "To be honest, detective, I don't think that Fran was trying to kill herself."

"You're more than likely right. There was no note, either. It was probably an accident. A strange one, but an accident nonetheless. Still, you'd never believe the weird things people do to kill themselves."

Harry didn't trust herself to speak.

"Celia Roberts mentioned that they'd been drinking before the film, so perhaps Ms. Matthews was tipsy and lost her balance. But

I'll hold off until we get the coroner's report. I also want to have a little chat with her lawyer to see what's in her will," he added. "It wouldn't do to made a decision prematurely, would it?"

"I suppose not," Harry said, mainly because he seemed to expect it of her.

"How long are you going to be here?"

"I'm not sure."

"Perhaps you'd better give me your Canadian address, then."

Harry did.

"Call me if anything comes up," he added, closing his notebook and slipping it into his pocket.

If she was going to tell Detective Manley about what Raven had seen, now would be the appropriate time. Harry didn't like withholding what might be important evidence, but it would sound so lame coming from her. What could she tell him? That this woman I know who wishes to remain anonymous thinks she saw someone give Fran a helping hand over the balcony rail? He would want to know who the anonymous witness was. Or, worse yet, he would believe it was Harry and suspect her of being a meddling neurotic, especially since no one else had come forward with the same information. And what did she know? Nothing. Even Raven wasn't certain what she'd seen.

"That's it, then," the detective said, holding out his hand.

Harry was surprised. She reached up and took it, but instead of shaking her hand, Manley grasped it tight and pulled her from the chair. Harry was completely taken aback. "Why, thanks."

"Don't mention it. I nearly strained a muscle getting out of that miserable excuse for a sofa." A smile lifted the corners of his lips and disappeared so swiftly that Harry wondered whether she had imagined it.

"Thank you for your time," he said.

"You're welcome."

"I'll see myself out."

Harry watched him leave, wondering whether she had misjudged him. Perhaps he was a lot smarter than he acted, like Columbo in the old TV series, who played dumb to trick suspects into letting their guard down. Maybe she had just made a colossal mistake in not telling him what Raven claimed to have seen the evening Fran died.

The house felt empty, but Harry still searched it, knocking on doors and peering into empty rooms. She half-expected to find Richie and Buck in their bedroom or the kitchen, but they weren't. She returned to the study, folded up the sofa bed and put her clothes in her suitcase. She was about to sit down on the sofa when she noticed the papers that had spilled onto the floor earlier that morning. She went down on her hands and knees and retrieved them. A phone bill missing its return envelope; a dunning letter from a major credit-card company; a legal-sized manila envelope which had been torn open, the documents pulled out and then carelessly shoved half back inside. She was about to add it to the pile of bills when she noticed "Last Will and Testament" written on top of the first sheet of paper.

Harry was electrified. She got up so swiftly that she bumped her head on the edge of the desk. Detective Manley had said he was going to check with Fran's lawyer, while all along a copy of her will had been sitting in plain view. The police obviously hadn't bothered to search the house; since they thought Fran had died accidentally, they believed that they had no reason to conduct more than a cursory investigation.

Harry sat on the sofa and pulled the photocopied document from the envelope, glancing up to make sure the door was closed. She didn't feel guilty about going through Fran's private papers, but she didn't want to be caught snooping. She swiftly scanned the will, ignoring the legalese to ferret out the salient points. It soon became evident that Fran hadn't managed to accumulate much in her fifty-three years of life. In addition to her personal possessions, a few antiques and a large number of keepsakes which likely had more sentimental than financial value, her only real asset was her house in the Castro. Harry flipped impatiently to the last page, reading swiftly, and then let the document tumble to her lap, barely crediting what she had read.

What kind of a woman would leave half-shares in her house to two of her ex-lovers, more specifically, to Raven Stone and Moira Chelso? A woman who didn't believe that blood was thicker than water, for one. A woman who thumbed her nose at convention, for another. A woman who liked cosmic jokes, perhaps. Harry picked up the will, turned to the final page again and looked to see when it had been signed. Only two weeks ago, she realized, her heart racing. Motive for murder, or simply coincidence? Determining who had killed Fran would be infinitely more complicated if she had radically changed her will from one version to another. Had Fran updated her will, or just modified it? Was there an earlier will?

Harry sat down in the steno chair and conducted a methodical search of Fran's desk. She started with the drawers, disturbing dozens of pens missing their caps, dusty rubber bands, mounds of paper clips, a rusty pair of scissors, outdated credit cards. She rifled through disorganized files, and when she found nothing of importance, began sifting through the documents on top of the desk. She unearthed receipts, several unpaid bills, letters, empty envelopes, cheque stubs, faculty newsletters and memos from the University of California, articles clipped from newspapers and notes Fran had written to herself, some of them enigmatic, some nonsensical, some even sexually explicit, but no will. She piled everything in three tidy stacks on the back of the desk and, for the moment, gave up. If Fran had kept a copy of her previous will at home, she must have destroyed it once she signed the new one. Or maybe she hadn't made a will before, although Harry couldn't quite believe that. Nearly everyone her age had a will.

Harry stuffed the will back into the envelope and dropped it on top of one of the piles on the desk. Then, reconsidering, she shoved it between several file folders. Not that anyone would come looking for it, she mused as she considered the unsavoury possibilities raised by her accidental discovery. Since Fran had likely told them what she intended, Raven and Moira Chelso had suddenly catapulted to the top of her list of suspects. And any of the people staying in the house could have gone into Fran's study when Harry was out and searched her desk, which meant that Celia, Richie and

Buck had had the opportunity to read the will. Neither could she discount Raven, who had spent last night in the study with her. Not only that, Raven had a set of keys. Harry wondered whether Fran had also forgotten to ask Moira Chelso to return hers once they broke up. Even Mandy could have found a way into the house, although her presence might have raised a few eyebrows. Actually, it was the same for Moira; anyone who discovered her snooping around would have wondered what she was doing there.

It was time to stop thinking and get cracking, Harry thought. Or *carpe diem*, as Celia had exhorted. She momentarily considered calling Detective Manley and telling him about Fran's will, but then decided not to bother. Manley had said he intended to contact Fran's lawyer today, so he'd have his own copy soon enough. And she still wasn't ready to inform him of Raven's suspicions. She retrieved Fran's will from where she had hidden it and stuffed it behind the dirty laundry in the outside pocket of her suitcase. Then she went downstairs. It was nearly noon, and she was starving. She decided to eat brunch out and then begin her investigation in earnest, tracking down and questioning potential suspects. If she waited passively for her housemates to turn up, she would soon begin to mope, but if she went out, she was bound to run into Richie, Buck, Celia, Mandy or Raven in one of the main theatres or on Castro Street. She made sure that her wallet was tucked in her inside jacket pocket and left, locking the front door with a key Richie had given her.

Suddenly a slender woman with long, thin black hair rushed up the stairs and approached her.

"Who are you?" she asked Harry, her voice gruff with distrust. "And what are you doing in this house?"

"I'm staying here," Harry responded, backing away from the woman's glare, not to mention her stale smell. The woman looked so affronted that Harry glanced past her to make sure that she wasn't alone. The sight of several groups of pedestrians strolling along the sidewalk and numerous people getting in and out of parked cars reassured her.

"Who are you?" Harry asked the older woman.

"Moira Chelso," she replied with great dignity.

Fran's ex-lover, Harry realized. One of her prime suspects.

"Give me the key," Moira demanded.

"What?" Harry instinctively slid the front-door key into her pocket, where it nestled securely behind Raven's now-crumpled card.

"The key," Moira said impatiently. "Give it to me."

"Why?"

"Because I need it to get in."

Did she know what was in Fran's will? Harry wanted to ask, but Moira was obviously furious with the world, which momentarily seemed to have Harry's name written all over it.

"I'm a bit confused, here," Harry said. "Don't you already have a key?"

Moira's expression shifted from outrage to disbelief to uncertainty to deviousness. "I know who you are. You're one of those bitches she was fucking every time she got out of my sight, aren't you?"

Harry stifled a sigh. Moira was obviously teetering on the edge of a violent episode and Harry wanted no part of it. "The first time I met Fran was three days ago," she said, shuffling sideways so that she was no longer trapped between Moira and the front door.

"Give me the key."

"Use your own," Harry said. She skipped down the stairs faster than a commuter navigating subway steps during rush hour and headed toward Castro Street. When she was far enough away to feel safe, she turned around, curious to see whether Moira was going to let herself into the house. To Harry's disappointment, she was slowly walking down the stairs. But that didn't mean Moira didn't have a key. Maybe she just hadn't brought it with her.

"You'll be sorry!" Moira warned in a sing-song voice.

Undoubtedly Harry would, and more than once before her life was over. But not about this.

"I bet you'd be interested in reading what I've got here," Moira shouted, waving a piece of paper at her.

"If it's all that important, leave it in the mailbox," Harry shouted back. It might be another copy of Fran's will, but she simply couldn't deal with Moira in her present state of mind. Harry turned onto Castro Street and lost herself in the crowd. Despite the cool weather, her skin was covered with nervous sweat.

Harry moved to the inside of the sidewalk and leaned against a wall. Moira was obviously unbalanced. Was this her way of mourning Fran, or was she truly deranged? Harry remembered Fran's blunt cheerfulness and thought it not inconceivable that Fran would have been capable of relating to a mentally ill lover. She also recalled Fran's inattention to her charred scrambled eggs and realized that Fran simply might not have noticed a slow and perhaps subtle deterioration in her lover's behaviour. Or perhaps Moira had taken a turn for the worse after Fran had ended their relationship. On the other hand, Fran might have broken up with Moira because she was disturbed. Now that Fran was dead, who really knew? Harry wasn't certain she would get a straight answer from Moira, especially about something like that. All of which meant what? Just because Moira was unbalanced didn't mean that she had murdered Fran, no matter how tempting — and simplistic — it was to think so. The problem was, she would rather suspect Moira than Raven. And while financial gain was a strong motive for committing murder, it wasn't the only one. There was also jealousy, not to mention unrequited lust, the desire for revenge or just plain anger.

Harry's stomach growled, bringing her back to earth. Nourishment first, and then she would attempt to regurgitate what had just happened in a more palatable form. Disgusted with her lousy pun, she slipped into the first restaurant she passed, took a window seat so she could watch the world go by, and resolutely ordered bacon, eggs, toast and coffee. The leather-clad waitress countered with eggs Benedict and espresso. Since it was nearly the same thing, just packaged differently, Harry readily agreed.

"What a coincidence." Buck picked up his bottle of club soda, his pack of cigarettes and lighter and walked over to Harry's table. "Do you mind?"

"Of course not." In fact, she was relieved at how easy it had been to find one of the very people she wanted to question.

Buck slid into the cane-backed chair opposite Harry and leaned his bare elbows on the table. "I figured if I sat here long enough, somebody I knew would walk in."

That had been Harry's idea exactly, but she didn't mention it. "Where's Richie?"

"He said he was going to check out one of the funeral homes in the Castro and then meet me here around lunchtime."

The waitress served Harry's espresso. "Your eggs Benedict will be ready in a couple of minutes."

Harry nodded.

"You look upset," Buck commented.

"I just met Moira Chelso. Why didn't you tell me what she was like?"

He had the good grace to look contrite. "I honestly didn't think about it. And I'm sure Richie didn't either," he replied, tapping the end of an unlit cigarette on the table.

Harry added sugar and drank her espresso. It was hot and strong and sent a spurt of energy through her body. "Do you have any idea why she would want my key to the house?"

Buck snorted. "Who the hell knows? Frankly, she's not all there."

"How long has she been like that?"

"I'm not certain," Buck replied, lighting his cigarette and blowing smoke out the open window. "Fran and Richie weren't particularly close, so she didn't tell him much about her relationships with women, although I got the impression that she had a hell of a lot of them. But from what I gather, her affair with Moira was not particularly successful or long-lived."

The waitress served Harry's eggs Benedict. The food looked delicious.

"I suppose you want me to put this out," Buck grumbled.

"Yes," Harry said as she picked up her knife and fork.

Buck sighed and stubbed his half-smoked cigarette out in the ashtray.

"Did Fran never mentioned that Moira was mentally disturbed?" asked Harry.

"Well, yes, I guess she did. Not to me, but to Richie."

"Is that was why they broke up?" Harry forked another piece of eggs Benedict into her mouth. The eggs were partly runny, exactly how she liked them.

"I suppose so."

"You don't seem to know much about it." Harry gestured to the waitress for another espresso, and Buck pointed to his empty club-soda bottle.

"Look, I told you, Fran and Richie weren't close," Buck said rather defensively. "Anyway, what difference does it make now?"

Harry had no intention of answering that question. Instead, she posed one of her own. "Have you seen Moira since we got here?"

"Sure."

"At the screening of *Blueberries*?"

Buck nodded. "Actually, I was rather surprised she was there."

Harry sat back as the waitress removed her empty plate. She returned seconds later to serve Harry's espresso and Buck's club soda. As soon as she was out of earshot, Harry asked, "Was she acting strange?"

"As crazy as a bedbug," Buck confirmed. "And she didn't smell great, either. I pity the people who were sitting next to her — I bet she was talking to herself during the movie."

"Did you and Richie speak to her that night?"

"No. I mean, why should we have? I'd never met her before, and neither had Richie. Fran pointed her out to us. And, to be honest, after I saw her I wasn't motivated to engage in idle chit-chat."

With such distinct memories of Moira so recently imprinted on her mind, what could Harry do but nod?

"Hey, there's Rich," Buck said, standing up and waving to his lover, who was hovering just inside the door. "Do you want a coffee or a soda?"

"Coffee. Desperately." Richie hurried over to join them, kissed Buck and then sat down. "I'll have café au lait, please," he told the waitress.

"Did you go to the funeral home?" Buck asked.

"Yes," answered Richie. "I told them that we weren't sure when Fran's body was going to be released, but they said that there would be no problem in doing the service on short notice."

"That's good," Buck nodded.

"But listen, I've got great news. I was poking around in Fran's bedroom and found a copy of her will in her bedside table," Richie replied. He pulled a bulky envelope from his jacket pocket and dropped it on the table.

"And?"

"Read it and see." Richie sounded satisfied, which puzzled Harry.

Buck picked up the envelope, opened it and pulled out several folded sheets of paper. He flipped through them quickly and then smiled. "It's what you expected. She left everything to you."

Richie nodded.

"Let me see that," Harry said, her tone sharp.

"Sure," Buck nodded. He handed the will to Harry and then lit a cigarette.

Harry held her breath as she checked the date on Richie's photocopy of the will. Richie's was dated two years ago, which meant that the one she had discovered on Fran's desk bore the more recent date and was undoubtedly Fran's legitimate will.

"I'm afraid I've got bad news for you. There's another will."

"Another will?" Richie looked dumbfounded.

"And it's a lot more recent than the one you have," Harry added.

"What the hell are you talking about?" Buck sounded confused, and Harry didn't blame him.

The waitress chose that particular moment to deposit Richie's café au lait on the table.

"I accidentally came across a copy of Fran's will this morning when I was picking up some papers I'd knocked on the floor," Harry explained as soon as the waitress returned to the bar. "It was dated two weeks ago."

Richie opened two packets of sugar and poured them into his café au lait. "And I suppose you're going to tell me that my name isn't mentioned in a major way in this new will of yours."

"No, it isn't."

Richie looked as if he had been poleaxed.

Buck stared at his lover for a moment and then asked Harry, "Let me have a look at it."

"I haven't got it with me," Harry responded, "but I'll show it to you as soon we get back to the house."

"If you've got it, then the lawyer's got it," Buck said morosely.

"This is unbelievable," Richie muttered.

"I take it you expected to inherit Fran's house," said Harry.

"Well, I *am* her only close relative," Richie replied. "But apparently I wasn't close enough. I hesitate to ask, but I have to know: Who did she leave it to in the end?"

"Look, Celia and Mandy are outside, and Celia's waving at us," Buck interjected. "They've got somebody with them."

Harry stood up and glanced out the window, surprised to see Raven deep in conversation with Celia. Mandy was trailing along behind them like a dog on a leash. What was Raven doing with Celia and Mandy? And what was she so intent on saying to Celia, and with such an earnest expression on her face? Not that Harry was jealous, or anything. Oh, all right, she *was* jealous. And she didn't know to what extent she could trust Raven. She hated to admit how ignoble it felt to be so intimate and yet so remote from her lover. That was what came of jumping into bed with someone she had just met and knew nothing about except that Raven was sensual, uninhibited and ... young. The last was beginning to sound like a dirty word.

"Darlings, how wonderful to see you all," Celia proclaimed as she rushed into the restaurant. She sat in the empty chair on Harry's right, gave her an affectionate peck on the cheek and crossed her shapely legs, which were clad in black leggings.

Hello, Harry thought. She had beheld those legs many times, but rarely had she seen Celia in such an ebullient mood. She obviously had something to celebrate, and all Harry could do was hope it wasn't at her expense.

Raven commandeered the chair to Harry's left. "I missed you," she whispered, kissing Harry on the mouth, nibbling on her lips for a split second.

"Me, too," Harry whispered inanely. There was something about Raven that made her head spin. For one dizzy moment, she wondered whether Raven's lipstick contained a hallucinogenic and then dismissed the thought.

Mandy hovered outside the inner circle and finally filched a chair from the table adjacent to theirs. She insinuated it between Richie and Buck, both of whom scowled at her.

"Harry was just about to tell us whom Fran left the house to," Richie said.

"How does she know?" Celia asked.

"She found Fran's will," Buck replied.

"Fran's *latest* will," added Richie.

"You mean there was more than one?" Celia inquired, looking startled.

"I'll explain later." Richie sounded impatient. "So, Harry, who's the lucky person?"

"There are two of them, actually," Harry stalled, glancing at Raven for help. From the look on Raven's face, it was clear that none was forthcoming. Either she didn't know, or she wasn't telling. "Fran left the house to Raven Stone and Moira Chelso."

"**R**aven Stone? And Moira Chelso?" Richie looked as if he had been kicked in the teeth. He turned to Raven. "She left the house to *you*?"

"Half of it, yes," Raven replied. "Harry, how did you discover what was in Fran's will?"

"She was poking around my sister's desk this morning —"

"I was not poking around," Harry said, interrupting Richie. "Some papers fell on the floor and I picked them up. One of them happened to be Fran's will. How did you find out?"

Raven raised her eyebrows. "Why, Fran told me, of course. And she gave me a copy of the will once it was drawn up." She reached inside her string vest and into the inner pocket of her sleeveless linen top and pulled out several legal-sized sheets of paper that had been folded several times, and handed them to Richie. "Go on, see what it says."

"I don't particularly want to," Richie muttered.

"Me neither," said Buck.

"I'll certainly volunteer," Celia offered.

"I'll read it," Harry hastened to say, taking the will from Raven. Celia's theatrical presentation of its contents would do nothing but raise the level of tension around the table. "Fran lists quite a few keepsakes that she wants given to friends. And, Richie, she left some antiques to you, including her kitchen table and chairs, a buffet in the living room, a china cabinet, a couple of dressers, a set of fine china and —"

"I don't give a shit about that," Richie interrupted, his voice harsh.

"It's not my fault that you're only getting the antiques," Raven said to Richie. "Yours, either, actually."

"What the hell do you know about it? My sister left half of her estate to a woman who belongs in a loony bin, not to mention you," Richie said bitterly.

An uncomfortable silence ensued. Celia broke it by glancing at her watch and exclaiming, "Look at the time! I've got a movie starting in a few minutes."

"Let's hit the trail, Rich," Buck said, rising from his chair.

Raven stood up. "I'm off, then. Are you coming, Harry?"

Should she? Did she want to? Harry rose before she had made up her mind. "I'll see you back at the house," she said to Richie and Buck.

"If *she* lets us in," Richie said, gesturing toward Raven.

"Come on, Richie, give her a break," Harry said.

"Why should I?" Richie's tone was so belligerent that Buck lit a cigarette and moved toward the door, leaving his lover standing there alone.

"Look, don't be any more of a jerk than you have to," Raven said sarcastically.

Richie flushed. "Are you finished?"

"Are you?"

"Let's go." Harry grasped Raven's hand and tugged.

Raven went willingly. Harry felt uncomfortable holding hands in the street, but Raven didn't show any signs of letting go, and no one paid any attention to them.

"Do you want to go back to the house?" Raven asked.

"No. Not really." Harry was still trying to digest the fact that Raven had known all along that she was going to inherit half of Fran's estate and that she hadn't told her. What else didn't she know? Was she going to have to decipher Raven's secrets one by one? "Let's go somewhere and have a coffee."

"But everything's so noisy around here," Raven protested. "There are tens of thousands of tourists in town for the Film Festival, not to mention Pride Day celebrations. We'll never be able to carry on a decent conversation in any of these bars or restaurants, not at this time of day. Let's go to the house and make a pot of coffee. We can sit in the kitchen and talk."

"All right," Harry conceded.

Neither of them said anything until they reached the house, although their clasped hands kept their silence from developing into total estrangement.

"Richie is certainly upset," Raven remarked as she unlocked the door.

"He thought he was going to inherit this house. He feels that his sister betrayed him."

"It wouldn't surprise me in the least if she had. Sometimes Fran would give you the shirt off her back, while at other times she was as stingy as hell," Raven said. "She could be kind and understanding, or bitchy and insensitive. She was like a chameleon, although there was one constant — she liked to control things. And people."

"Was she manic-depressive?"

"I don't think so," Raven responded. "She could play people like a virtuoso. That's what she did to me, anyway. And I wouldn't doubt she did the same thing to Moira Chelso."

"Why did you stay with her for two years, then?"

Raven gave Harry an amused look. "Because I was in love with her, silly. And because she was great in bed."

Harry flushed. "What were you and Celia talking about?"

"Nothing much. We just happened to run into each other on the street. I find her amusing. She's such a femme. And so imperious, not to mention impervious."

Harry following Raven along the hall to the kitchen. "And attractive?"

"She is, isn't she?" Raven remarked, giving Harry a mischievous grin.

Harry gave up and sat down at the kitchen table. She watched Raven grind the coffee beans and fill the percolator with distilled water from a jug in the fridge, thinking how comfortable she looked in Fran's kitchen. She certainly knew her way around.

"The coffee will be ready in a few minutes," Raven said. She plugged in the percolator and removed two mugs from the top shelf of the kitchen cupboard. Then she opened the fridge, took out a carton of skim milk and carried it and the mugs to the table. "Harry, you have to stop being such an idiot. I haven't been with Celia. In the biblical sense, I mean."

"But I thought you found her attractive."

"That doesn't mean anything," Raven replied, resting her hand on Harry's knee. "Look around you. There are tens of thousands of attractive lesbians in San Francisco, many of them much more beautiful and interesting than Celia."

They didn't bother to wait for the coffee. Raven took Harry to bed, or perhaps it was the other way around. Neither of them could tell, but it didn't matter. The end result was the same.

A knock on the door woke Harry from a light sleep.

"Don't answer it," Raven said. She clasped her arms around Harry and snuggled closer.

"But what if it's important?" Harry's voice was muffled against Raven's chest. "And I'm awake anyway, so I might as well see who it is."

Raven sighed and moved away.

"Just a minute," Harry shouted.

"It's about time," Richie called back.

Harry reached out and switched on the lamp. She picked up her watch and glanced at it, surprised to see that it was nearly eleven o'clock. She and Raven had slept for most of the evening. She retrieved her jeans from the floor, slid into them, and pulled a tee-shirt over her head. Rarely was she ready to face the world braless, pantyless and barefoot, but what the hell; her sexual life seemed to be regressing to the sixties, so why not the rest of her? If only the flab would recede accordingly.

Raven pulled the covers over her head. "I'll just hide right here, if you don't mind."

"Go back to sleep," Harry said, admiring the shape of her body under the sheet. "I'll be back soon." And this time it would be to ask questions, not to frolic in the hay, Harry resolved. She padded across the carpeted floor and opened the door.

"I need to talk to you," Richie said, his voice low. He craned his thick neck and glanced past her into the bedroom. "Is *she* in there?"

"Raven? Yes." Harry pushed past him and closed the door.

"I'm amazed," he commented.

"Well, keep it to yourself." Harry meant it as a joke, but it didn't quite come out that way.

He grasped her by the hand and said, "Listen, I need your help."

"What for?" Harry would have preferred to freshen up, to pass a washcloth over her face and run a comb through her tousled hair, but Richie hustled her down the hall and past the bathroom before she had the opportunity to break away.

"You'll see," Richie said as they went downstairs.

Buck, Celia, Mandy and Moira Chelso were seated around the kitchen table. The coffee percolator was sitting at one end of the table beside the open carton of skim milk and a cracked china bowl filled with brown sugar. Celia looked petulant, Mandy her usual timid self. Buck was puffing furiously on a cigarette and the ashtray in front of him was full of butts. The room was awash with the fug of cigarette smoke and bad temper.

"She has a copy of the will saying that she inherited half the house," Richie said, pointing at Moira Chelso. "Everybody in the world has a copy of that will except me, but that was my darling sister's way. Give the boy an unpleasant surprise? Why not? It might make him lose his temper, which would be good for a laugh. It's like being haunted from beyond the grave. But that's beside the point. The problem is, Moira says that, since it's her house, she's going to *stay* here."

"And who's to say I can't?" Moira grinned and filched a cigarette from Buck's open pack, glancing at him to see if he was going to protest. Buck ignored her and puffed unperturbedly on his cigarette, although a vein in his forehead was pulsing, making Harry wonder about the tenor of the conversation before she arrived.

"And she's decided that she wants *my* room," Celia sputtered. "I mean, why doesn't she take Fran's if she's so intent on moving in?"

"Because I want your room, that's why." Moira's tone was one of sweet reason. "And it's my house, so I should be able to choose first. If cutie-pie there wants to stay, let her move into our dearly departed Fran's room. It might be haunted, but cutie-pie doesn't look the type to believe in ghosts. You have to have some *imagination* to believe in otherworldly spirits, after all."

"The whole situation is impossible, and I resent being tossed around like a sack of potatoes. It's highly insulting," Celia sputtered. "I don't see what choice I have but to leave."

"Now, Celia," Mandy said in a misguided effort to placate her.

"I mean it. Perhaps I'll move in with you for the duration," Celia threatened.

Mandy's expression brightened, grew hopeful.

"Actually, where are you staying?" Celia asked.

The expectant look on Mandy's face was replaced with one of trepidation. "In a women's bed-and-breakfast between here and downtown."

"Is it by any chance located in a bad part of town?"

"Well, not exactly —"

"I should have known." Celia sighed. "But it's not really your fault — I don't imagine you could have afforded to stay anywhere else."

Mandy looked upset, but she didn't say anything. When is she going to pick herself up off the floor and tell Celia where to shove it, Harry wondered. Everyone except Moira looked uncomfortable; she seemed to have missed the whole conversation. But no one was going to come to Mandy's defence. They might feel sorry for her, but people didn't like a loser.

Harry sat down in the only empty chair, which was across from Moira. She poured herself a coffee, but it was the dregs from the pot and as black as ink. All she could smell was sour coffee and stale sweat wafting from Moira's direction. It was not a fortuitous combination.

"You'll never find a hotel room in the Castro during the festival," Buck warned.

"Well, maybe I'll move downtown, then," Celia said. "God knows I feel like I've worn out my welcome in this house."

"This one's a real live wire, isn't she?" Moira commented with a laugh.

Celia glared at her.

"Anyway, I've changed my mind," Moira declared. "I've decided to move into Fran's room after all. I'm not unacquainted with ghosts, and Fran and I had many an amusing conversation while she was alive, so why not after she's dead? And I couldn't let cutie-pie desecrate Fran's memory by sleeping in her bed. Fran would roll in her grave if she knew."

"I've already been in that bed, thank you very much," Celia snapped.

"But you weren't invited to take up permanent residence in it, were you?"

Celia flushed but said nothing.

"I can't believe this is really happening," Richie groaned, reeling across the room. "Does anyone want more coffee? I could put on another pot."

"Not really. I've had more than enough for one day," Buck said. "Why don't you see if there's any juice in the fridge?"

"There's booze in the bottom cupboard to the left of the fridge," Moira said hopefully.

Richie opened the fridge and retrieved two cartons of juice, one orange, the other apple. Then he went down on his haunches and rummaged in one of the cupboards for several seconds. When he stood up, he had a bottle of gin and another of brandy in his hands.

"They're not mine, but help yourselves anyway," he said, depositing them on the table.

Buck stood up, plucked a carton of apple juice from the table and filled his empty coffee mug. "I hope it hasn't fermented."

"I'd prefer to have juice, but only if it's fresh," Celia said. "And I'm not going to drink that awful plonk, that's for sure."

"Fran prided herself on buying the cheapest booze she could find," Moira claimed.

"So it seems." Celia stared with distaste at the labels on the brandy and gin bottles and finally poured an inch of orange juice into her cup. "I suppose it's too much to hope for an ice cube or two."

Moira snorted.

Celia ignored her and got up and walked to the fridge. She opened the freezer door and was met by a nearly solid wall of ice.

"Plenty of ice there." Moira cackled.

"Never mind." Celia gave a theatrical shudder. "I suppose it's cold enough to drink anyway."

"Harry?" Richie asked, holding out the brandy bottle. It had a store-brand label on it.

Harry shook her head and watched him pour a generous serving into a cup. She had tried store brands because they were so cheap, but most of them had been harsh enough to permanently damage the lining of her digestive system.

"I'll take this," Moira said slyly, a grimy hand darting out and closing around the gin. She hugged the bottle to her body for a moment and then unscrewed the cap and half-filled the cup in front of her.

"What are we going to do, Harry?" asked Celia.

"Why are you asking her?" Moira demanded suspiciously. "She doesn't look like she could fight her way out of a paper bag."

Harry ignored Moira's comment. "I don't understand; what do you think I can do?"

"Help us figure a way out of this mess," replied Richie.

Did they think she was a miracle worker? "But if Fran really left this house to Moira and Raven, then there's not much anyone can do."

"Fran must have been out of her mind," Celia muttered.

Moira's laugh was distinctly unpleasant, making the hair on the back of Harry's neck stand up.

"Look, hire a lawyer and see if there's some way you can challenge her will. That's the only thing I can suggest," Harry said.

"I was afraid you were going to say that." Richie sounded despondent.

The kitchen was beginning to smell like a booze can. Harry watched Richie and Moira drink Fran's cheap liquor. Celia was thumping her fingers on the table, an irritated look on her face, while Mandy was sitting with her eyes closed, although Harry didn't think she was asleep.

Any one of the people seated around the table could have killed Fran, although some of them had more substantial motives than others. Both Moira and Raven had known about the provisions of Fran's new will. Moira's motive was likely the strongest, since she obviously needed a roof over her head, not to mention the security of owning property in one of the trendiest districts of San Francisco. Harry wondered whether Moira was homeless. She certainly smelled as if she could be living on the street, but she didn't look dirty enough, and there were no greasy shopping bags piled high around her feet. She hadn't been carrying anything other than a large purse when Harry had seen her that morning, either. Moira probably lived in a tiny room in a run-down rooming house and shared a washroom that had defective plumbing and no hot water with several other people. Still, being poor and a little insane didn't mean Moira had killed her former lover.

As for Raven, all Harry knew was that she was a waitress and likely worked hard for her money. Nor was there much future in her occupation. But that didn't mean Raven had started out that way; she could easily come from a well-to-do family. There were certainly a lot of lesbians who were downwardly mobile for political reasons, and perhaps Raven was one of them. For all Harry knew, she might be capable of changing her lifestyle with a snap of her fingers.

Richie had been certain he was going to inherit Fran's house, and Harry tended to believe his protestations that he knew nothing about the provisions in Fran's latest will. However, that would mean that Richie had a strong motive for murdering his sister, especially if he was desperate for cash. Although Richie was a talented and respected actor, he worked sporadically, as did many Canadian performers. And Buck had mentioned that parts were getting fewer as Richie aged. How could she find out about Richie's financial situation? And Buck's, she added mentally, because Buck would benefit indirectly if Richie were to inherit a property worth a large sum of money. Buck had a steady job, but nurses didn't make that much, especially after the cutbacks of recent years. If he had known that Fran had modified her will in Moira and Raven's favour, then he likely wouldn't have killed her.

As far as Harry could tell, Celia didn't have a financial incentive to want Fran dead, but she had been sexually involved with the murdered woman. The question was, how intense had their relationship become in such a short period of time? And how jealous a woman was Mandy? Had she struck back at Celia through Fran?

Harry sighed. She was going around in circles. But she knew that the moment she started asking questions, everyone would become suspicious and clam up. They would think she was prying and wouldn't understand why. If only Raven would tell the police what she had seen the night Fran died. "I'll be back in a couple of minutes," Harry said. She rushed upstairs, hurried into her room, turned on the desk lamp and sat on the bed beside the slumbering Raven.

"Wake up. I need to talk to you."

"Huh?" Raven mumbled.

"Pay attention, Raven. It's important."

"Harry, it's the middle of the night. Can't it wait until morning? And can't you turn off that damn light?"

"No. Everyone is downstairs in the kitchen, and it might help me discover who killed Fran if you admitted that you saw someone push her off the balcony."

"I already told you that I wasn't willing to say anything to the police."

"But you wouldn't be telling the police. Look, it's incredibly difficult for me to question people when they have no idea that a crime has been committed. They think I'm just prying into their private affairs."

"The answer is no."

"What are you afraid of?"

"What makes you think that I'm afraid of anything?"

"Raven, what did you really see?" Harry stared into her lover's eyes and encountered nothing but innocence, but she wasn't deceived. Raven wasn't the first women she had known who knew how to use her eyes to her best advantage. "You can tell me."

"I didn't see anything."

"Don't you trust me?"

"That's the wrong question to ask, Harry."

Unfortunately, Raven was right. What did they know about each other, really? Raven had motive and opportunity, and despite her seemingly laissez-faire attitude about sex, Harry knew very little about her.

"Were you disappointed when Fran told you that you were going to inherit only half the house?" Harry asked.

"Why should I have been? I never expected to inherit anything, so it was a pleasant surprise."

"Have you seen Moira recently?"

"No, although I do know her," Raven answered. "I think it's cool that Fran left what she had to people who needed it."

There was that, Harry thought. She had been blessed with middle-class parents who had supported her until she was capable of making a living. They had also accepted her lesbianism, although they didn't understand it, and her father refused to discuss it to this day.

"If you know Moira, then you must realize that she's one step removed from being a street person, and she's more than a little crazy," Harry said.

"I suspect that she's just fallen on bad times since she and Fran broke up."

"Maybe." But Harry didn't really believe it. Moira's proclivity for madness didn't seem to have overtaken her suddenly, although perhaps she was more in control of her symptoms when she was in a relationship. Sometimes the creepy things that nibbled on your soul in the middle of the night could be blunted by the presence of another person in your bed, not to mention your heart.

"Back to what you saw in the theatre that night."

"I told you everything I know," Raven insisted.

"Don't you want to find out who murdered Fran?"

"Why is that so important to you?"

Was Raven serious? Harry stood up, went to the window overlooking the backyard, and opened it. Everything was so dark and silent that it was difficult to believe that Castro was just up the street.

"I mean it, Harry."

"I know you do. But I don't understand you."

"The feeling is mutual."

The ensuing silence was as chilly as the damp night air rushing into the room through the open window.

"Listen, do what you want," Raven capitulated.

"Are you sure?"

"No. But you're going to anyway."

By the time Harry went back downstairs, Richie and Buck were the only people left in the kitchen. "Where did everyone go?" she asked.

"Moira staggered off toward Fran's old room, clutching the bottle of gin she commandeered. Celia went up to bed, while Mandy seems to have taken up residence in the living room, although having had first-hand experience with the sofa, I don't envy her," Buck replied.

"She might have started in the living room, but I bet she's already upstairs with Celia," Richie remarked.

"You might be right," agreed Buck.

"I usually am," Richie said.

Harry sat down. "I have something to tell you."

"You and everybody else, it would seem. Come to San Francisco, lose your friends, not to mention your inheritance." Richie's tone was glum, his words slurred. Cheap brandy would do that to you, Harry mused. He would be lucky if he could crawl out of bed in the morning. Too many gay people drank too much, she thought, and not for the first time.

"Have a drink," he said.

"Actually, I think I will. But juice, not brandy."

Richie stood unsteadily and splashed apple juice into an empty coffee mug. Harry took the mug from Richie and sipped. It was warm, but at least it moistened her dry mouth.

"So, what do you want to tell us?" Buck asked, placing an elbow on the table and resting his chin in his hand. He looked tired.

"Raven thinks she saw someone push Fran over the railing," Harry said.

The sound of shattering glass assailed her ears and the smell of cheap brandy blossomed throughout the kitchen. Richie cursed and went down on his hands and knees to clean up.

"You've got to be kidding!" Buck protested.

"I'm afraid I'm not."

"Did she see who it was?"

"No."

Richie stood up, holding shards of glass in both hands. He carefully deposited them on the table and sat down.

"It makes sense, doesn't it? Fran wasn't the type to take a dive," Buck said.

"So Detective Manley mentioned that to you, too."

"What do you think?" Buck responded with a cynical grin. "After all, cops like Manley probably prefer accidental or suicidal death to murder."

After her last conversation with Detective Manley, Harry thought he was more complicated than that, but she didn't say anything.

"But nobody had a *reason* to kill Fran," Richie said. "She fell, that's all. She was probably a little drunk. It was just a stupid, idiotic accident."

Harry took another sip of juice. "Maybe. But Raven had the distinct impression that there was someone standing near Fran just before she fell, and that he or she shoved her."

"Raven's young, and she's got an overactive imagination." Richie's face was flushed.

"You don't like Raven very much, do you?" Celia asked, startling the three of them. They had been so wrapped up in their conversation that they hadn't heard her come into the kitchen.

"That has nothing to do with it," Richie replied.

Celia was wearing a rose dressing gown that was cut low to display a rather significant décolletage. She poured herself a glass of apple juice and sat down.

"Perhaps not," she said. "But you don't seem overly fond of Moira, either. You shouldn't hold their inheritance against them. After all, as Raven said earlier, it's not their fault. But then you're only human, and you must find it difficult to deal with feeling so much anger against someone who's dead. It's easier to take it out on people who are alive, isn't it?"

"I don't have to sit here and listen to this," Richie snarled. He stalked from the room. Buck gave Celia a dirty look and hurried after him.

"What did I say?"

"Never mind." Harry sighed. Celia's grand entrance had foiled her intention to interrogate Richie and Buck.

"Where is Raven, anyway?"

"Sleeping." Had Celia overheard what Harry told Buck and Richie? If so, why wasn't she asking any questions? It wasn't like Celia not to centre in on the main chance and milk it for all it was worth. "Didn't you hear what I said about Fran being murdered?"

"Of course I did," Celia said. "It's just a lot to absorb, that's all. But I wouldn't believe everything Raven says if I were you. You see, I saw her when I was downstairs."

Harry's heart dropped. "Did she go back upstairs before you did?"

Celia shrugged. "Who knows? I wasn't watching. Look, I think you should be prepared for the worst. Raven's probably more ambitious than she lets on. Think of it, Harry; she's working as a waitress and, with the economy the way it is, that might be the best job she's ever going to get. And then one day Fran tells her that she's going to inherit half of this prime piece of real estate. What if Raven decided to hurry things along a little?"

"But she was sitting in the last row when the lights came on," Harry protested feebly.

"Perhaps she was," Celia agreed. "Perhaps she was indeed. I didn't see her on the stairs when I went up. I didn't see her leave the lobby either, although I wasn't looking for her."

Something about the way Celia answered caught Harry's attention. Had Celia lied earlier about whom she was meeting in the lobby? "Were you by any chance planning to meet Raven and not Fran?"

"You shouldn't be so suspicious." Celia laughed. "I wouldn't mind having a little fling with Raven, but it's clear that she's not interested in me. But you have to face the fact that Raven could have given Fran a shove. She was her lover for two years, and who knows how she felt when she and Fran broke up? Perhaps she held a grudge all this time. Or maybe Fran was dangling her on a hook, going to bed with her every once in a while but not letting their relationship resume. And don't forget, she stands to inherit half of a valuable piece of property."

As if she could forget, Harry thought sourly. "But why would she say she saw someone push Fran if she was the one who did it? Why would she risk putting suspicion on herself?"

"How would I know?" Celia shrugged. "Maybe she feels guilty and wants to be caught. Anyway, I'm going back to bed. Hopefully Mandy's succeeded in crying herself to sleep by now. God, listen to me — I sound like an uncaring bitch, and I'm not that way at all. Oh, all right, so I'm half an uncaring bitch," she added when she saw the sceptical look on Harry's face.

"You could have pushed Fran yourself," Harry said.

"Don't be ridiculous," Celia scoffed. "Why would I want to do that? I barely knew the woman."

"You were her lover."

"Get serious, Harry. We met briefly during the Gay Games in Vancouver, but I had no further contact with her until we arrived here three days ago," Celia responded. "Now you tell me, am I the type to fall so madly, passionately, terminally in love that I'd have any reason whatsoever to murder someone?"

Harry wasn't going to let Celia bedazzle her with words, even though they made a fair amount of sense. If there was one thing she had learned in the past few years, it was that nothing was impossible in a murder case. "Who else was on the stairs with you?"

"Elvis," Celia responded as she rose from her chair. "He just loves women's porn, especially the lesbian variety. That's why he's staying undercover. Imagine if the blue-haired set learned of his penchant for dirt, and perverted dirt, at that? Why he'd lose all his fans, not to mention his status as a near-deity."

"Celia!"

"Oh, all right. Moira, Richie and Raven were in the lobby part of the time I was there. Richie and I waved at each other but didn't speak. He was on his way to the men's room. Perhaps there's an epidemic of weak bladders going around. I mean, it's as good an explanation as any, isn't it?" Celia added factitiously. "Ta-ta, darling. See you in the morning. Say hello to the little angel for me, will you?"

Harry stifled a caustic remark and watched Celia stride from the room, moving like a panther on the prowl. Thank God she wasn't attracted to Celia. It would be like signing her emotional death warrant. She put her mug of warm juice on the table and got up. Her stomach was rumbling with hunger, and her mouth tasted foul. She walked to the fridge, opened the door and rummaged inside, uncovering half a loaf of stale bread, a hunk of mouldy Cheddar cheese and several pieces of lettuce which would be edible if not crisp if she tore off the blackened ends.

There was no one she could trust, she thought as she brushed crumbs from the top of the toaster and popped two slices of bread into it. Therefore, there was no one with whom she could discuss her suspicions, she concluded as she opened several drawers until she found a paring knife to use to scrape the mould from the cheese. Not one single person in whom she could confide her fears that Raven had killed Fran for financial gain, she brooded, retrieving two unevenly browned slices of bread that the toaster eventually ejected, and coating them with the yellowish dregs from the bottom of a jar of mayonnaise. Once upon a time she had been able to discuss her speculations about murder suspects with Judy, but those days were long gone. She set the empty jar in the sink and ran water in it. Then she spread several scraps of wilted lettuce on one piece of toast and sliced the wedge of cheese, placing the thin slices on the lettuce. She covered her meagre offering with the other piece of toast and took her sandwich to the kitchen table, which was littered with mugs, cups and saucers, overflowing ashtrays and shards of broken glass.

"I thought I smelled civilization, or at least something to eat," Richie said. He was dressed only in a white singlet and white boxer shorts decorated with bright flowers, but Harry decided not to feel embarrassed if he didn't.

"There's no more cheese, the lettuce is left over from the last century and the bread's first cousin to cardboard," Harry told him just before she chomped into her sandwich and chewed vigorously. Not that she would protect it with her life, or anything.

"I'd settle for toast if I could find some butter," he muttered as he ransacked the fridge.

"Good luck," Harry mumbled, her mouth full. "Fran must have lived mostly on air and bottled water."

"She ate out a lot," Richie said, triumphantly waving a tub of margarine in his hand. "Toast it is."

Harry decided to wait until he finished making toast before interrogating him. She hadn't expected him to fill the toaster three times, but it did give her the opportunity to eat her own sandwich. By the time he sat across from her, his plate piled high with greasy toast, her plate was empty save for a few crumbs.

"Nirvana." He sighed. He rolled two pieces of limp toast and stuffed half of the carbohydrate hot dog into his mouth.

"Are you sure you didn't know about Fran's new will?" Harry asked abruptly.

"Mppph —"

Harry leaped to her feet, ready to catapult over the table and perform the Heimlich manoeuvre, but after depositing the contents of his mouth into a napkin, Richie took a ragged breath and stared at her.

"Give a man a chance, why don't you?"

"I might feel sorry for you if you were sitting down to a gourmet meal, but under the circumstances, perhaps you ought to thank me, especially if you've got a cranky gall bladder."

"You're just saying that because *you* got the cheese."

"Stop prevaricating and answer my question." Harry sat back and crossed her arms. "First of all, did Fran ever come right out and say that she was leaving you this house?"

"Yes, and more than once," Richie replied, pouring himself some cola. "She could be devious, but in this instance I actually believed her. I mean, I had no reason not to. I was her only living relative other than a few distant cousins neither of us had met more than a couple times in our lives. It's been so long since I've seen any of them that I probably wouldn't recognize them. Fran always said that she'd leave me whatever she had, although she invariably added that she didn't have much. Even when she bought this house, she didn't think it would appreciate a whole lot. She used to say that it was dumb luck that she bought in the Castro District and not some other area."

"And she never mentioned that she was going to update her will."

"Never." Richie shook his head and eyed the four remaining pieces of toast on his plate, but he left them untouched.

"Have you any idea why she wouldn't tell you she'd decided to leave the house to Raven and Moira?"

Richie shrugged and pushed his plate away. "Maybe she thought I'd be angry and didn't want to deal with it. After all, how could she know she was going to die so suddenly? None of us think our demise is imminent. Or perhaps she planned to tell me during my visit but didn't have the opportunity before she died. We were pretty busy, you know."

"Why do you think she changed her will?"

"I have no idea."

"Really? Nothing untoward happened between the two of you?"

Richie looked uncomfortable.

"Out with it, Richie."

"It was just more of the same crap as before." He sighed. "She really wanted me to move down here, and every time we were alone, she started pestering me. And the more she pushed, the more ambivalent I felt. And Buck wouldn't even discuss it."

"Why did you go downstairs during the movie?"

Richie pushed his plate of toast aside and picked up a nearly empty bottle of brandy. "Join me?" he asked, pouring himself two fingers.

"No, thanks."

He emptied his glass and then glanced at the doorway. "You have to promise to keep this to yourself."

"Of course," Harry responded automatically.

"Shortly after the movie started, I went down to relieve myself. While I was in the washroom, I was approached."

It took a moment for Harry to comprehend what he meant, but it finally sunk in. She didn't know quite what to say.

"Don't look at me like that," he said. "I'm not an angel. I never have been."

"So you and this other fellow had —"

"Sex," he said gently. "It's not a dirty word, you know."

"Of course not," Harry said. She didn't understand anonymous sex, but she tried not to look down on Richie or her other friends who indulged in it.

"And after we had sex, I went back up to my seat," Richie continued. "And that's where I was when Fran fell. Or was pushed, if Raven's story is to be believed."

"Did you see anyone else when you were downstairs?"

He shook his head. "No. There were a lot of people around, but I wasn't especially looking for anyone."

"Why didn't you say anything about this to the police?"

Richie gave an aggrieved shrug. "What difference would it have made? When the detective questioned me, I had no idea that someone might have attacked Fran, and I was offended that he believed she had committed suicide. So I thought, what the hell, why should I tell this guy anything? I figured that where I was and what I'd been doing just before Fran fell was none of his damn business."

"How do you feel about that now?"

"The same, basically," he replied, looking uncomfortable. "I mean, no one is sure that what happened to Fran wasn't an accident."

"But what if it wasn't? What if someone actually did kill her?"

"Then it was likely someone she knew," he said. "But it wasn't me."

Harry looked at him and raised her eyebrows.

"Fran had a pretty full life, you know. And she wasn't a particularly nice person. I bet she had a lot of friends — and enemies — we don't know much about. The theatre was filled with people that night, and one of them might have had a reason to want to hurt her."

"What you're saying is that there's a cast of hundreds."

"Dozens, at least."

"Many of whom we don't know."

"And you're not even sure it was murder. Look, I don't want to believe that my sister was killed. To tell the truth, I'd prefer it to have been an accident. Since the AIDS epidemic started, I've watched friends and acquaintances drop like flies. Everybody I know has had unprotected sex, so I've become somewhat philosophically attuned to chaos theory. I mean, look at who's HIV-positive and who isn't. How does that relate to how they've lived their lives, how many times they had sex and with whom? Very little, in the end. And that's hard to take."

"I can understand that," Harry said, thinking of Barb.

"So, in a strange way, I can relate to accidental death, no matter how stupidly it happens. I'm more comfortable with it than with murder, but then, I suppose most people are," Richie said. "On the other hand, if the murderer was one of the people who stand to inherit this house, I might be able to challenge Fran's will. Then again, who knows? Maybe everything would go to the innocent one. It depends on California law, about which I know nothing."

"Me neither."

"So what do you want to do?"

Harry didn't respond immediately. "I don't really know."

"Look, it's late," Richie said after glancing at his watch. "Why don't we sleep on it? I'll see you in the morning."

"Good night, then," Harry said, rising from the table. Suddenly she wanted to talk to Raven. She walked swiftly down the hall, took the steps two at a time and hurried to her room. "Raven?"

There was no answer.

"Raven? Wake up."

There still wasn't any answer.

Harry slid her hand along the wall, found the light switch and flicked it. "Damn," she swore at the empty room. Her bed had been abandoned. Its sheets were dishevelled, its blankets thrown back. Raven's clothes were no longer on the floor.

She was too sleepy to find Raven tonight. She undressed and slid between sheets that were still warm from Raven's body. She pulled the covers up around her neck and fell asleep.

The day dawned clear and fogless, and when the sun rose, so did the temperature. Harry couldn't sleep. She breakfasted early in a hole-in-the-wall just off Market Street, where she forced down a dry bagel and a fruit plate in which seedy grapefruit sections and several overripe slices of banana predominated. There was also, rather cruelly, one tiny, delicious piece of kiwi. Being a glutton for punishment, she downed two cups of bitter coffee.

After that inauspicious beginning, she headed off to revisit some of the tourist destinations of San Francisco, which, unfortunately, she couldn't help but identify with Judy. She took a ride on a cable car and made her way to Fisherman's Wharf. The weather was hot and sunny, and Fisherman's Wharf, although more commercialized than the last time Harry had been there, was still delightful, especially when she by-passed the most blatant tourist traps and made her way to the wharfs where the fishing fleet still docked. She stared out over the water and breathed in the moist, salt-tinged air. Being around large bodies of water usually calmed her soul, probably because she had grown up in a small fishing village nearly surrounded by the Atlantic Ocean. But instead she felt lonely. She wasn't used to doing things by herself. Her sense of loss and her feeling of being adrift emotionally, compounded by her insecurity about Raven, was too strong to overcome. She needed to talk to Raven, to try to resolve her distrust, and, yes, her growing sense of having been used.

Harry went to Union Square, telling herself that she wasn't really looking for Raven. But, in the end, she couldn't stop herself from going from restaurant to restaurant, ostensibly in search of good food rather than her lover. Unfortunately, she found neither and ended up skipping lunch altogether. She couldn't eat. She knew that finding Raven would restore her appetite, as would identifying Fran's killer. Unfortunately, what had extinguished her appetite in the first place was the thought that they were one and the same.

By mid-afternoon, Harry's feet were sore and her heart heavy. As she walked between the high-rise caverns of the business district, she shoved her hands into her jeans pockets. Her fingers closed around Raven's card and she pulled it out. It was crumpled, but still legible. Harry entered the first phone booth she came to, stuffed a quarter into the slot and dialled Raven's number.

"Hello?"

"It's me."

Raven hung up.

Harry found another quarter and dialled again.

"I have to talk to you."

"I think not." Seconds later, the dial tone hummed in Harry's ear.

Harry searched her pockets and came up with one last quarter. "Please don't do this to me," she muttered. She pushed the coin into the slot and dialled. There was no answer. Harry let it ring six, seven, eight times, and was about to hang up when she saw a cab cruise slowly by, looking for a fare. She waved at the driver, who pulled in to the curb. Harry let the phone dangle, rushed to the cab and hopped into the back seat.

"Phone broken?" The cab driver asked.

"Yes," Harry lied.

"Typical," the cabby replied, turning around to look at Harry. She had a round face, and her skin was deeply tanned. In another few years it would feel like leather. "Where to?"

Harry gave her Raven's address.

The driver checked her rear-view mirror and eased out into traffic. After a few minutes, she turned off the busy street and drove swiftly through a semi-industrial area, and then into a residential neighbourhood that contained a mix of bungalows and apartment buildings. Harry wondered if she should ask the cab driver to wait in case Raven had seen through her feeble ruse of leaving the pay phone ringing and had vacated her flat.

The cabbie pulled up in front of a low-rise apartment building. "Here we are."

Harry paid her and got out.

"Want me to wait?" the driver called through the open window.

"No, thanks," Harry said.

"I'll stick around for a few minutes, just in case," the driver shouted.

Harry rushed up the steps, opened the door and slipped inside. She glanced at Raven's card and pressed the buzzer for 305, but there was no answer. Was Raven playing possum or had she gone out? Harry made a deal with herself. If the inner door was locked, she would give up. If it was open, she would continue on.

It was open. Harry took the elevator to the third floor, reading the graffiti as the elevator slowly rumbled upward. Most of the messages, which had been scribbled on the metal walls with felt-tipped pens or Magic Markers, weren't very funny. The rest she didn't understand. She walked down the hall and knocked on Raven's door. There was no answer, but Harry was almost certain that she heard movement inside.

"Raven!" she shouted, pounding on the door. "Raven! Open up!" When the door finally opened, Harry's whole body felt bruised. She stood there trembling, trying to catch her breath.

"How long were you going to keep that up?"

"As long as it took."

"Until the cops got here, you mean," Raven said, turning away. "The only reason they're not here already is that my neighbours probably think you're a cop making a drug bust. No one else makes that much noise in the middle of the day. I bet everyone in the building is busy flushing their dope down their johns right this very moment."

Harry followed Raven into her one-room apartment, which was bright, clean and fresh-smelling. The walls looked newly painted and the worn hardwood floors were covered with carpets. There wasn't much furniture, but what there was was in good condition. An apartment-sized white leather sofa and matching chair sat to one side of the room, a round glass-topped table between them. On the facing wall was a tiny dining-room table. The galley kitchen was in a nearby alcove. At the far end was a single bed covered with a duvet and a pillow in a matching case, and behind that what Harry assumed was the door to the bathroom. There was no television, but next to the sofa was a black metal stand holding a stereo and CD player. Except for the CD player, none of the furniture or appliances looked new. But they fit well together, and they had obviously been purchased with thought and care.

And everywhere there were plants. Several large spider plants hung from the window, flowering plants sat on every available surface, and there was a small tree in the corner next to Raven's bed. Its upper branches nearly touched the ceiling.

"You have a nice apartment," Harry said.

"I'm sure you didn't come here to tell me that."

After years of dealing with Judy's irritability, Harry had next to no patience with moody women. She crossed the room and took up residence on the sofa.

"Aren't you going to offer me something to drink? Lunch? A little late-afternoon romp between the sheets?"

Raven looked perturbed. "I wish you hadn't told everyone what I saw."

"But you said I could."

"I know, but I still thought that you'd respect my wishes." Raven's tone was sullen. She walked into the kitchen and opened the fridge. "Will orange juice do?"

"Yes, thanks. If you were adamant about not wanting anyone else to know, you should have made that clear to me. I'm not a mind reader."

Raven put two glasses of juice on the glass table. "I thought you understood how I felt. In the first place, I don't know exactly what I saw. Perhaps Fran was off balance and someone walked too close to her. Maybe she was planning to go downstairs but misjudged the distance between her seat and the stairs because she'd had a little too much to drink. There may be no way of knowing for sure, and I didn't want to make a fool of myself. And I really didn't want the police to get wind of it."

A likely scenario, Harry thought. Raven wasn't the type to worry about making waves.

"That's why I didn't want you to say anything to anyone." Raven drank half her juice and returned her glass to the table. Harry thought she looked nervous.

"I'm sorry," Harry said, although she knew she'd do the same thing again. "However, I also have a bone or two to pick with you."

"What are you talking about?"

"First of all, you never mentioned Fran's will. And second, you didn't tell me that you weren't in your seat during part of the movie."

"It never occurred to me that you would be interested in the will."

"How could you have thought that? The fact that Fran so recently changed her will in your and Moira's favour is incredibly important."

"If you say so," Raven commented lightly. "And yes, I went downstairs during *Blueberries*. I already mentioned that I thought the movie sucked. I also told you that all I could think about was you, and there I was, stuck in that damn theatre for another couple hours while you were sitting somewhere else. I went down to the washroom, and then bought something to drink. I wasted a little time standing around in the lobby, drinking my cola and people-watching. I saw Moira standing in a corner, talking to herself. She didn't smell so good, so people were going around her. I didn't particular want her to see me because I didn't want to stop and talk, so I averted my face and rushed by."

"And you didn't see anybody else you knew."

"Richie was there," Raven said. "He was pretty intent on getting to the men's washroom, so I don't think he saw me, either."

"And?"

"Just as I was about to return to the balcony, I saw Celia."

"And did she see you?"

Raven nodded.

"Did you talk with each other?"

Raven nodded again. It was like pulling teeth, Harry thought. Something had happened between them.

"She's attracted to me."

"So she mentioned. She also said that you weren't interested," Harry said.

Raven threw back her head and laughed.

"You weren't, were you?" Harry was uncertain now. Celia was an attractive woman, after all.

"Of course I was," Raven said. "You would have been too if someone put the moves on you like she did on me. She kissed me, Harry. Good and hard."

Harry's mouth dropped open.

"She was coming on to me in a big way," Raven said. "She said she was paying me back for what I did to you in the bar, but that wasn't it at all. I think that the movie probably made her horny and she got a little carried away."

"I'll say," Harry muttered.

"And to be honest, I responded," Raven added. "My *body* responded, I mean. In the heat of the moment, kissing her felt good. I didn't want to tell you because I knew that she was your friend. Once I got over the shock of what had happened, I told Celia to get lost. She took it well. Her type usually does. Then I went back up to the balcony. The stairs were packed, and in case you're interested, I didn't see anyone I knew on them. But I wasn't really looking."

"Did you notice whether any of the others returned to the balcony?"

"No."

"Where were you when the lights came on?"

Raven fixed her eyes on Harry's. "In my seat."

There was a moment of strained silence.

"You suspect me of having pushed Fran, don't you?" Raven demanded.

"I didn't say that."

Raven got up and went to the window. "But that's what you mean, isn't it?"

Although she hated herself for doing it, Harry let the silence between them thicken. When that didn't work, she got up, approached Raven and put her hand on Raven's shoulder.

"Don't."

Harry left her hand where it was.

"I said, don't!" Raven wheeled around, dislodging Harry's hand. "You think that you have the right to dig around in people's private affairs and harass them until they tell you what you want to know, even if it has nothing to do with you. You're smart, Harry, but I suppose you know that. But one of these days, you're going to fall flat on your face and there won't be anyone there to pick you up."

"I'm simply trying to find out what happened to Fran," Harry said, taken aback by Raven's vehemence. "You should be pleased that someone cares. She was your lover, after all."

Raven walked over to the stereo and turned it on. A CD began to play, one which had been released just before Judy had broken up with her. Harry had repeatedly played its melancholic torch songs while Judy had packed her belongings and moved them out of the apartment box by box.

Raven sat down on the sofa. "I'm sorry I lost my temper. I know you're not trying to hurt me on purpose. Look, what I told you before was true."

"Up to a point," Harry said. But she couldn't help wonder why Raven left out some fairly essential facts. "How well do you know Moira?"

"Fairly well," Raven replied. "Fran didn't believe in isolating her lovers from one other. She thought they should all be friends, like one big happy family. That was okay by me. I never have been able to understand why women cut themselves off from their former lovers. You lose a lot of memories that way."

"Sometimes it hurts too much to stay in touch," Harry said, thinking about Judy.

"But people get over it eventually, and once that happens, there's no reason for them to avoid each other," Raven said. "Anyway, I think Fran was relieved that we remained friends. You've seen what Moira's like. As you can imagine, their relationship turned sour pretty fast. Fran was quite broad-minded and more than a little eccentric at times, so she had a lot of tolerance for weird behaviour. But once the honeymoon ended, Fran swiftly got tired of Moira. Fran would call me and I'd go over and mediate between them, or keep one or the other of them company."

"That doesn't sound like it was much fun."

"Sometimes it wasn't," Raven agreed. "But Moira could be really sweet. And nobody can deny that she's an interesting woman, insane or not."

They sat in silence for a long time. Raven eventually got up to close the window to keep out the chilly air which had come in with the fog. She put on a new CD, a jazz pianist Harry didn't know.

"Do you want some soup?"

"No, thanks. I should be getting back."

"I'm a suspect, aren't I?"

"Yes." Harry felt miserable saying it, but it was the truth and there was no point lying about it.

"I'll call you a cab."

"Don't bother."

"Get off your high horse," Raven snapped, reaching for the phone. "This is pretty good neighbourhood. It's usually safe out there for a tourist. But you really don't know your way around, and I don't want your rape or murder on my conscience."

"Fine." Harry felt humble, grateful that Raven wasn't angry enough to toss her out on the street to fend for herself. Raven insisted on walking her to the front door and waiting there with her, and the ten minutes it took for the cab to come were among the longest in Harry's life. She wanted to tell Raven that she was sorry, but she knew it would be useless. The only way she could apologize would be to stop suspecting her of having pushed Fran over the balcony, and that she couldn't do.

"Goodbye, Harry," Raven said as the cab turned the corner, passed a vacant lot and pulled up in front of Raven's apartment building.

"But, Raven —"

"Are you such a masochist that you would sleep with a woman you suspect murdered her former lover?"

Trust Raven to cut right to the quick, Harry thought. She opened the back door of the cab, slid in and pulled the door shut after her.

"Address?" the driver asked.

Harry didn't feel like going back to the house right away so she told him to take her to the corner of Castro and Market. He put the car in gear and pulled out. Harry promised herself that she wouldn't look back, but she couldn't stop herself from doing so.

But Raven was gone. Except for the thickening fog, the sidewalk was empty.

"Give me a break," Harry muttered angrily as the cab sped away. Not only had the driver disgorged streams of religious patter of the far-right variety, some of which verged on being homophobic, but Harry suspected that he had also taken a roundabout route to the Castro District so he could milk a few more bucks from her. Really, she was such a wimp. She should have told him to stop and got out in a royal huff, but she could never bring herself to do that when she was in a cab, no matter how infuriating the driver was. Except for once, when she had felt physically threatened by a Montreal cabby who had started telling her about a skin flick he had recently seen and had then made blatant sexual advances toward her. But never mind, she told herself. She was back in the Castro. She tugged on the sides of her jacket and strode along the street, searching for a familiar face. Unfortunately, the one she found was not the one she had been looking for.

"Hey, you!" Moira Chelso shouted, rushing from a doorway to confront Harry. "I know you, don't I? You're Raven's latest paramour. You were at the house last night when young Richie broke out the gin."

Paramour? Harry stifled a grin and said, "Yes. I'm Harriet Hubbley. We met yesterday."

"Hmm. Young Richie said that you do some sort of detecting and that you'd somehow discovered that Fran had likely been murdered." Moira nodded sagely. "I often fancy that I'm a detective of the inner world, but the evidence isn't always conclusive. But never you mind. You're just the person I want to see. Would you care to sup with me this evening?"

Moira smelled like herbal soap. She had obviously taken a shower, and her long hair was dishevelled but clean. She was wearing different clothes, and since her matching cotton blouse and skirt were much too large for her thin frame, Harry suspected that she had borrowed them from Fran's closet. But whether she smelled like rose petals or a garbage dumpster, whether she looked like a bag lady or a svelte fashion plate, she was odd.

"Come on, I don't bite," Moira urged. She reached out and closed her long fingers around Harry's arm. "And I'm quite a charming dinner companion, you know."

Should she or shouldn't she? Moira had been in the theatre when Fran had been killed, and perhaps she would be willing to talk about what she'd seen. Then, too, she could have been the one to give Fran a quick shove. Perhaps it was worth a bit of misery over dinner to find out, Harry thought.

"It's early, but why not?" she said.

"Time means nothing where gourmet dining is concerned. You're certainly fortunate that I know this city like the back of my hand. Some places serve crap on fancy plates and empty your wallet while they're doing it. But there's a marvellous seafood restaurant just around the corner, which I highly recommend." Moira slipped her arm through Harry's and led her away from Castro Street.

Think of it as an adventure, Harry told herself. And a challenge to make sense of what Moira said. She let Moira steer her to a restaurant with an ornately carved wood door. "Here?"

"I rarely eat out, my dear, but when I do, I refuse to patronize greasy spoons," Moira said, her tone haughty. She pushed the door open and stalked in, leaving Harry to chase after her. "No smoking, a window, a table large enough to spread our elbows on, and mind, not too close to anyone wearing perfume," Moira was telling an attentive waiter as Harry caught up with her.

Harry gave the waiter a wan smile.

"And this is Harriet, my darling, darling niece," Moira said brightly. "She looks that way because she has just survived a painfully long flight from Sri Lanka. Darling, have you successfully parked the Lincoln? Towncars are so difficult to squeeze into San Francisco's teensy-weensy parking spots, don't you agree?"

Niece? Sri Lanka? A Lincoln towncar? And what was wrong with the way she looked?

"This way, ladies."

Harry momentarily pondered whether one denimed dyke and one escapee from a mental hospital who was dressed in ill-fitting clothes equalled two ladies and then gave it up as a lost cause.

"What are you doing?" she hissed the moment they were seated.

"Lying through my teeth," Moira said, sounding cheerful. "I can't whistle, you know."

Harry unfurled her menu and hid behind it.

"Champagne? Caviar? Lobster? Filet mignon? All of the above?" Moira mused.

Hiding obviously wasn't going to work, especially since Harry had the distinct sensation that she was going to be paying the bill. "How about a bottle of white wine, a Caesar salad and a nice piece of broiled or grilled fish?"

"Sounds good to me," Moira responded.

Harry gestured to the waiter and ordered for the both of them.

"Such a loving niece to always take care of her aunt," Celia said *sotto voce* as the waiter walked away.

"Stop it," Harry chastised her.

"Can't an old lady have a little fun?"

"First of all, you're not old, and, second, I'm not having any fun," Harry replied.

"Well, go all hoity-toity on me, then," Moira gently rebuked her. "It always did run in the family, so I shouldn't be surprised. Honestly, I don't know what's worse — insisting on reality for no good reason or having no sense of humour."

"You mean that you *want* me to be your niece?" Harry asked as the waiter uncorked their bottle of wine.

"But, dear, you *are* my niece," Moira explained patiently. "I know you've come a very long way, but do try to *concentrate*, darling."

Harry realized that the waiter was looking askance at her and clammed up until he had finished pouring their wine and walked away.

"Don't do that to me," she whispered, downing half her glass of wine.

Moira looked amused. "You're so cute when you're upset. Of course, that runs in the family, too."

Harry refrained from speaking while the waiter served their bread and salad, but as soon as he was gone, she said, "Moira, let's talk about the night Fran died."

"Do we have to? It depresses me, and I was so enjoying myself."

"You must have cared very deeply about Fran," Harry sympathized, forking a piece of lettuce and a crouton into her mouth. The tangy salad dressing was scrumptious, so she ate more.

"On the contrary, I was no longer the least bit fond of her," Moira replied. "Oh, I was quite infatuated when we met — who wouldn't have been? She was gorgeous — a brilliant, vital, quintessential specimen of womanhood. She could be charming when she wanted to, but, unfortunately she also had it in her to be mean and vicious. Everyone thinks she broke up with me, but it was the other way around. She thought she could treat me like dirt because of my condition. I took her abuse for a while because I thought that eventually things would change. But it just got worse, and so I walked out and never went back. I might act like I belong in a nuthouse, but I'm not a masochist. I lost most of my stuff, but I didn't care. I had my independence again, my freedom, my self-respect. That meant a lot more to me than all the junk I'd accumulated. I know I'm a nut case, but nut cases have rights, too."

"I would guess so," Harry said.

"I'm a certified loony, with documents to prove it," Moira said. "I've got my release papers right on me, just in case somebody gets the wrong idea. I don't want to spend one more night than I have to in the local hoosegow or the state mental hospital, although I don't suppose I should worry about that any more. In the old days, once they got their claws into you they used to throw away the key. But with all the budget cuts, they can't afford to keep people like me locked up. They don't want to know about my problems unless I go completely nuts and walk out into the middle of traffic or shoot up the neighbourhood with a machine gun."

"It's like that everywhere," Harry said, thinking of the hundreds of people who had been institutionalized on a long-term basis and then been released from Montreal-area mental hospitals without the necessary support systems in the community.

"My parents committed me because I was exhibiting 'homosexual tendencies,' as they called it in those days. They caught me in bed with my best friend, you see, and we were engaged in more than a little hanky-panky. My parents found a shrink who would go along with them, and faster than you can say 'commitment,' I was."

"But that's horrible!" Harry exclaimed. She finished her salad and wished there had been more of it. She hadn't eaten enough leafy green stuff in the past few days.

"It certainly was," Moira said wryly. "I've never been the same since I received that series of shock treatments. I think they fried my brain."

"That's disgusting," Harry said heatedly.

"Yes, it is. But you have to maintain your sense of perspective, not to mention your sense of humour, child." Moira waved her fork at Harry. "Otherwise you won't get through life intact."

"Look, you can't be more than a couple years older than me, so stop calling me 'child,'" Harry insisted.

"Not until you start calling me 'auntie.'" Except for her lank hair, she looked sedate enough to be someone's aunt, but it would be a cold day in hell before Harry called her "Auntie Mo." "And stop looking so stubborn."

The waiter chose that particular moment to swoop down, remove their salad bowls and serve the main course. The fish looked perfectly cooked, the rice pilaf plump and steaming, the vegetables crunchy. Harry pushed the broccoli aside; it gave her gas.

"You were going to tell me about the night Fran died," she said, sampling the fish. It was moist and delicious.

"Let me eat my dinner in peace and then we'll talk," Moira said.

Harry slowly devoured her meal, savouring each mouthful. Moira ate every last morsel, finished the wine, emptied the bread basket and used all the pats of butter.

"This is the best damn meal I've had in months," Moira declared. "Of course, the paltry welfare cheque I get doesn't buy much after I pay the rent."

"But that's changed now," Harry reminded her.

"Changed? Because I stand to inherit half of Fran's house? You've got to be kidding," Moira scoffed.

"I don't understand."

"That's because you've always had money in your pocket and food in your mouth. You've got middle class written all over you, although there's nothing wrong with that except for a certain paucity of the imagination when it comes to what it means to have nothing," Moira said. "Are we ready for coffee? Garçon! GARÇON!"

Harry wouldn't have been any more embarrassed if Moira had actually snapped her fingers.

"Café latte, cognac and something decadently chocolate," Moira told the waiter.

"Certainly, madam." He made a few notes on his pad, removed their empty plates from the table and took them away.

"Subservience turns me on," Moira said.

"Really?"

"Actually, no," Moira admitted. "Especially if it's real."

Harry thought of Celia and Mandy and nodded.

"Anyway, if you think that inheriting Fran's house is going to change my life, you're wrong," Moira said. "I ask you, where are Raven and I going to find the money to pay the taxes on a property located in the Castro, not to mention the electricity, repairs and the incredible number of bills that fly in the door the minute you own a piece of real estate?"

"The location is fantastic for a bed-and-breakfast," Harry commented.

"Are you crazy? Could you see me running a B and B? For bag ladies, maybe, but they'd end up paying with lice and bed-bugs," Moira retorted.

Harry grinned.

"But that's neither here nor there. Now, what else do you want to know?" Moira asked.

"What happened that night."

"You can't leave it alone, can you? But I guess that's why you're a detective."

Harry didn't bother to correct Moira's misconception about her profession. Besides, she might not see any difference between a physical education teacher and a private investigator. When she thought about it, Harry realized that, in the past year, she had spent more time investigating than instructing, which was likely why she had love handles around her middle.

"Fran bought me a pass to the Film Festival," Moira said. "She sent it in the mail, actually. You're probably asking yourself why she would do that since we broke up six months ago, and the answer is because she knew how much I disliked erotic movies. That's because they turn me on, drive me wild, make me want to get down and dirty, which is very frustrating. You look confused. Are you sure you're really paying attention?"

Harry nodded.

"A niece should always pay attention to her aunt," Moira said for the waiter's benefit. He served their dessert and coffee and placed two bulbous brandy snifters on the table.

"I wish you would stop playing that game," Harry said once the waiter left.

"I know you do." Moira smiled agreeably and dug her fork into the rich chocolate cake on her plate. "But I enjoy being an actress, even if I am unsung. You should have some cake — it's scrumptious. Divine, in fact. If I don't watch out, I might grow into Fran's clothes. But never mind. My nervous system is too active for me to put on weight. Listen, if you're not going to eat your cake, pass it over."

Harry handed Moira her plate.

"And your cognac?" Moira asked hopefully.

"That I plan to drink," Harry said, protectively closing her hand around her snifter.

"Oh, well. I can always order another," Moira said. "Now, where was I?"

"Fran sent you a pass." Harry poured cream in her coffee and added sugar.

"Yes. Otherwise I wouldn't have been there. I rarely get to go anywhere these days. Everything costs too much. I was a bit startled by the movie's subject matter, but with such a title, who could tell it was going to be erotic? I mean, *Blueberries*. It sounds like one of those films made by an airhead of a dyke, you know the kind. Lesbians in wispy blue costumes leaping in unison through tall grass or an environmental tale about a farm collective growing organic blueberries or a modern-day, feminist morality play about a coven of middle-aged witches cooking blueberry pies or creating a quilt with pie-shaped pieces. The variations are endless if you let your mind roam freely. But not erotica, for goodness sake. Flower petals, artichokes, even cherries, but blueberries, no."

"I was surprised, too."

"Naturally," Moira remarked. "Who wouldn't have been? Unless you acted in the damn thing, which, now that I think about it, must have been an interesting proposition. Do people really get paid for screwing on screen?"

"I think so," Harry replied, trying to stifle a laugh.

"I wonder whether they get paid by the orgasm," Moira ruminated.

"I doubt it, somehow. Moira, why don't you tell me about that evening? I know what the movie was about, I was there too," Harry said, trying to move the conversation along.

"Of course," Moira said. "That damn film made me horny as hell. Talk about an intolerable situation — why anybody thinks it's fun to sit in a theatre surrounded by hundreds of other horny people when all you want to do is go to bed with someone, I'll never know. But that's neither here nor there, since I don't have a girlfriend at the moment and, as you can imagine, darling niece of mine, women are not lining up for the privilege of hopping into the sack with me."

Harry hid behind her cognac glass.

"Still, I thought I would try my luck cruising the restroom," Moira said casually. "So I went downstairs and hung around a little, but I didn't get any action. Everybody was scoring but me, so after a while I got depressed and left."

Scoring? In the women's washroom?

"You look shocked," Moira commented. "Have you never cruised a washroom? No? Not even when you were a desperate teenager?"

Harry tried to imagine cruising the ladies' one-holer in the Woolworth's or going to it in one of the tiny cubicles in the women's washroom in the skating rink in her home town, population three thousand. She couldn't. She supposed that she had never been quite that desperate.

"I don't believe it — my darling niece turns out to be a babe in the woods. You don't take after me, that's for sure."

Harry felt somewhat deficient. "The opportunity never arose."

"Never mind," Moira said, waving her off. "Shall we have another cognac?"

"Not for me, but you go ahead."

Moira captured their waiter's attention and ordered another drink. "Now, where was I? Oh, yes. When I was downstairs in the lobby, I saw Raven rush by. She looked intent on her mission, so I didn't interrupt. Or perhaps she just didn't want to talk to me at that particular time. That happens more often than I care to admit."

Harry felt uncomfortable.

"And young Richie was in the lobby, and then, later, I saw Raven again with that bitch Celia. They were so busy fooling around that they didn't notice me go by. You should speak to Raven about that. It's not proper for her to be fooling around with someone else."

"Celia was coming on to her, that's all," Harry said, thinking that she would be all too pleased to talk to Raven if only Raven would talk to her.

"I'm sure you would know, my dear." There was a pleasant but guarded expression on Moira's face. "Anyway, I think you could have dropped a bomb beside them and they wouldn't have realized I was there."

"Then what?"

"I decided to go back to my seat, even though I wasn't enjoying the movie. Sitting through the rest of it was better than the alternative, you see."

"Which was what?"

"Going back to my room, which is no more than a grimy hole in the wall, a soiled closet a dung beetle wouldn't stay overnight in. You couldn't possibly imagine what a relief it is to sleep in a clean bed with no rats running across my pillow in the middle of the night." When Moira saw the look on Harry's face, she asked, "Does that shock you?"

Harry nodded.

"Why do you think so many people who live in rooming houses spend most of their time on the street?" Moira asked.

"I hadn't thought about it," admitted Harry.

"And why should you?" Moira nodded. "It's no good cluttering your mind with useless facts or worrying about things you can't change."

Moira certainly had the knack of letting her off the hook while making her feel guilty at the same time.

"Did you see anyone you knew on your way back to the balcony?" Harry asked.

"Not a soul." Moira downing her second cognac. "But then, it was dark and I was watching my step. I was sitting in the back row, so it was a long way to go."

"Was Raven there?" Harry asked.

"I have no idea. I was looking at the screen at that point."

Harry hadn't expected a definitive answer, but it would have been nice to get one.

"I don't know where the rest of them were, but I was in my seat when the deed was done," Moira added.

"What?"

"Don't play cutsey with me, child," Moira said. "It seems I'm to inherit half of Fran's house whether I want it or not, which makes me suspect *numero uno* — or *dos*, depending on whether you have more dirt on Raven than on me. Since she's your girlfriend, I'm sure you'd rather pin it on me. No hard feelings, I'd do the same thing if I was in your shoes. It's only natural."

Harry had forgotten who she was dealing with for a moment.

"Harriet, don't let me down. I may be nuts, but I'm not dumb," Moira said.

"Sorry." Harry hadn't thought she was prejudiced against the mentally ill, but perhaps she was wrong. "It's just that most people aren't so forthright about things. But you're right. Everyone who was there that night is suspect."

"Including you."

"Yes. Although I didn't do it."

"That makes two of us."

"Can you prove it?"

"You're a tricky little dyke, aren't you?" Moira chuckled, oblivious to the waiter's presence.

"Anything else, ladies?" he asked.

"No, thanks," Harry responded, not waiting for Moira to reply. "Just the bill."

"Don't sound so depressed," Moira said.

"It's just that I'm not certain whether Fran was actually murdered."

"Well, I am," Moira said.

Harry was startled. "What?"

"She *deserved* to be murdered," Moira said with great equanimity. "That's how I know. Everybody came to despise her sooner or later, and people who are hated deserve to die violent deaths. The real proof that there is no justice in this world is that most of them don't. Look at how Fran treated people. She bragged to me that, when Richie was a child, she used to call him a fat slob just to make him cry."

"How cruel," Harry murmured.

"Yes. He was a chubby little boy, so she made fun of him. And take Raven: For reasons known only to herself, she desperately wanted to live with Fran, but Fran wouldn't let her move in. She said she needed her privacy and that Raven would be like a millstone around her neck. What a crock of shit. Why, that house is so big that people have to make a date if they want to see each other. But the worst thing was that Fran treated Raven like a child. By the time Fran chewed her up and spit her out, Raven barely had enough confidence to reply when she was spoken to."

"You're exaggerating," said Harry.

"Unquestionably," replied Moira. "It would take a lot more than the likes of Fran to put a woman of Raven's worth down for good. But she hurt that child in the worst ways. I know, because she did the same thing to me, and likely every other woman she took to bed. Oh, Fran was a cruel woman. She had a cold heart. So it was only natural for her to die in a brutal fashion."

Perhaps that was as good a reason as any to conclude that Fran had been murdered, Harry reflected. She tossed her credit card on the bill, and a few minutes later, they left the restaurant.

"That was a delicious meal." Moira sighed, grasping Harry's arm.

"Yes, it was."

"We must do it again sometime."

"You're right."

They rounded the corner and climbed the stairs to Fran's house. Harry used her key to open the door.

"I think I'll go right up," Moira said. "All that food has made me feel sleepy."

"Me, too," Harry said. It wasn't late, but she could use a good night's sleep. She followed Moira up the stairs and down the hall. "Auntie Mo."

Moira turned and cocked her head, a pleased expression on her face. "Yes, niece-of-mine?"

"You're not really crazy, are you?"

"Ah now, child, that would be telling." Moira opened the door and swept into Fran's old room.

Harry grinned. What a cagey woman, she thought. She was so good she should give lessons.

Harry hated crossword puzzles, jigsaw puzzles and algebraic equations where x equalled one thing, y another, not to mention z. She also despised the kind of questions they asked on Grade Five tests, like if A and B were twenty-five miles apart, and if Jim left A at ten o'clock and travelled at twenty miles per hour and Gina left at ten-thirty and went thirty miles per hour and Michael left at ten-forty-five and went forty miles per hour, who arrived at B first? Your average high-school graduate with a driver's licence would realize that the question was unrealistic since no one was speeding, and anyway, Harry didn't care whether Jim, Gina or Michael arrived first. If she had to, she would bet on Gina just because she was a woman. But if make-believe puzzles both mystified and annoyed her, what made her think she could solve a real one?

Harry was wide awake, even though it was before dawn. The sheets were nubby and irritated her skin, something she hadn't noticed when Raven had been there with her. She gathered the covers around her, but she was too chilly to get up and close the window. She could hear heavy rain falling, and somewhere nearby there was a loud, steady drip. It seemed to be marching in time to the beat of her heart.

Who had killed Fran? Raven, Moira, Celia and Richie had been downstairs during the movie, but all of them except Celia professed to be in their seats when the lights came on, and not one of them could — or would — say whether any of the others were seated.

She would have to forget about where and think about why. Harry sighed and turned over, wishing for distraction. But there was nothing but the sound of the drizzle. A door slammed somewhere outside, and then a car engine sputtered into life. The rain, the slowly breaking dawn and her solitude made her feel lonely. She had a feeling that she was going to become accustomed to that particular emotion before long. She turned her thoughts to the problem at hand; at least it diverted her attention from her personal difficulties.

The problem was, *everyone* had a motive to want Fran dead. Worse yet, some of them had more than one motive. Jealousy, financial gain, revenge, unrequited love, hatred, one of the above, some of the above, all of the above.

Harry decided to look at things from a different angle. What had she learned about the murder victim? That Fran was a schemer given to playing nasty tricks on other people, that she had a bad temper, that she had treated Moira and Raven cruelly, that she had played loose and dirty with her lovers. What else? That, to all intents and purposes, she had betrayed Richie and, by extension, Buck, by changing the provisions in her will. What didn't she know? Whether Moira still loved Fran and sought revenge. Ditto for Raven. Whether Richie would kill for financial gain. Ditto for Buck and Moira and Raven. Whether Richie would kill because he hated his sister. Whether the rest of them would kill because they despised Fran. Whether Mandy would kill because she was overcome with jealousy. Whether, whether, whether. Greed, hatred, jealousy. The desire to take back something Fran had stolen, like self-respect, or to regain control of something Fran had confiscated, like the future.

Someone walked by Harry's door without pausing and then went downstairs. Feeling petulant, confused and not inclined to stay in bed one second longer, Harry jumped up, grabbed her kit-bag and headed for the bathroom. A few minutes later, she returned to the study and got dressed. She checked to make sure the photocopy of Fran's will was still safely tucked behind her dirty laundry, and then left. She walked past the bathroom and knocked on Richie and Buck's door.

"Come in," Buck answered.

Harry opened the door and went in. Buck was sitting on the edge of the bed, pulling a brown sock on one of his bare feet. He was alone. It must have been Richie she'd heard on the stairs, then.

"Why didn't you want to move to San Francisco?" Harry asked. She had hoped to startle him, but he didn't appear to be fazed.

He put his socked foot on the floor and crossed his other leg over his knee. "Because I like living in Vancouver."

Harry closed the door and leaned against it. "Try again."

Buck slid his sock over his foot and adjusted the heel. "My shoes are around here somewhere," he said. "Under the bed, probably."

"Answer my question, Buck."

"What, is it Detective Hubbley of the SFPD now?" he said mockingly. Then he gave a slight shrug. "I don't know why you're bothering about Fran's death. She was *not* an agreeable person. In fact, she was rather detestable. And that was precisely the reason I didn't want to move down here and live with her. I was positive that she'd manipulate Richie and make both our lives miserable."

"That was all?"

He bent down, searched under the bed for his shoes, and then reached in and retrieved one. "Isn't that enough? I didn't want Rich to fall under her control."

"But wouldn't you be much better off financially if you took a nursing job in the States?"

"I suppose so," he admitted, pulling out his other shoe. "Jeez, it looks as if no one has dusted under here since the house was built."

"And wouldn't Richie have a shot at a lot more parts in movies and on TV?"

"Perhaps," Buck answered. He rubbed the tops of his shoes on the mat and then put them on.

Harry was exasperated. "What's the matter with you, Buck? Why are you acting like this?"

"Because you're behaving the way you are," he said with a false smile. "And don't give me that look. You obviously think Richie had something to do with his sister's death, and I resent it."

"Richie thought he was going to inherit this house, and —"

"So what?" Buck interrupted. "Millions of other people will one day inherit relatives' houses and they aren't planning to resort to murder to get a head start."

"I wasn't finished," Harry said. "I think Richie discovered that Fran had changed her will, and that made him very angry indeed."

The corner of Buck's mouth twitched. "I honestly don't think he knew. It's true that Rich was often mad at Fran about one thing or another. That was the type of relationship they had. In fact, that was the kind of relationship Fran seemed to have with everybody.

I think she must have got off on it in some perverted way. But, no matter what, Rich wouldn't have hurt a hair on her head."

Buck sounded so sincere that Harry knew he believed what he was saying. She decided to switch to another, much blunter, tack. "Although your enthusiasm for Vancouver is admirable, it's also quite unbelievable. You have another lover there, don't you?"

A vulnerable expression crossed Buck's face, and Harry pounced before he could recover. "And Richie doesn't know anything about this other man, does he?"

Buck looked miserable. He got up, went to the dresser and stared at himself in the mirror. His gaze was drawn to Harry's reflection, and when their eyes met, he began to laugh. "I look as guilty as sin, don't I?" He spun around to face Harry and leaned against the edge of the dresser. "Yes, there's another man. And no, Richie doesn't know about him. His name is Joel, and he's all the things that Richie isn't: Thoughtful, kind and considerate. Richie has always been self-centred and temperamental, but that's who he is. He has other qualities that drew me to him. He's outgoing, charming, well read, intelligent and loyal. Besides, I knew about the drawbacks when I got involved with him."

"So you don't want to move to California because you're afraid you would lose Joel."

"That's right." Buck nodded. "I didn't go looking for someone else, it just happened. His father had a heart attack, and when he was well enough to leave the intensive-care unit, he was transferred to the ward I happened to be working on. Joel visited him nearly every day. I was attracted to Joel, but I have a rule of never mixing business with pleasure. People are too susceptible to suggestion when they're seriously ill or when someone they care about is hospitalized. Not only that, there are too many opportunities for error. It wouldn't do to make a pass at someone who turned out to be heterosexual, for example. It would be a sure-fire way to lose your job"

"But you broke your rule for Joel."

"Not at all," Buck insisted. "He realized immediately that I was gay, so we spent a fair amount of time talking. He was quite close to his dad, and he was afraid he was going to lose him. He needed a shoulder to cry on, and I ended up providing it. Plus I tried to reassure him that his father was going to recover, that time at least. Sure, we were attracted to each other, but that was as far as it went.

We never spoke about our feelings for each other while his father was in the hospital. When his dad was discharged, I figured I'd never see him again. People come into your life, stay for a while, and then disappear. But a few weeks later, I ran into Joel at a gay-rights march. We discovered that we belonged to the same gay group, and it seemed natural to go out for coffee after meetings. I told myself that we weren't actually dating, but I suppose we really were. I just didn't want to admit it to myself."

"And you didn't mention it to Richie," Harry surmised.

Buck shook his head. "No, although I should have. If only I had casually said something about Joel when I was telling Richie about the demonstration — that I'd run into a fellow I'd met at the hospital, that I had coffee with him after the march — but I didn't. After that, I knew it would sound suspicious if I referred to him. Rich would want to know where I'd met him, how long I'd known him, why I hadn't mentioned him before. It seemed too complicated. I kept telling myself that it was okay to have a friend, that there was nothing wrong with what I was doing, but deep down I knew I was rationalizing. If Joel was just a casual friend, then why was I keeping our meetings a secret? The problem was, Joel was becoming more than a friend to me. He and I soon discovered that we had a lot in common. We both liked sports; doing outdoors stuff, like going fishing and hunting; and hanging out in cafés and sports bars. We felt easy with each other, as if we'd been buddies all our lives."

"And eventually you became lovers."

Buck looked troubled. "That's right."

"How long has this been going on?"

"Over two years."

"And Richie doesn't suspect anything?"

"No. Joel and I have been very careful."

But Harry was certain that, on some level, Richie knew. That would explain his insecurity about Buck, which was so thick you could cut it with a knife. "And nobody else knows?"

"No," Buck said, his voice cracking slightly.

He was lying. Harry stared at him for a moment, her mind working rapidly, and then said, "Fran figured it out, didn't she?"

The corner of his mouth twitched. "She made a lucky guess."

"Did she threaten to tell Richie?"

"What do you think? She pulled me aside that first night at the Café Bar and said Richie was upset and drinking too much. She wanted to know what I'd done to him," Buck said bitterly. "When I told her that I hadn't done anything, she accused me of lying. She said that if I really loved Richie, I'd agree to move to San Francisco. Then she came to the same conclusion you did — that I wasn't staying because I loved Vancouver but because I was in love with another man. She said that if I didn't agree to move down here, she'd tell him the truth."

And there, in a nutshell, was Buck's motive for killing Fran. "What did you say?"

"That I'd think about it."

"And?"

"She was satisfied with that, at least for a couple of days. She knew that she was asking me to choose between Richie and Joel, and I think she'd have been pleased if I'd decided to leave Richie," Buck replied. "I've felt so guilty ever since Joel and I became lovers that in some ways it would be a relief if Rich found out about it. Life with Joel would be so comfortable, you see. He really loves me, and I care deeply for him. And yet there's still something strong between Richie and me, and it's hard to turn your back on five years. But he's not an easy man to live with."

Harry wondered momentarily whether Judy had gone through a similar struggle in the months leading up to their separation, and then put that consideration from her mind. She would never know, so there was no point thinking about it. "What did you tell Fran in the end?"

"I didn't have a chance to tell her anything — she died before I made up my mind," replied Buck.

He must have known that such a solid incentive for wanting to silence Fran made him a suspect. But he said nothing about it, and neither did Harry.

"I've got to go," he remarked. "Rich is making breakfast, and he's probably wondering where I am."

"Fine." Harry nodded, getting up off the bed as if she was going to follow him. He dashed from the room, closing the door behind him without a backward glance. She listened to his footsteps echo on the hardwood floor and heard him rush down the stairs.

She took a deep breath and began to search Buck and Richie's bedroom, trying to stop her knees from trembling. She had to keep her wits about her and not leave behind traces of her hurried exploration. She went through the dresser. The top and bottom drawers were empty, and their personal belongings were in the two middle drawers. They were filled with tee-shirts, socks and underwear, the flowered boxer shorts obviously Richie's, the more trendy bikini briefs Buck's. There were a couple of shirts and several ties, and that was all.

She turned to the two bedside tables. The first contained a paperback novel, several sections of the *Vancouver Sun* newspaper which they must have brought with them, and an open package of condoms. Harry shut the drawer and moved to the second table. It was empty. She went to the closet, where she found several pairs of jeans draped over clothes hangers and two sports jackets. She ran her hands into all the pockets, but there was nothing but some spare change and a lot of lint. There were two suitcases on the closet floor. They were both unlocked, so she went through them one after the other, but she didn't find a damn thing.

She zipped up the suitcases, stood them upright, and backed out of the closet. Where would Richie hide something, she wondered. She closed the closet door, walked over to the bed, got down on her hands and knees, lifted the dust ruffle and peered under the bed. Buck had been right; dust bunnies abounded. She wished she had a flashlight, but, even without one, she was fairly certain there was nothing there. She got up and looked around the room. Under the mattress, perhaps? She slid her hand under it and worked her way from the top to the bottom, and then switched sides. Halfway down, she struck pay dirt. It was a thick, legal-sized envelope with the seal broken. She pulled out the documents, put them on the bed and went through them, astonished to see copies of eight different wills. She arranged them in chronological order and quickly realized that Fran had made a new will every two or three years. She had also alternated between leaving everything to Richie and bequeathing all of her belongings to various women whose names Harry didn't recognize. As far as she could tell, the only will that was missing was the one she had discovered in Fran's study. What a bombshell! The implications of this find were enormous.

Harry was in the process of returning the wills to the envelope when she heard footsteps in the hall. She frantically stuffed the envelope under the mattress and looked around. Where could she hide? She momentarily considered slipping under the bed but decided against it, knowing that the dust would cause her allergies to flare up. It would never do to sneeze if she wanted to go undetected. As the footsteps halted outside the bedroom door, she bolted for the closet. She barely had time to secret herself inside and shut the door. It was pitch black, so she closed her eyes, hoping that, when she opened them again, her eyes would have become accustomed to the dark and she would be able to see daylight in the cracks around the door. She took a cautious peep, but so such luck.

The bedroom door opened.

"So that's what she said," Buck was saying.

"It's not true. I didn't know anything about her new will," Richie replied.

The bedroom door closed. Harry had a hard time stopping herself from hyperventilating. She was not overly fond of small spaces, having locked herself in a closet when she was a child. She moved sideways until she was behind Richie's and Buck's clothes, although they were scant cover should one of the men open the closet door.

"I know you didn't," Buck said.

She heard the bedsprings creak as one of them sat down. Oh, Lord; what if they made love? How could she not announce her presence if they began making out? Could she stoop so low?

"Buck, look at this!" Richie said excitedly. "Somebody's been through my bedside-table drawer!"

"How can you tell?" Buck asked.

"I'm positive that the *Vancouver Sun* wasn't on top," Richie replied. "I tossed it in the drawer when we arrived and I haven't touched it since. But last night I was reading my book, and later I opened that package of condoms."

Someone closed the drawer and then there was a short silence.

"Why would somebody search our room?" Buck asked.

"I don't know," Richie responded. "Perhaps they were looking for money."

"But there isn't anything of value in here," Buck said.

"You and I know that, but a thief wouldn't. Listen, did Harry leave when you did?" Richie asked.

"Yes. She was right behind me."

"Well, then, whoever it was must have come in here after Harry left," Richie said. "That was the only time the room was empty."

"You know, it could have been anybody in the house. Celia, Moira, Mandy or even Raven, depending on whether she spent last night with Harry. I could go back downstairs and see who was here overnight," Buck offered. "Perhaps Harry saw someone in the hall when she left our room."

"That sounds like a good idea," Richie replied.

Harry heard the door open and close. Had they both left, or was Richie still there? She strained to hear something and was rewarded when the bedsprings squeaked.

"Shit!" Richie muttered to himself. "The envelope."

Harry grimaced in the dark. There hadn't been time to replace the envelope precisely where she'd found it. The bedsprings squeaked again and then there was silence. Harry imagined Richie creeping toward the closet; a hand reaching out; the door suddenly opening; and Richie reaching in and grasping her arm, shoulder, hair, and pulling her from the closet. She supposed it was too much to hope for a secret passage that would lead her from the embarrassment of discovery.

But nothing of the sort happened. Harry heard the door close and footsteps recede. When she was absolutely certain that she was alone, she stepped forward and hurriedly turned the doorknob, feeling as if she was going to suffocate if she didn't get out of that tiny hole. She burst into the bedroom, taking deep breaths to still her racing heart. Only when she was out in the hall and rushing toward the study did her trembling cease.

She threw herself on the sofa in the study and lay quietly until her heart stopped thumping. It was foolish to feel so nervous. After all, nothing would have happened if Richie and Buck had discovered her there. She would have been incredibly embarrassed, but she couldn't imagine either of them hurting her, even once they realized that she had tossed their room and found the wills. She turned on her side and told herself to stop rationalizing. If either — or both — of the two men had been involved in Fran's death, they could have treated her very badly indeed. But she had to drop this line of thought. Fear would only paralyse her, stop her from doing what she had to do. She got up and went into the bathroom and splashed water on her face. Just as she was drying her hands, the door opened.

"Oh! Sorry!" Mandy said, her face reddening.

"It's my fault," Harry said. "I forgot to lock the door."

"I'll come back later."

"No, I'm finished," Harry assured her. "But, listen, have you got a minute? There are a few questions I want to ask you."

Mandy looked as if she was going to bolt, so Harry moved to cut her off.

"It's nothing special, I'd just like to know if you went to *Blueberries*," Harry said, keeping her voice gentle as she followed Mandy down the hall.

"Didn't Celia tell you that I did?"

"Sort of, in a roundabout way," Harry answered. "But I just wanted to hear it from you. Where were you sitting?"

"In the balcony." Mandy rushed down the stairs and Harry followed her. "I wanted to sit near Celia, but my ticket was for another row."

"So what did you see?"

Mandy opened the front door. "What do you mean, what did I see? The movie, of course."

"You didn't get up? Go downstairs to the washroom or to buy something to eat or drink?"

"No. Of course not. The movie only lasted for half an hour."

"You didn't notice anybody moving around?"

Mandy looked at her as if she was crazy. "Of course I did — people were acting like they had ants in their pants."

"I mean, did you see anybody you knew wandering around?"

Mandy shook her head. "No. Look, Celia told me that you think Fran was murdered, but I don't know anything about it. I didn't hear anything, I didn't see anything, I didn't do anything. So if you don't mind, just leave me alone."

Harry raised her eyebrows. "Don't you care who killed Fran?"

"Why should I? I didn't know her."

"No one deserves to be murdered."

Mandy snorted, turned away and walked through the open doorway. So much for that, Harry thought, watching her run down the stairs. She probably would have got as much information from the bloody film projectionist. The more she learned, the more questions Harry had. She sighed, closed the front door and trudged up the stairs to her room. Eight wills! Nine counting the latest, and apparently final one, she had discovered on Fran's desk. Fran had played off her lovers against her brother, changing her will with great regularity. What an underhanded way of controlling people. And she had obviously given copies of each of her wills to Richie, which meant that he knew that his periods of grace lasted no more than two or three years. Had he finally tired of this charade and put an end to it by doing away with his sister?

Not only that, did Raven and Moira know that *their* periods of grace were limited until Richie got back into his sister's good graces or until Fran's next set of lovers managed to make it into the winner's circle?

Harry was so exhausted from her near misadventure in Buck and Richie's room that she stretched out on the sofa in the study and napped for two hours. She was roused from a sound sleep by the ringing on the telephone on the desk, but somebody picked it up before she could answer it.

A few minutes later, Celia burst into the study. "Raven's been mugged."

Harry's mouth grew dry and her stomach cramped. "What happened? Where is she? Is she all right?"

Celia reached out and put her arm around Harry's shoulder. "That was someone from the hospital. Apparently Fran's number was in Raven's wallet. It seems that she was attacked on her way to work this morning. They wanted her to stay for observation for a while, but she wouldn't. One of the nurses was worried about her, so she called to see if someone could go to her apartment and spend some time with her."

"Did they say how badly she was hurt?"

"She's been beaten up, but she's all right," Celia replied, giving her a reassuring hug.

"I'm going to see her," Harry said, not caring whether Raven wanted her there or not.

Celia picked up the phone. "I thought you'd want to. I'll call you a cab."

"Will you come with me?" Harry asked Celia as soon as she gave the dispatcher the address and replaced the receiver in its cradle.

Celia looked surprised. "What on earth for?"

"I don't think Raven will let me in," Harry admitted. "She's angry with me."

"So you want me to run interference. To pretend that I'm alone so she'll buzz me in and you can sneak in after me."

"More or less." Harry tried to sound nonchalant.

"I'm not sure if I want to particulate in such duplicity," Celia mused, a flash of amusement flickering in her eyes.

Harry hated begging, but in this case she would if she had to. She was desperate to see Raven. She hadn't realized how much she cared for Raven until she heard that the younger woman had been attacked.

"Come on, Celia. I can't stand not knowing whether she's all right."

"Well, I could certainly find that out for you if I went by myself," Celia said with a grin.

"What kind of a friend are you, anyway?"

Celia laughed. "One who likes to tease. Come on, don't you know I wouldn't refuse you something as important as this? Now, let's get a move on. The taxi's probably here by now, and time's a'wastin'!"

Harry let Celia shepherd her into the cab, and from the cab to the sidewalk in front of Raven's apartment house. Harry grasped Celia by the hand and led her up the staircase and into the building. She pressed the buzzer several times in quick succession.

"Yes? Who is it?"

"Celia Roberts. The hospital called Fran's house and told me what happened, so I thought I'd drop by to see how you're doing."

There was a rather long silence before Raven replied. "Come up, then."

The buzzer sounded and Celia opened the door. "I told you she was home. Now go make up with her. And find out what happened."

"And whether it has anything to do with Fran's murder," Harry said grimly.

"You don't think —"

"I'll know more once I've spoken to Raven," Harry interrupted. "Aren't you coming up?"

"You know what they say about three being a crowd — well, it's absolutely true," Celia said. "Actually, with someone like Mandy, even two is a crowd, but that's another story. More like a broken record, in fact. But listen, I have something I simply have to confess. Otherwise I'm going to go bonkers. Remember that night at the movie, when I said I went down to the lobby to meet Fran? Well, I just happened to run into Raven while I was there."

Harry knew what Celia was going to say, but she certainly wasn't going to make it easy for her. "So?"

Celia was staring so fixedly at the floor that Harry wondered if she was attempting to follow the swirling patterns in the marble tiles from one corner of the lobby to the other.

"I made a pass at her," Celia muttered. "I didn't intend to, it just happened. It must have been the effect of that damn movie."

"Raven already told me about it."

"And you're not angry?"

"Not any more."

"That's a relief," Celia admitted, giving Harry's arm a squeeze. "I was worried that you were going to hold a grudge. But it didn't mean anything, and I immediately regretted it. Listen, why don't you go upstairs? I'll see you back at the house later."

Harry watched her climb into the cab. Celia might be a bother at times, and she was certainly audacious, but she also knew how to be a friend. There was a solidity about her which came to the fore when someone she knew was in trouble or needed emotional support. Harry wondered where that steadfastness went the rest of the time, and why Celia chose to act so tempestuous. She must ask her one day. Not that she'd get a reasonable answer.

Harry decided to take the stairs. She was out of breath by the time she reached the third floor, but she hurried to Raven's door. She was about to knock when it opened.

"Hello, Harriet."

"How did you know it was me?"

"Celia wouldn't have come to visit," Raven said, turning away. She was walking stiffly and holding her right arm tight against her body. "You might as well come in."

Harry followed Raven into the apartment, wanting to take her in her arms. But there was an aloofness about Raven that made Harry keep her distance. She cleared her voice and asked, "How do you feel?"

"What do you think? I was mugged."

"But are you all right?"

"Why shouldn't I be?" Haven answered testily. "Someone knocked me down and kicked me around a little, that's all."

"You could have been killed!"

"Don't be silly — it happens to people all the time. I have a sore kidney, a couple of bruised ribs and black-and-blue arms, but nothing's broken and the rest of me's okay," Raven said.

Harry wanted to shake the flippancy from her voice. "Don't act like this, Raven."

"Like what? Do you want some juice? I was just about to pour myself some."

Perhaps Raven's mood had nothing to do with her, Harry thought. Perhaps her bravado was simply a defence mechanism she had erected to protect herself. She followed Raven into the kitchen. "I'd love a glass of juice. Apple, if you've got it." She watched as Raven removed a pitcher of apple juice from the fridge and stopped herself from reaching out to help when she saw the younger woman flinch. She was an independent little cuss, and Harry had to respect that.

Raven handed her one of the glasses of juice and led her to the living room. Harry sat on the white leather sofa and watched Raven lower herself into the leather easy chair opposite her. She looked away when Raven cringed.

"All right, so it hurts like hell." Raven sounded angry about conceding anything to Harry, as if admitting her fragility was a sign of weakness.

"You did see a doctor, didn't you?"

"I didn't have any choice in the matter," Raven replied. "A Good Samaritan came along and scared off the mugger. I was flat on my back on the sidewalk, so he called an ambulance before he disappeared, and they carted me off to the nearest hospital, where I was poked and prodded and x-rayed and generally made to feel worse than I did when they took me in. They told me that nothing was broken, that technicolour bruises would blossom over a large part of my body and that I'd feel like hell for a while. I find that that last bit was particularly true."

"Did you see who beat you up?"

"No. It was just before noon, and I wasn't expecting to be jumped at that time of day. Most muggers prefer to work at night. I feel kind of stupid about the whole thing, actually. I've lived here for years. I moved in shortly before Fran and I started dating, and that was four years ago. I've always been pretty street smart. Even when I'm exhausted or I've got a lot on my mind, I'm aware of what's going on around me. So when that thug came out of the alley beside the building and hit me from behind, my first reaction was one of shock. It was only when I tripped and went down that I started being afraid. Even when I was on the ground, I was mad as hell. But I couldn't get up — I was too busy protecting myself from being hurt somewhere vital."

"Was it a man or a woman?" Harry asked.

"I have no idea. I was attacked from behind. Once I was down, all I wanted to do was to shield my head," Raven replied. "Whoever it was packed a mean kick."

Harry saw red. If Raven's assailant had been within striking distance, her fists would have been flying. She took a drink of juice and tried to settle herself down. "What did the person take? Your wallet?"

For the first time Raven's discomfort seemed to stem from something other than her physical injuries. "Nothing."

"Nothing?" Harry's mind raced. "What, didn't you have anything of value on you?"

"I had two twenties in my wallet, plus a couple of credit cards and my bank card," Raven replied. "And whatever jewellery I had on. A watch that wasn't worth much, a silver necklace, silver hoop earrings."

"Real silver?"

"Yes."

"And they weren't taken?"

"I wasn't even frisked."

Harry pursed her lips. "Why would someone mug you without stealing every penny in your pocket and every piece of jewellery you were wearing?"

"How should I know? I'm neither a mugger nor a mind reader. Maybe he gets his kicks from beating up people. Maybe the Good Samaritan interrupted him before he could strip me of my valuables. I just don't know. I don't have any special truths about this particular event," Raven replied.

Perhaps Raven didn't have any special truths, but she certainly must have instinctive ones. Harry slowly finished her apple juice, trying not to look underhanded as she drew out the silence. She was prepared to see Raven get up and water her plants, which looked droopy, or prepare lunch, for which Harry would be thankful, since she was hungry. Raven might also tell her to get the hell out, for which she was not the least bit prepared. Perhaps it was going to come down to which of them was more stubborn.

"Don't think I don't know what you're up to," Raven remarked, looking more tired than angry.

"I'm not up to anything."

"You're not going to say 'I told you so'?"

"I've never in my life said that."

"You don't really think that I was worked over because I saw someone push Fran over the railing, do you?"

"I don't know," Harry admitted. "Whoever mugged you didn't take anything, which doesn't make sense. You could be right, though; the mugger could have been interrupted before he or she had a chance to rob you."

"But I can't identify the person who pushed Fran," Raven protested. "I don't even know if it was a man or a woman. So why would anyone see me as a threat?"

"Perhaps Fran's killer thought he or she had committed the perfect crime, until the person found out what you'd seen," Harry suggested. "Or it could be that the killer thinks you can identify him or her but that you just haven't gone to the police yet. Maybe whoever it was thinks you're not sure exactly who it was but that something will eventually jog your memory. Or maybe the killer wants to be absolutely certain you won't be there to testify."

"But, Harriet, I haven't a clue who it was."

"The killer doesn't know that."

Raven probed Harry's face with her eyes and then nodded, apparently satisfied about something. "Okay, I'll tell that police detective what I saw the night Fran got killed."

Harry's mouth dropped open for a split second, but she closed it immediately. "That's great," she said, her tone mild. "Why don't you call them now? Ask for Detective Manley and tell him you have evidence you want to pass on to him regarding Fran's death."

Raven looked hesitant. "Right now?"

"Why not?"

Raven slowly got up and walked to her bed. She gingerly sat down on it, opened the drawer in her bedside table, reached inside and withdrew a telephone book.

"Why don't you just dial nine-one-one?"

"I don't want to call that much attention to myself," Raven responded. She made the mistake of giving a shrug and flinched.

Harry rose from the sofa and went to sit beside Raven on the bed. "Let me," she said, taking the phone book from Raven. She searched through the book for the general, non-emergency number for the police, dialled and asked how to get in touch with Detective Manley. The operator gave her the correct precinct number, which Harry then dialled. She spoke with the desk officer, who told her that Detective Manley wasn't in the building. Harry left a message for him to contact Raven on an urgent matter and then hung up.

"I'm sure he'll call soon."

Raven curled up on the bed and closed her eyes. "I'm exhausted."

"No wonder, after what you've been through," Harry said. "Why don't you have a nap?"

"Will you stay for a while?" Raven asked, opening her eyes for an instant.

"Yes," Harry murmured, stretching out beside Raven. She put her arm around Raven's waist. "Tell me if that hurts."

"No, it's okay." Raven's voice was groggy.

"Did the doctor give you something for the pain?"

"Yes — I took a pill just before you got here. I'm glad you came."

Harry kissed the back of her neck. "I couldn't have stayed away."

"You're sweet."

Harry was touched. She couldn't remember the last time anyone had said that to her. "Sleep, then."

She waited until Raven had drifted off and then slowly moved away and got up. She covered Raven with a comforter that had been folded on the bottom of the bed and went into the kitchen and poured herself another glass of apple juice. She didn't think Raven would mind if she helped herself to something to eat, so she made a sandwich with two pieces of sourdough bread, which she lightly coated with Dijon mustard, a leaf of lettuce and a thick slice of mild Cheddar cheese. She put her sandwich on a plate, and her plate and glass of juice on a tray, and carried her mid-afternoon lunch to the sofa.

What she hadn't told Raven was that she had no intention of leaving until Raven had given her statement to Detective Manley.

Once the pain receded and the effect of the painkillers abated, she would likely realize the danger she was in. Until then, someone had to watch over her in case her assailant decided to come back and finish the job, and that someone was Harry.

She finished her sandwich, drained the juice from her glass and settled in for a long afternoon.

It was after nine. Not wanting to disturb Raven's rest, Harry hadn't turned on the stereo or the overhead light. Before it had grown too dark to see, she had browsed through several feminist and lesbian magazines, but there was no longer enough light to read. She stretched, got up and approached the bed. Raven was curled up on her side and facing the wall, the comforter pulled tight around her neck.

Harry moved to the window and looked out. There wasn't much of a view, just the long brick wall and the curtained windows of the adjacent building. A rickety fire escape ended a few feet below Raven's window, its metal base rusted, several stair slats missing.

The window was within stepping distance of the fire escape. Harry was contemplating the relative lack of security when the front-door buzzer rang, startling her. She glanced at the bed. Raven groaned in her sleep and turned over. Harry crossed the room in the dark, bumping into the back of the easy chair. Where was the intercom? She switched on the kitchen light just as the buzzer rang again.

Perhaps it was Detective Manley. She scanned the kitchen and finally located the intercom. It was built into the wall next to the fridge and, just as she reached it, the buzzer sounded a third time.

She pushed the button. "Yes?"

There was only silence.

Harry released the button and pushed it again. "Who's there?"

Nothing but silence.

She stared at the intercom as if it could tell her who was downstairs. The stillness expanded inside her until she thought she would burst. And then she was suddenly certain that the person who was ringing the doorbell was the same person who had killed Fran and mugged her young lover. Perhaps if she hurried, she could catch the killer in the lobby but still locked out of the building.

She dashed to the door and charged down three flights of stairs. She came to an abrupt halt when she realized that the lobby was in utter darkness. Either the light bulb was burnt out or it had been removed or broken. Someone could be hiding in the shadows and she wouldn't know it until the person was on top of her. She pressed herself against the wall, shivering when the damp plaster sent a chill through her body. It occurred to her to be afraid. Raven was asleep and the building felt deserted. Where were the other tenants? She hadn't met any of them on the stairs or in the lobby. She hadn't even heard voices from behind closed apartment doors. For a terrifying moment, she had the distressing sensation that she, Raven and Fran's murderer were alone in the building, and that she was being stalked like an animal. She heard a noise from the lobby, as if someone had stepped on a discarded newspaper.

"Detective Manley?" she yelled.

When there was no answer, she darted across the hall and hugged the opposite wall. Detective Manley would have responded to her shout, as would an innocent visitor. And speaking out had undoubtedly given away her position. She slowly moved backward until she reached the first-floor corridor. If only she had a flashlight so she could see where she was going, or some sort of weapon with which she could defend herself.

There was a sudden racket, and then the lobby door crashed shut. When someone rushed up the stairs, Harry realized that, by retreating from the area directly in front of the staircase, she had left the coast clear to Raven's apartment.

She ran after the figure on the stairs. She took the steps two at a time, barely pausing on each landing to catch her breath. As she rounded the landing to the last flight of stairs, she stumbled. She went down heavily, catching herself on her right wrist. Pain shot through her arm, making her feel sick to her stomach. Her wrist was stinging and her breath was coming in pants, but she recovered and doggedly went on. She forced her aching muscles up the last flight of stairs, cursing her thoughtlessness in leaving the door to Raven's apartment open. She should have searched for a key and locked it before she went downstairs. Even better, she should have stayed where she was rather than rushing off to the lobby. What a fine protector she had turned out to be.

Harry burst into the apartment. A figure was bent over Raven.

"Don't you touch her!"

The figure bolted for the window and tried to open it with gloved hands. When it wouldn't budge, the intruder kicked out the glass and disappeared between the jagged shards hanging in the frame. She heard a heavy thud and assumed that the intruder had landed on the top step of the fire escape.

"Damn!" Harry muttered, rushing forward. She stumbled over fragments of broken glass and peered out the window, careful not to cut herself. The fire escape wobbled as the intruder neared the ground. Harry thought about leaping through the pointed spears of glass and following, but the intruder had too much of a head start. She wouldn't even get to the bottom before he or she disappeared.

Instead, she turned her attention to Raven.

"Are you all right?"

Raven sighed and her eyes fluttered open.

"What the hell's going on here?" a gruff male voice interrupted.

Harry turned, balling her fists despite her aching wrist, ready to ward off another intruder. Then the overhead light came on.

"Detective Manley?"

The detective glanced from Raven to Harry to the broken window and the glass on the floor. "What are you up to, Ms. Hubbley? And what's the matter with your arm? You're bleeding. How did you cut yourself?"

Harry looked at her wrist and saw blood trickling down the back of her hand. The flesh around her wrist bone was puffy and swollen, and from her experience as an athlete and physical education teacher, Harry recognized a sprain when she saw one. She realized that the detective thought she had cut her arm while breaking the window and that perhaps she was the one who had tried to hurt Raven.

"There was an intruder," she said. It was only then that she became fully aware of the danger both she and Raven had been in. Her knees were so weak that she sat down hard on the edge of the bed.

"Harriet?" Raven groaned, trying to sit up. "What was all that noise? And who's that?" she added, looking suspiciously at Manley.

"It's the detective," Harry said. "We left a message for him before you went to sleep, remember? As for the noise, someone just tried to break in. Whoever it was escaped through the window before I could prevent it."

"Christ!" Raven exclaimed, sitting up. "Did the person attack you? Was it the same one who beat me up?"

"I wasn't attacked," Harry assured her. "I fell chasing him or her up the stairs and sprained my wrist. I must have cut it on the step's metal edging, but it's not serious. As for whether it was the same person who mugged you, I don't know. Do you need another painkiller? No? Then let's talk with the detective."

"All right," Raven said, her voice conveying her reluctance.

Harry gave her shoulder a brief squeeze of reassurance and rose from the bed. "I'll just wrap something around my wrist while Raven gets up," she told Detective Manley. She went into the kitchen, turned the tap on cold and ran water over her wrist. Rivulets of diluted blood washed down the sink. She averted her gaze and turned off the tap.

Detective Manley gazed attentively at her wrist. "You might need a few stitches," he commented.

"Perhaps," agreed Harry. She picked up a dish towel which was draped over a cupboard door and wrapped it around her arm, trying to ignore how painful it felt. "Let's sit down and we'll tell you what happened," she said. She led the detective to the easy chair and then sat beside Raven on the sofa.

Raven recounted the story of her mugging, and then Harry went on to tell him about her encounter with the intruder. By the time she finished, he had a thoughtful look on his face.

"But why would someone mug you, steal nothing and then try to break in?"

"I think my Good Samaritan interrupted the mugger. Unfortunately, he left once he'd called nine-one-one."

"It's too bad that he didn't stick around," Manley said. "He might have been able to give us a description of your assailant."

"Maybe he'll show up once he's had time to think it over," Harry suggested. "Or perhaps he'll call."

"Maybe." But Manley didn't sound convinced.

"There's something else I have to tell you," Raven said. "It was my distinct impression that someone pushed Fran Matthews off the balcony in the theatre that night."

Harry had to hand it to Detective Manley; he took it well. He didn't look surprised, he didn't even ask Raven why she had withheld information. "Tell me what you saw" was all he said. He led Raven through the events of that night and made copious entries in the notebook he had removed from his jacket pocket. "Now tell me about being mugged."

Raven did, and then she said, "Unfortunately, I couldn't see who it was."

"That's not unusual, even in the daytime," the detective said with a nod. "Ms. Hubbley, were you able to identify the person you chased into this apartment?"

"No. Someone buzzed three times but didn't say anything, so I went downstairs. With hindsight, I can see that that was a stupid thing to do." Harry's voice full of chagrin. "For one thing, I left the apartment door open, assuming that the intruder was locked out. *I* didn't buzz the person in, but I should have known that someone in another apartment would."

"People do that all the time," the detective remarked. "It's incredibly stupid, but there it is."

"I also gave the intruder the opportunity to get upstairs before me. I chased him or her in here, and that's when the person broke the window and went down the fire escape," Harry added.

"You could have been seriously injured," Raven interjected.

"So could you, and it would have been my fault," Harry responded.

"Was the intruder a man, then?" the detective asked.

"I don't know," Harry admitted. "It was dark in the lobby and I never got a good look. The only light in the apartment was in the kitchen, and that isn't very bright."

"I use forty-watt blubs to conserve energy," said Raven.

"The intruder was bending over Raven when I shouted, and then he or she kicked out the window and jumped to the fire escape. By the time I got to the window, the person was nearly on the ground and it was too late to follow after," Harry explained.

"And too dangerous," the detective commented. "You did the right thing by staying here. Now, give me your impressions. Was the person shaped like a male or female, tall or short, fat or thin, young or old?"

"Whoever it was was fast, that's for sure, but that's all I can tell you," Harry said. "I couldn't see him — or her — at all when I was downstairs, it was just too dark. And on the stairs it was impossible."

"And once you were in the apartment?"

"As I said, it was dark. Everything happened so swiftly that I simply didn't get a good look," Harry said apologetically. "Actually, the way the intruder ran up three flights of stairs and then leapt onto the fire escape, he or she had to be in good condition. But as to whether the person was tall or short, I have no idea. I never got close enough to see except when we were both in the apartment, and at that point the intruder was bending over Raven. The only thing I can tell you was that the person wasn't fat."

As Detective Manley nodded, Harry felt Raven's hand slip into hers. She squeezed it tenderly, and then held it firmly in her own, despite the detective's presence. Even a minimum amount of contact between them made her feel better.

"Could you see what he or she was wearing?"

"Not really," Harry said hesitantly. "The person's clothes were dark in colour, though."

Detective Manley scribbled something in his notebook. He looked frustrated.

Harry felt inept. "I know it's not much to go on, but I didn't see more than that."

"Never mind." Raven squeezed her hand, and Harry gave her a grateful look.

"Well, thanks for the information, ladies," the detective said. He put his notebook in his jacket pocket and rose from the sofa.

"Will you be reopening your investigation of Fran's death?" Raven asked.

He reached for the doorknob. "Probably."

Before Harry could ask him why it wasn't a certainty, he opened the door and left.

"You mean that I talked to a police officer against my better judgment just for a 'maybe'?" Raven nearly jeered.

"I'm sure he was simply being cautious," Harry said, trusting that she was correct.

Raven picked at the dish towel covering Harry's wrist. "Was the detective right? Do you need stitches?"

Harry hoped not. She was suddenly overcome by fatigue. "No," she said, even though she didn't really know.

"Let me see."

Harry gingerly unwound the cloth and they both stared at the oozing cut on her wrist.

"It needs stitches." Raven said glumly.

"You're right. But tomorrow," Harry said. "I can barely keep my eyes open."

"Are you sure? It might get infected."

"Not overnight. But what are we going to do about that window?"

"Let's tape a piece of cardboard over it for now," Raven said. "I suppose I should clean up the broken glass first, so we don't cut ourselves on it."

Between the two of them, they managed to sweep the glass into a dustpan and deposit it in the garbage can. Then Harry held the cardboard while Raven fastened it with tacks and packing tape.

"This isn't really very secure," Harry commented.

"I know. But it's the best I can do."

"You should get a thick screen or bars."

"Hey, if someone really wants to get in, nothing's going to stop them. Anyway, that's it," Raven said, cutting the last piece of tape. "Of course it won't keep anybody out, except for the bugs and the mice, but I'll call the hardware store and order a new piece of glass first thing in the morning. Now, let's get something to eat and go to bed."

Harry didn't think she was hungry until she followed Raven to the kitchen, where she swiftly put together a cheese omelette and sourdough toast with orange marmalade, and two mugs of hot chocolate. By the time Raven cut the omelette in half and spilled it onto two plates, Harry's stomach was growling. After they finished eating, Raven rinsed their plates and stacked them in the sink. Then they joined hands and wordlessly walked toward the single bed. Harry slipped out of her jeans and crawled under the comforter in her panties and tee-shirt, cradling her wounded wrist in her other hand, as Raven slid in and curled up against her.

Harry and Raven woke early, Harry because her wrist was throbbing and Raven because her whole body was stiff and sore. They both knew that the first order of business was to get Harry's wrist stitched up, so, after they ate a quick breakfast, Raven took her to the local hospital. Because she wasn't an American citizen, it took more time to complete her insurance documents than it did for the doctor to stitch up her wrist, tell her that she had a light sprain, give her an tetanus injection and write a prescription for a mild painkiller.

"Come back in a week to have them out," the nurse said as Harry prepared to leave.

"I won't be here a week from now," replied Harry.

"Then have your family doctor remove them," the nurse suggested.

Raven looked perturbed. "You're leaving in a couple of days?"

"We're supposed to drive to Vancouver after Pride weekend and then I'll be flying back to Montreal shortly after that," Harry said.

Even though they were still in the hospital, Raven grasped her hand. "But what's going to happen to us?"

Harry hadn't given it a second thought. She hadn't planned on becoming involved with someone on such a short vacation, and she had been so preoccupied with investigating Fran's death that she hadn't spent any time pondering the future of this new relationship. She was accordingly dumbstruck by Raven's question.

"Why do you have to leave so soon?" Raven asked.

"I suppose I don't," Harry replied slowly.

She and Raven left the hospital lobby and walked to a cable car stop, where they sat on a bench. The weather was cool but sunny, although neither of them noticed.

Harry hadn't realized how much she cared for Raven until her young lover had been mugged. Didn't she owe it to herself — and to Raven — to explore the boundaries of their attraction to each other? But wasn't it too soon to become involved in another intense relationship? She wasn't even over Judy. Still, people didn't necessarily drop into one's life at the most opportune times. Often, it was just the opposite.

"Celia said that you'd come into a large sum of money when an old friend of yours died."

"That's true, but I'm not rich, not by any stretch of the imagination."

"But you don't have to rush back to Montreal to work, do you?"

"No, I don't." But she wasn't in love with Raven, and she certainly wasn't like a teenager enamoured with the idea of being in love. And she wasn't trying to escape the residual sorrow she felt over the break-up of her twelve-year relationship with Judy. The attraction between her and Raven was mainly sexual, although she wasn't about to underestimate its seductive power. But if she prolonged her visit to San Francisco, and she and Raven spent more time together, would she fall in love with her? The potential was there, of that she was certain.

"My girlfriend of twelve years left me a short time ago," Harry said, wishing she had told Raven about Judy before. "As you can well imagine, I'm still getting over her. But I do care about you."

"I care about you, too," Raven responded.

People were gathering at the cable-car stop and Harry didn't want the whole world to overhear their conversation. "Why don't we walk a little?"

Raven got up and grimaced, pressing her arm against her ribcage. They walked slowly away from the crowd. "Will you stay on in San Francisco so we can get to know each other better?"

When Harry hesitated, Raven said, "You don't have to answer right away. All I want is for you to think about it. Meanwhile, I'm going to take the cable car when it comes. It'll get me nearly home."

Harry was relieved. She supposed Raven had seen the ambivalent expression on her face and didn't want to force the issue. "Why don't you take a cab?" Harry suggested. "You're obviously still in a fair amount of pain."

"You're right. I'm exhausted," Raven admitted. "I'm going to call the hardware store around the corner from my apartment building and ask them to replace the glass in my window, and then I'm going to take one of those painkillers the doctor prescribed and sleep for the rest of the day."

"Good," Harry nodded. "Why don't we get together later this evening? If you feel like it, that is."

Harry was treated to a momentary flash of Raven's provocative grin.

"Oh, I'll feel like it, all right. I'll call you when I wake up. Look, there's a taxi," Raven said, waving her hand. As the cab stopped, she gave Harry a quick kiss on the lips and hobbled stiffly toward it.

What was love all about, anyway? Harry had been jealous when Celia had made a play for Raven, and she had been nearly frantic when she'd believed that Raven had been badly hurt. She had been in a relationship for so long that she had forgotten how difficult it was to differentiate between love and desire.

Harry felt sad and not a little sorry for herself. She sat down on the bench and watched a streetcar sluggishly climb a hill and disappear over the top. Who had killed Fran Matthews? The same person who had attacked Raven? Had the mugger intended simply to warn her, or had he or she meant to kill Raven? Was that why the person had made a second attempt? She decided to return to Fran's house and try to find out where everyone had been last night just after dark. She glanced at her watch, rose from the bench and hailed another passing cab.

She paid the cab driver, a taciturn man wearing a soiled baseball cap, and used her key to open the front door. She locked it behind her and headed for the kitchen.

"The prodigal daughter arrives," Celia said.

Harry couldn't believe her luck; four of them were seated around the kitchen table — Buck and Richie, Celia and Mandy. The only person missing was Moira. Someone had been grocery shopping. There was a platter of steaming scrambled eggs, a plate piled high with croissants and toasted bagel halves, a butter dish, jars of peanut butter and jam, and a jug of orange juice on the table. The coffee percolator was chugging along on the counter, and the aroma of freshly brewing coffee filled the air.

Richie reached for a bagel and the jar of peanut butter. "Why didn't you warn us about the police?"

Harry went over to the cupboard, took out a dinner plate and sat down at the table. "Were they here this morning?"

"*Very* early this morning," Celia remarked, serving herself a large heap of scrambled eggs. "What happened to your wrist?"

"I ran into something hard and sharp. It won." Harry took the platter from Celia and scooped a generous portion of eggs from it with a soup spoon. "I'll tell you about it later. What did the police want?"

"They put us through hell, questioning us about our movements the night Fran died. It was downright gruelling," Richie grumbled.

"They wanted to know detail after excruciatingly boring detail," claimed Celia. "They got us out of bed indecently early and made us sit around in our jammies waiting to be questioned. Of course I was speaking generically since I don't really wear pyjamas. I prefer to dress as if I'm going to have company in my bed, even when I'm fairly certain I won't. But a negligée is not my preferred attire for being meticulously cross-examined by a pack of dour detectives, even when I'm wearing a matching wrap. They didn't let us talk to each other, either, which was really stupid since we've had days to coordinate our stories. Should any of us want to, that is," she added as a pensive afterthought.

"They were just trying to put us at a disadvantage," Buck said. "It's a police tactic, that's all."

"Be that as it may, I still think it's uncivilized," Celia grumbled.

"I wonder whether Raven told the police what she saw or whether there was another witness," Buck mused aloud.

That was a good question, but Harry wasn't going to answer it, at least not right away. "Would you mind telling me where you were last night around sunset?"

"That's one of the questions that damn Detective Manley asked, and he didn't say why he wanted to know either," Richie griped.

The scrambled eggs were moist; Celia must have made them. She was a damn good cook, which never failed to amaze Harry, who considered it practically obscene for someone so thin to be a gourmet chef.

"Look, if you tell me where you were, I'll spill the beans about last night."

"It's a deal," Celia said promptly. She grabbed a croissant and began spreading a thick coat of marmalade on it.

"What about the rest of you?" Harry asked. "Do you agree?"

"I suppose so." Buck sounded cautious. Harry noticed that he hadn't eaten anything since she had arrived, although he had downed two cups of black coffee. His red-rimmed eyes were weary and Harry wondered if he'd had a little too much to drink last night.

"Richie?"

"Fine, fine." Richie sounded impatient.

"Mandy? What about you?"

"I haven't got much to tell," Mandy said. "I went out to dinner by myself and then to the Castro Theater to one of the Film Festival movies. It was great — I'm sorry the rest of you missed it. It was about —"

"I'm sure it was wonderful," Harry interrupted gently. "Did anyone see you there?"

Mandy looked at the other people around the table and then shook her head. "No. I chatted a little with the woman sitting next to me, but I don't know who she was. She was older than me, had long brown hair and was wearing glasses, but I didn't get her name. I mean, I didn't have any reason to ask her who she was, you know?"

Celia looked as if she wanted to say something condescending, but she didn't. Harry admired her for her forbearance. "So you don't have an alibi."

"No, and frankly I don't see why I need one," Mandy said. "I didn't even know Fran Matthews."

But Mandy was obsessed with Celia, and she could have been jealous about Celia's affair with Fran, Harry reflected. "What about you, Richie?"

"I was a good little boy," Richie said. "I stayed home last night and watched the ball game on TV. And no, I don't have an alibi. Since everybody else was out, I was alone for most of the evening. The phone didn't even ring. Is there more coffee?"

"Enough for a cup or two," Celia said, passing him the percolator.

"I'll have some too," said Harry. She took a clean mug from the table and filled it. "Where were you, Buck?"

"Out."

"You agreed to tell me where you were," Harry reminded him, taking a sip of her coffee. When she realized it was perfectly brewed — not too mild, not too strong, not too bitter — she drank half of it.

Buck shrugged. "So I did. I went out to dinner and then to a couple of clubs. I felt like having a night out on the town and exploring San Francisco a little."

"Yes," Harry said encouragingly.

"Harry," Celia hissed.

"What?" Harry turned to Celia, who was making faces at her.

"Do you really need it spelled out for you?"

The light dawned: Buck had gone cruising, and Celia was intimating that he had been successful. Harry thought of Buck's relationship with Joel and wondered what had motivated Buck to search out another man. From her recent conversation with him, Harry would have thought that his life was complicated enough. Perhaps he simply wanted Richie to think that he'd been cruising. Or perhaps he had been up to something else altogether.

"I got back around dawn," Buck volunteered.

"Fine," Harry said. If he had been cruising, he wasn't going to provide details of his escapades in front of Richie. "So Celia, what were you up to?"

"I was out," Celia said. "I had dinner by myself at a wonderful vegetarian restaurant on a side street just off Castro, and then I went to a movie at the Roxie. I saw a deep, philosophical film that dissected gay and lesbian life with a scalpel. It was quite stimulating, food for intelligent thought."

Harry raised her eyebrows. She knew Celia well enough to tell that, when she started babbling about philosophy and intelligent thought, she was talking through her hat. "What was the movie called?"

Celia looked pained. "I don't remember. I'll have to look it up in the schedule. It was good, though."

"I'll bet." Harry nodded. "What was it really about?"

"Women," Celia replied nonchalantly.

"And what?" Harry asked.

"Life."

Celia was trying to make her to laugh, but she wasn't going to succumb. "So you don't have an alibi, either."

"Now you know: None of us can prove where we were," Buck said. "It's your turn to come clean."

"Yes, that's right. What the hell is so significant about our whereabouts last night?" asked Richie.

"Raven was mugged yesterday morning," Harry began.

"I already told everyone that," Celia interrupted impatiently. "But I don't see what that has to do with us."

"Her assailant came back last night just after dark," Harry continued, "apparently to finish what he or she started." There was a momentary silence, and then everyone began talking at once. Harry finished her coffee while their heated conversation wound down.

"And your wrist? Why is it bandaged?" Celia asked.

"I was chasing the person and fell."

"Didn't you see who it was?" Richie wanted to know.

"No. It was too dark."

"It could have been any one of us," Buck deduced.

"Or it could have been someone we don't know," Mandy declared.

"I doubt it," Buck said.

"None of us has a good alibi," mused Celia.

"That's right," Harry said grimly. While she had their undivided attention, she put her cup down with a none-too-gentle thump, pushed her chair back and stood up. "And I imagine the police were the first to realize it. So if anyone wants to have a little chit-chat, I'll be in my room."

Harry walked away. Her desire to turn around and scrutinize the expression on their faces was so strong that her back began to itch, but she resisted the urge. She had baited the hook, and now she would reel someone in. Maybe. Perhaps her belief that they would tell her their secrets was as much of a deceit on her part as their pretentious lack of alibis was on theirs.

She went upstairs, took a shower, dressed in clean clothes and waited for visitors. When no one came after an hour, she began to regret having offered to wait. Patience was not her long suit; she would never have made a good cop, social worker or priest. She rummaged through Fran's desk until she found a blank sheet of paper and a black marker, scribbled "Gone fishing" on it, taped it to her door and walked down the hall to Fran's old room. She hesitated for a moment before knocking, not certain that she was ready to deal with Moira. Maybe she'd never be ready to deal with Moira, she mused, rapping forcefully on the wood door.

"Come," Moira commanded imperiously.

Harry opened the door and went in. The decor was surprisingly stark, the furniture austere. The walls were painted white, and the bed was queen-sized and lacked a headboard. There was one bedside table, also painted white, and a matching four-drawer dresser. The only other furniture was a small wooden desk and matching chair. The bed was covered with a starburst quilt, the room was lit by two wall lamps on either side of the bed, and everything smelled strongly of fresh eucalyptus.

"Moira?"

"I'm in the closet, child."

Harry stifled a grin and approached the walk-in closet. "At your age? And with your experience?"

"Don't be snide. I'm just studying my vastly expanded wardrobe," responded Moira.

"Where's your sense of humour?" Harry teased. "Perhaps being a property owner has turned your head."

"Actually, it's shocking how many clothes Fran had," Moira said. "And although I haven't asked her, I don't suppose Raven will want any of them. They're not exactly her style."

Harry gazed at the clothes hanging in the closet, amazed to see how many dresses, blouses, pants and sweaters Fran had owned.

"See what I mean?" Moira asked.

Harry nodded. "Yes. But I didn't come to see you about Fran's clothes."

"I know. You want to ask me some questions, don't you?"

"That's right. But let's get out of this darn closet. I've never been comfortable in cramped spaces."

"A gal after my own heart," Moira said.

Harry kept her mouth shut to be certain she wouldn't end up with her foot in it.

Moira sat on the bed and patted the space beside her. "So what do you want to know?"

Harry sat down beside Moira, who reached out and took Harry's hand in hers.

"You have such strong fingers," Moira observed, stroking Harry's hand.

It was disturbingly erotic. Harry gently disengaged her hand and made a conscious effort not to take a deep breath. She didn't want to offend Moira, but she couldn't afford to be distracted, either.

"Actually, I came by to ask you where you were last night around sundown."

Moira's response was prompt. "Why, I was praying to the goddess. Doesn't everyone at that time of the evening? How else would any of us make it through the night?"

"And where were you when you were doing all this praying?"

"Ah, child. You have such doubts."

"Don't manipulate me," Harry grumbled, springing from the bed.

Moira rose and grasped her arms. "I would never try to manipulate you, of all people. You must believe that. I have the greatest respect for your intellect, for your emotional capacity, especially to suffer. That I understand implicitly. You cause yourself harm, child, when you don't give yourself credit for who you are."

Harry closed her eyes, and this time she couldn't stop herself from taking a deep breath. As soon as she was able to speak, she said, "Perhaps you're in a position to say that, but I'm sorry, I'm not able to deal with it. And that wasn't the question I asked, so stop running interference."

"My, aren't we getting tough." Moira chortled. "And tetchy." She whirled away, her body twisting around, her hands fluttering in the air above her.

"Stop changing the subject. Where were you last night?"

"I'll tell you if you tell me," replied Moira.

Harry didn't like the way this conversation was developing. She felt a certain affection for Moira, and she didn't particularly want her to have been the one who had murdered Fran. But now that Raven was no longer a suspect, Moira was unquestionably the person who'd had the most to gain by Fran's death.

"I was with Raven."

"And I was with myself," Moira chirped. "You see, child, I don't need other people around to entertain me. I'm quite capable of amusing myself. Not everyone has that capacity, of course, and that rather torpid police detective, what's his name? Manley? Well, he was quite cheeky about it. He wanted to know why I wasn't at the Film Festival last night. Was I in mourning for Fran? No? Well, then, why wasn't I out having a good time? He just didn't seem to understand that I was perfectly capable of having a sublime time without going out and mixing with other people, and that the tales in my head are much more interesting than most of those which appear on the big screen."

"Do you mean that you spent the whole evening here?"

"Where else would I be?" Moira said, giving Harry an ingenious smile.

"In this room?"

"Most of the time," Moira answered. "I didn't keep notes of my whereabouts, but I'm certain I must have traipsed off to the bathroom now and again, and I did nip downstairs for a bite to eat. Not that there was much in the fridge, but beggars can't be choosers, as we all know."

Harry walked over to the dresser. It was covered with bottles and jars of creams and potions and an ornate comb, brush and mirror. Everything was covered with a layer of dust. Harry glanced at herself in the mirror. Despite the pounds she had gained in the past year, she looked gaunt. It was those raccoon eyes, she thought as she turned away.

"Did you see Richie last night?"

"Ah, young Richie. I do believe I ran into him in the upstairs hall at one point," Moira said, looking pensive. "He was dressed in leather chaps and a leather vest. Such an unfortunate affectation; it cheapens the overall effect, although I'd never tell him that."

Had Richie planned to go out and then changed his mind? "Do you remember what time that was?"

"Unfortunately not," Moira said with a shrug. "I had a few wee drops of gin to grease the creative processes, and once they were off and running, I had absolutely no interest in the time. After all, I had no prior commitments, I wasn't expected anywhere and I had a roof over my head, food in my belly and a bottle of gin in my room. So no, I don't have any idea when he and I crossed paths. But, although I didn't see him leave, from the way he was dressed, I assumed he was on his way out."

"What time did you go to bed?"

"Bed? What an extraordinary concept," Moira responded. "I didn't go to bed, child. Oh, I'm sure I had a nap or two, but I didn't go to bed as defined by normal standards. No face washing, teeth brushing, undressing, silk negligées, tuckings of sheets up to the neck. No, none of that. It's much too formal for someone like me. Should I decide to participate in that type of falderal, I would surely suffer from insomnia the minute my head hit the pillow. Better to let sleep descend unawares, like a welcome gift from the goddess."

It was worse than Harry thought; if Moira didn't know when she had slept, no wonder she couldn't pin down when she had seen Richie.

"But you were here all evening."

"Yes," Moira said firmly. "Of that I have no doubt. Now, stop acting like such an inquisitor and tell me what this is all about."

Harry's wrist had started throbbing again, but she didn't want to take a painkiller because she knew it would make her groggy and she didn't have time for that. She sat down on the bed and gingerly placed her arm in her lap.

Moira sat down beside Harry, put her arm around her shoulder and gave her a generous hug. "You're hurting child, so get whatever it is off your chest so you can have a good rest."

Harry described what had happened to Raven and to her the night before. "So then Detective Manley came and took our statements, and earlier this morning I had my wrist stitched up."

"You've had a rough time," Moira sympathized. "Why don't you stretch out on the bed and have a nap?"

"I think I'll go back to my room, if you don't mind," said Harry. She didn't really think that Moira was up to anything, but, if she was, Harry didn't have the energy to deal with it. Still, Moira was uncharacteristically quiet as Harry rose from the bed.

"Have I offended you in some way?" Harry asked.

Moira chortled and leaned back on her elbows. "Offended me? What in blazes are you talking about? I think it's wonderful. To be truthful, not that many women have been so attracted to me that they felt uncomfortable just innocently sitting beside me on a bed. And don't look so shocked, child. It's no sin to be enchanted by a crazy woman."

Harry was so astounded that she couldn't even croak.

"Of course, Fran was captivated by me, but she never wanted to show it. She was so intent on controlling people that she refused to display her real feelings. She thought that sentiments like love, affection and sexual desire were signs of weakness. She liked the strong emotions, like anger, hatred and lust. She had an interesting life, of course, but not a complacent one. I don't think anyone should be surprised that she met a violent end. Now stop standing there with your mouth wide open and go and get some rest."

The meekness Harry evinced as she left Moira's room was heartfelt. Her emotions felt as sore as the cut on her sprained wrist.

She wanted to sleep forever, but a nap would have to do. She opened the door to the study only to find Richie sitting in the steno chair.

18

Richie was so intent on studying the documents in front of him that he didn't hear her come in.

"Find anything interesting?" she asked. "Or something useful in overturning Fran's will?"

Richie jumped to his feet and spun around. "I hope you don't mind, but since no one else has looked through Fran's papers, I thought I would," he said rapidly. "Besides, there's some personal stuff here that she wouldn't have wanted other people to see."

It sounded like a lot of guff to Harry, but she let him get away with it. "Tell me, Richie, why did you put on your partying duds last night if you were intending to spend the entire evening at home?"

He blinked.

Harry perched on the edge of her bed and went on the attack. "Could it be that you went out at some point to cruise the Castro and that you didn't want Buck to know about it?"

"It was Moira, wasn't it?" Richie sighed. "It had to be her. She was the only person I saw last night. She seemed so drunk that I didn't think she'd remember running into me, but I guess I was wrong."

"What time did you see her?" Harry asked, ignoring her aching wrist.

"It was late, sometime after eleven."

"And you went out right after that?"

Richie got up from the steno chair and began to pace. "Yes."

"Where did you go?"

"To a bar on Castro."

"Cruising?"

"I had a date."

"Not with Buck," Harry surmised.

"No, not with Buck."

"Don't make this too easy for me," Harry griped. "Who was it?"

"The fellow I met in the washroom at *Blueberries*," Richie admitted, looking ill at ease. "His name is Carlos. He gave me his phone number that night, and when Buck told me he needed a night out alone, I decided to give Carlos a call. I wasn't in the mood to be by myself, not with everyone else going off. I didn't feel like being a wallflower. Carlos and I spent the night together. We visited a couple of bars and had a few drinks, and then we went to some pretty raunchy clubs."

"Sex clubs?"

Richie nodded.

"I hope you were careful."

"Don't lecture me, Harry."

"All right. I hope you had a good time while being careful. What time did you get home?"

"Just a little before Buck."

"This morning, then."

"That's right."

"So the only person who was here all night was Moira," Harry mused aloud.

"You couldn't ask for a more useless witness," Richie commented.

Harry nodded but didn't say anything. The thought of criticizing Moira made her feel guilty, disloyal. "Did you actually watch the ball game?"

"Yes."

"What was the score?"

"Hell, I don't even know who was playing," Richie professed. "I was angry with Buck because I didn't want to be alone. I might not have had many warm feelings for my sister, but she was the only sister I had, and let's face it, I'm not perfect either. Her death upset me. And discovering that she was likely murdered didn't help. So I wanted Buck to stay with me, or to go with him, but he was adamant. He wanted to be alone. That happens every once in a while. He gets restless sometimes. He needs to escape, to get off by himself, to let off steam. It's all quite innocent, really — he just sits in bars, looks at other men and drinks too much. He's never cheated on me, of that I'm certain. Most of the time I don't mind being left at home, but last night I did." Richie sat back down in the steno chair. "We had words, and he left. I turned on the TV and there was a baseball game, so I sat down and watched it, sort of. I hate baseball, but I was stewing, you see, so I didn't care what I was looking at."

"And then you decided to go out."

"If you can't beat them, join them."

There was a knock on the door and Celia rushed into the study. "Raven's downstairs," she said.

"This house is turning into Grand Central Station," Richie joked.

"She's got a suitcase with her, too," Celia added.

"I stand corrected: It's turning into the Ritz Hotel," Richie continued, his tone glum. "But she owns half of the house, so she has as much right to stay here as Moira. In fact, she could decide to move in and no one could stop her. Unless she killed Fran."

Harry didn't want to think about that. She opened the door and the three of them left the study together.

"Actually, I'm surprised you didn't bring her back with you before," Celia commented.

"She wanted to get the window in her apartment repaired first," Harry explained. "But perhaps she couldn't."

Richie went into his room and Celia detoured to the bathroom, leaving Harry alone. She went downstairs. Raven was waiting in the hall just inside the front door. She was wearing black leggings and a thin, black sweatshirt with a vee-neck. There was a white silk scarf with a long fringe wrapped around her neck, as if to ward off a chill. She looked fragile and appealing and terribly young. A small suitcase sat on the floor beside her.

"I know we were going to see each other tonight, but I hope you don't mind me showing up a little early," she said as Harry took her in her arms and gave her a gentle hug. "No one can come repair my window and install bars on it until tomorrow, and I don't relish sleeping there by myself tonight. Even being there during the day with just a piece of cardboard tacked over the window was a bit too much for me to take. I'd feel more secure staying here with you until everything is fixed."

"Of course you can stay with me," Harry assured her. "I should have thought of it before. Let's get your things upstairs." She took Raven's suitcase in her good hand and led Raven upstairs and into the study. She dropped the suitcase just inside the door, ushered Raven to the steno chair and awkwardly opened the sofa bed with one hand.

Raven was hunched over, obviously in some pain. The look on her face reminded Harry of a wounded puppy.

"Have you got your painkillers with you?" Harry asked.

"Yes. But I took one before I left my apartment and I'm not due another for about five hours." Raven sat on the edge of the bed. "The problem is that I'm afraid of becoming more involved with you than I already am."

"I should have been more responsible," Harry conceded. "When you touched me that night at the bar, it was an incredibly intimate gesture, and I was extraordinarily attracted to you. Then Fran was killed, and once you told me you thought she'd been murdered, all I could think about was finding out who did it. I didn't think of us or our future together, which was a mistake."

"So where does that leave me?" Raven asked.

"The same place it leaves me, I suppose," Harry responded.

Raven shifted, stretching her obviously stiff muscles. "I don't like emotional limbos."

"Neither do I."

"So will you stay for at least a while?"

Ambivalence was tearing Harry apart. "We were strangers, when you touched my breast in a bar, and you climbed into my bed in the middle of the night after we'd been on one date. What you felt was mostly lust, and I responded in kind. Given that, how were either of us to know that we would begin to feel something more for each other?"

"Are you prejudiced because of my age, like Fran was?"

"I don't know," Harry said. "I don't think so, but I don't know for sure. I've never been involved with someone much older or younger than me. I won't lie to you — I have mixed feelings about staying. It takes time to fall in love, for passion to turn into something deeper and for trust to develop between two people. And I'm not entirely over Judy yet; she's often in my mind. I still feel sad that my relationship with her is over. I'm not coming to this new relationship with a clear mind or an entirely open heart, although I know that I do care for you."

"If you don't have to rush back to Montreal to work, then I can't see why you don't want to stay. I admire your honesty about your feelings for your former lover, but please give our relationship a chance," Raven said.

Harry rested her elbows on the desk and leaned her chin on her hands, wincing when her wrist began throbbing. She had lived for half a century, exactly twice Raven's twenty-five years, and yet this young woman made her feel as if she was less in command of her emotions — and her life — than she should be.

"I feel I'm letting you down, but I need some time to think about my future," she said to Raven.

Raven looked disappointed. "I suppose I'll have to accept that — for the moment, at least."

Harry was relieved; she'd been given a reprieve. "I don't know about you, but I'm exhausted. I'm going to take a nap. Would you like to join me?"

They cuddled together in Harry's bed, each of them nursing her wounds, both physical and emotional. Raven curled against Harry's back, and then one of the younger woman's hands cupped her breast. It was a gesture of intimacy, of comfort, and entirely lacking in eroticism.

Once they woke up, they were drawn into plans for dinner and found themselves following everyone to a Chinese restaurant on Market, where they started with won-ton soup. Plate after plate of steaming chicken, beef, ribs and fish arrived on their table. Richie ordered a jug of Panda beer, which they all tried, except Celia, who was adamant about drinking only wine.

After dinner, Celia prevailed, and they went to a nearby bar. Raven looked tired, Richie listless, Buck distracted. Despite the cheerful decor and upbeat music, Harry felt a growing sense of ennui.

"Who wants to dance with me?" Celia chirped. "Richie, why aren't you up there bopping around on the dance floor?"

"I'm so stuffed I can barely move," Richie said with a groan. "I'm going to have to go on a diet when we get home."

"There are a lot of good restaurants here, aren't there?" Mandy commented.

Richie gingerly patted his stomach. "Yes. And not only that, Chinese food always makes me feel like a pig. See? I'm beginning to get a paunch and we've only been here for a week. I have this habit of wanting to finish everything on my plate, which is a near impossibility when you're dining in a Chinese restaurant. I gave it the old college try, but I just couldn't get through that last bit of chicken chow mein."

"Well, tomorrow's another day, and I'm sure there'll still be some food left in the world when you wake up," Buck said somewhat cynically.

"Never mind," Celia chided.

Harry heard Richie snort and the tension around the table doubled. She reached out and took Raven's hand in hers and gave it gentle squeeze. Everyone but Celia was in a lousy mood. She thought about leaving, but she didn't want to be the first to break up the evening. She and Raven would have to stick it out.

Celia tapped Harry on the shoulder. "Come dance with me."

"Sorry, my hand's too sore," responded Harry.

"Raven?"

Raven gave Celia a dispirited look and shook her head.

"Am I the only one who isn't suffering from indigestion or a bruised body?" Celia asked. "Buck, what about you? Or have you mysteriously sprained an ankle or chipped a tooth or suffered an unsightly hangnail?"

"No." Buck chuckled. "At least I don't think so. The last time I looked I was all in one piece. But why don't you dance with Mandy? She's tapping her foot so hard that she's going to wear a hole in her shoe."

Harry stifled a grin; Celia looked as if she wanted to throttle Buck, but Mandy was already on her feet, an expectant look on her face.

The evening wound down slowly, and by midnight everyone was beginning to flag. They walked home in silence. Since Harry and Raven were exhausted, they went straight upstairs.

Harry watched Raven undress. Her body was beautiful, although the purple bruises which covered it enraged Harry all over again. Raven turned off the desk lamp and slid in beside Harry. Their exploratory kisses soon became intense, but Raven pulled away just as Harry was beginning to rise over her.

"God, I'm horny," Raven moaned. "I wish we could make love, but I'm too sore."

Harry put her rising passion on the back burner. She should have realized that Raven was still too badly injured to make love, while all she had was a sore wrist. Harry turned over on her back. "You're not the only one who's horny."

She heard Raven chuckle. "Maybe tomorrow."

Harry lay still, her body rigid at first. More than anything else in the world, she wanted to turn over, put her arms around Raven and hold the younger woman close to her, as if body contact would somehow heal Raven's physical wounds.

"May I hold you?"

"Of course," Raven whispered.

Harry shivered with desire as their skin touched.

"Why don't you let me make love to you?" Raven asked, her fingers fluttering across Harry's belly.

But Harry felt too shy at the thought of Raven giving her undivided attention to her passion. "No, it's all right. Let's just sleep."

Raven's hand stilled, then moved to Harry's hip. Moments later, her deep, regular breathing signalled to Harry that she had fallen asleep. Although she was tired, Harry felt restless. She was about to begin going through the known evidence again when Raven stirred and moved closer. Harry kissed her on the forehead, closed her eyes and drifted into sleep.

She dreamt that she and Raven were walking hand in hand through dense fog. They were in a dark house, and the lights wouldn't work. No, that couldn't be right. The interior of a house wouldn't be foggy. Maybe they were on the street and it was the middle of the night. There was obviously something wrong with the streetlamps, and the fog was blocking sight of the houses on either side of the road. Or perhaps they were strolling on a deserted beach, although, strain as she did, Harry couldn't hear the waves lapping against the shore. What she did hear were shouts in the background, but she couldn't make out the words. But Raven thought that fog was romantic, so who was she to complain?

Harry wiped at the air in front of her, thinking that the fog would clear soon. It didn't. It got thicker, and then she began coughing. She rubbed her nose but still the fog caught in her throat. She sat up and opened her eyes, which immediately began tearing. It was smoke, not fog! She felt for Raven's shoulder and gave it a rough shake.

"Raven! Wake up! The house is on fire!" Harry's head was aching and she couldn't stop coughing.

"Fire?" Raven said, already hacking. "Oh, Christ! Where are my clothes?"

"Forget your clothes. We've got to get out of here!"

"But, Harriet, I'm naked. Turn the light on, will you?"

Harry unthinkingly reached out and switched on the lamp. It didn't work. She nearly tripped over the steno chair and remembered that her jeans and tee-shirt and Raven's were draped over the back. She grabbed her clothes and put them on.

"Where are you?" she called to Raven.

"Right here." Raven coughed. "This is really bad, Harriet. I can't breathe. We could die in here."

Harry could barely breathe either, but she wasn't about to give up. She handed Raven her clothes. "Let's try for the door. Get down on your hands and knees. Grab onto me and don't let go."

They crouched down. The air was less smoky near the floor. Harry took several shallow breaths, trying not to cough, and made sure that Raven had a good hold on her belt. Then she struck out for the door, trying to ignore the pain that stabbed at her wrist every time she put her weight on it. Her head was splitting, her throat was raw, her eyes and nose were running.

"Here it is," she croaked.

"You're supposed to make sure it's not hot before opening it," Raven whispered.

Harry ran her hand over the door. It didn't seem to be hotter than the air around them. She gingerly brushed the metal doorknob with the tip of a finger. When her finger wasn't singed, she grasped the doorknob with her hand and opened the door a crack. "Do you think there's more smoke out there than in here?"

"No. I don't know. Maybe," Raven said. Her voice was hoarse and simply talking brought on another paroxysm of violent coughing.

"Let's go," Harry muttered, leading the way. They scurried along the hall, their heads nearly touching the floor. Harry held her breath until she couldn't stop herself from breathing and then began to cough. "We have to warn the others," she managed to say.

"Maybe they already got out."

Harry paused at what she thought was Richie and Buck's door and banged on it. She was about to reach up for the doorknob and open the door when she realized that she could be making a fatal mistake. The fire could have started in any one of the bedrooms. What if she inadvertently let it out? She was nearly at the end of her strength now, and Raven couldn't be in much better shape.

"Let's go," she said grimly. "The best thing we can do is get out of here and call the fire department."

The smoke seemed denser near the stairs. "Is there another staircase?" Harry asked. Her throat was so hoarse that she could barely speak.

"No."

"Then we'll have to keep going."

It was awkward and slow but they made it to the bottom without falling.

"Oh, Christ," Harry groaned. "I can see flames just inside the front door. There's a back door, right?"

"Through the kitchen."

The smoke grew denser as they groped their way down the hall to the kitchen, but as soon as they pushed through the swinging door, it diminished drastically. Harry slumped on the floor, gasping for air. Tainted as it was with smoke, it still tasted wonderful.

"Come on, Harriet. Keep going."

She couldn't. Not a muscle in her body would move, although she tried.

"Harriet! Stay with me!"

Her body was racked with a fit of coughing. The smoke was getting thicker in the kitchen.

"Where the hell is the fire department?" Raven railed. "You've *got* to try to move. You've just got to!"

"Go for help," Harry croaked. "I'll be along."

"I won't leave you."

"Go," Harry insisted. There was no point in the both of them dying.

Raven's fingers stroked Harry's face and then she was gone. Harry's head sank to the floor, which felt refreshingly cool. She panted through her mouth, but it was futile. There wasn't enough oxygen left in the house to sustain a mouse. Seconds later, she passed out.

19

" **W**hite looks good on you, but you've got to do something about your hair." Celia moved a chair from beside the window, put it beside Harry's bed and perched on it. She was wearing a pair of bleached blue jeans and a matching jacket with a black tee-shirt, all obviously new.

"It seems to me that you said the exact same thing thirty years ago, when I had my tonsils out and you came to visit me in the hospital." Harry's head hurt, her voice was hoarse and her throat was dry and inflamed, but she was alive, and there was real air to breathe and an oxygen mask nearby should she need it.

"Well, you certainly look as good now as you did then, although you've got a little extra padding around the edges," Celia joked.

Harry laughed, which provoked a painful fit of coughing.

"Oh, Harry, I can't believe that you nearly died."

Harry didn't believe it either, but since she was very much alive, she didn't particularly want to think about it.

"Where's Raven? Is she all right?"

"She's in a room down the hall," Celia responded. "She's also suffering from smoke inhalation, and she has some burns on her hands and arms."

"She saved my life," Harry said.

"You saved each other's lives," Celia corrected her. "You got her to the kitchen, and she went for help when you collapsed."

"What about everyone else? Was anyone injured?"

"Not really, apart from a few scrapes and bruises," Celia answered. "We thought that you and Raven had got out. Richie banged on your door and shouted your name a few times, but there was no answer. And the smoke was getting thicker and thicker, so we couldn't wait any longer. Mandy and I came down with Richie and Buck — the four of us were in various states of distress and undress, hacking from the smoke, trying to hide bits of exposed flesh. When the fire department arrived, a kind medic thoroughly checked us over and gave us blankets. Moira wandered by, completely dressed right down to the gin bottle in her hand, and after offering her bottle around, she rambled off again. We thought you and Raven had got out and we just hadn't run into you yet in all the confusion. What a horrible mistake!"

"It's all right," Harry said, thinking about her decision not to spend more time trying to warn the other occupants of the house. Heroes certainly didn't grow on trees.

"I told Richie to open your door and peek in just to make sure you weren't there, but he said you couldn't possibly sleep through all the racket he'd made and the smell of the smoke. The bedroom doors weren't particularly airtight, after all, and we woke up when the smoke made us start coughing," Celia continued. "I'll never forgive myself for not having insisted that he take a quick look inside."

"I suppose that the painkillers Raven and I took prevented us from waking up sooner. But never mind — it came out all right in the end," Harry reassured her. "How did the four of you escape?"

"Through the front door."

"When Raven and I tried to do that, the flames were so thick that we had to turn toward the kitchen," Harry said.

"There were flames in the corner of the living room when we left the house. They must have spread from there into the hall. It was an old house, so I suppose the fire took hold rather quickly."

"Is it badly damaged?"

"Badly enough," Celia nodded, a glum look on her face. "I suppose there's insurance, but what with Fran having died so recently and the will not having been read yet, who knows when Raven and Moira will be able to collect. They're going to have a miserable time, initially, at least."

There was a knock on the door, which then opened. It was Detective Manley. "Ms. Hubbley? Could I ask you a few questions?"

"Certainly," Harry croaked.

Celia reached out, grasped Harry's hand, raised it to her lips and kissed it. It was then that it dawned on Harry how very close she had come to dying.

"I'll be back later," Celia said.

"Could you pick me up some clothes?"

"Sure," Celia replied. "Actually, I'd love to."

"My style, not yours," Harry warned.

"Don't worry," Celia laughed, giving her a wave.

The detective waited until Celia had closed the door behind her before he approached her bed. He sat in the chair Celia had vacated and took out his notebook and a ballpoint pen.

"Was it arson?" Harry asked before he had the opportunity to question her.

"Let's just say that it was a fire of suspicious origins," Manley responded rather formally.

"Why do you think that?"

"I'm the one who's supposed to be asking the questions," the detective reminded her.

"Detective, I nearly died in that fire, so I feel rather personal about it."

Manley looked down at the empty page in his open notebook and then flipped it shut. "We're nearly certain that it was arson. It started in two places, you see — just inside the living room, where, according to the arson investigator, it was bound to spread to the front hall, and in the back entry-way."

Harry's heart skipped a beat. "Do you mean someone was trying to block the exits?"

"It would seem so."

Somebody had tried to burn the house down, possibly to kill Raven. Or perhaps they had been intending to murder the whole lot of them. Harry sat in silence for a moment while she digested this bit of information.

"What would you like to know?" she asked the detective, her tone subdued.

Manley's questioning was thorough and orderly, and despite her headache and raw throat, Harry's answers were complete and exact. Manley took copious notes, and nodded frequently.

"I think that's about it," he finally said. "Are you sure you didn't hear Mr. Matthews and the others when they paused outside your bedroom door?"

"Both Raven and I were exhausted," Harry explained. "And both us had taken painkillers before going to bed. I was sound asleep and dreaming about fog. I did hear someone shouting, but it was coming from far, far away and I incorporated it into my dream."

He nodded.

"Detective, do you think that Raven's in any danger? She was attacked on the street, and then someone got into her apartment and tried to finish the job."

"We're still investigating her mugging and the subsequent break-in," he said. "Actually, we're not sure that they're related to Ms. Matthews's death."

"But —"

"Unfortunately, there were no witnesses to either," Manley interrupted. "I know you were there when someone broke into the apartment, but you couldn't identify the intruder, and he or she didn't hurt Ms. Stone. It could have been a botched robbery attempt. And the Good Samaritan who came along while Ms. Stone was being mugged still hasn't come forward."

"The intruder might have been planning to attack Raven, though," Harry insisted. "The person was bending over her, and it was only when I came rushing back into the room that he or she broke the window and escaped."

Harry and the detective stared at each other, obviously stalemated.

"You can't be sure the intruder wasn't trying to kill her," Harry contended stubbornly.

Detective Manley got up from the chair and tucked his notebook in his jacket pocket. "I want to assure you that I understand your concern. We're following this case quite closely, and I'll make certain we keep a close watch on Ms. Stone. If anything else occurs to you, anything at all, please call me."

"I will." That was that, Harry thought as she watched him leave. They weren't going to put a guard on the door of Raven's hospital room or monitor her apartment once she returned home. At least she'd extracted a promise that he would pay special attention to Raven. Actually, that might not be something Raven would appreciate, Harry thought wryly.

Except for a sinus headache, an extremely sore throat and lungs that felt somewhat singed, Harry didn't feel too bad. She wanted to see Raven, to assure herself that she wasn't seriously injured, so she got out of bed, holding her johnny gown together in the back. She couldn't prowl the halls dressed like that, not with her bare butt sticking out. But if her clothes hadn't been burned in the fire, they were likely so saturated with smoke that they weren't salvageable. She opened the closet door, relieved to see a dressing gown hanging there and a pair of slippers sitting on the floor. She put them on, left her room and made her way to the nurses' station.

"Could you tell me which room Raven Stone is in?" she asked the middle-aged nurse sitting behind a curved counter.

The nurse looked up from the chart in which she was writing. "Ms. Hubbley? You shouldn't be out of bed just yet."

"Well, I am," said Harry. "And if you'll tell me where Raven Stone is, I'll pay her a short visit and then I'll get back into bed."

The nurse looked taken aback.

"Ms. Stone is in the room to the right of yours. But don't exhaust yourself, Ms. Hubbley, and don't tire out Ms. Stone."

"Thank you very much," Harry said with a bob of her head. She hurried to Raven's room. Although the door was ajar, she knocked, and when there wasn't any answer, she entered her room. Raven was asleep. She was lying on her back, the covers folded neatly across her chest. Her skin was pale, nearly translucent, and her hands and arms below her elbows were swathed in white bandages. Richie was sitting quietly in a chair beside the bed.

"What are you doing here?" she asked in a low voice so she wouldn't wake Raven.

He looked more subdued than she ever remembered seeing him. And he didn't look particularly pleased to see her. "I came in a few minutes ago to ask her a few questions, but she was asleep. So I decided to do a little thinking on my own and wait for her to wake up."

Harry stared down at her lover, who gave no signs of stirring. "What were you going to ask her?"

Richie shifted in his chair. "I've been feeling guilty about not mentioning my suspicions about Moira Chelso. I wanted to find out what Raven thought about the woman."

"Do you think that Moira set the fire?"

"I don't know for sure. But I do know that she could have killed Fran," Richie replied.

Harry perched gingerly on the edge of Raven's bed. "What's your rationale for thinking that?"

"Moira's a little crazy and she plays hard and fast with the truth, so who knows what her ethical framework is?" Richie responded.

"Once Fran told her that she was going to inherit half the house, she could have decided that she didn't want to wait for nature to take its course. She could have been determined to go for the whole nine yards and get rid of Fran, and then Raven. She certainly had the opportunity to kill Fran, attack Raven and set the fire. Don't forget that she was fully dressed when she showed up outside last night."

But Moira claimed that she never went to bed, that she took catnaps when the urge hit. And the night she and Harry had eaten dinner together, Moira professed not to be all that thrilled about inheriting a half-share in Fran's house because of exorbitant taxes and other expenses. Then again, Moira could have been lying. She and Raven didn't have to keep the house, after all. They could have sold it for a bundle and lived on the proceeds.

"Anyway, think about what I've said. I'll leave so you can sit with her a while. I can always speak to Raven later." Richie stifled a grunt as he slowly rose stiffly from the chair.

"What happened to you?" Harry asked.

"Oh, it's nothing," Richie reassured her. "I just pulled a muscle or two getting out of the house last night."

"Did you have a doctor check you out?"

"Naw," he scoffed. "It'll go away in a couple of days. Besides, I didn't bother to get medical insurance before we came down. I haven't got any burns, and a few stiff muscles and assorted bruises aren't going to bother me for long. Anyway, I'll drop by and see you later."

Harry sat down in the chair he had vacated. "Where are you staying?"

"We were lucky — due to a last-minute cancellation, we managed to find a room in a bed-and-breakfast a block away from the house. Here's the address and phone number," Richie said, handing her a card. "We haven't got a phone in our room, but you can leave a message."

Harry took it from him.

"Unfortunately, it's for men only, so you'll have to find somewhere else to go when they discharge you," he added. "Celia's taken a room in a hotel downtown, and I think Mandy's bunking with her, so maybe you could get a room there, too."

Like Celia, Harry could afford to stay in a hotel. But she could also stay at Raven's, and it already felt quite homey to her. It didn't take much thought for Harry to decide that she wasn't going to leave San Francisco, not until Raven was back on her feet again. She also wanted to discover who killed Fran, who had attacked Raven and who had tried to burn them all in their beds last night. Perhaps she should just admit to herself that she had also decided to stay because she wanted to spend time with Raven, to give their relationship a chance.

"I'll be fine," she told Richie.

"See you later, then."

She nodded and watched Richie leave.

"Do you think Moira did it?" Raven asked, opening her eyes the minute the door closed.

"I honestly don't know. How long have you been awake?"

"Most of the time the two of you were talking," Raven replied.

"Why did you pretend to be asleep?"

"I have no idea," Raven admitted. "I was surprised to see him come in, and I didn't particularly want to chat. He and I hardly know each other, after all."

"So what do you think about his accusations against Moira?"

"I find it hard to think that she would harm anyone, but I suppose that's normal. I mean, if it was so easy to understand the motives of a killer, then the possibility of committing murder wouldn't be so far removed from the realm of possibility, would it?"

"I suppose not," Harry agreed, wondering not for the first time who Raven really was.

Raven lifted her bandaged hands and stared at them. "They look like big white mittens, don't they? I suppose I'll have to use some creativity in my lovemaking for a while. And I guess I won't be working as a waitress any time soon."

"Don't worry about that," Harry said. "We'll figure something out."

Raven used her elbows to move farther up on her pillow. "I won't say that I'm not worried, but I've got a little put aside."

"I can help, too, if you'll let me."

Raven looked touched. "Would you?"

What kind of lovers had Raven had in her short life? "Of course I would," Harry replied. As she bent over and lightly kissed Raven on the lips, she suddenly felt all choked up.

"I love you," Raven whispered.

Harry tucked her head in Raven's shoulder and closed her eyes. It was a bit too much for her to take in all at once.

"It's all right, Harriet. I don't want to push you further than you're able to go, but I just had to tell you how I felt," said Raven. "And it's not your fault that you don't feel the same way, not really. Sometimes the end of one relationship and the beginning of the next come too close together."

Harry sat up and impatiently brushed tears from her cheeks. Should she tell Raven that she wanted to stay or should she take more time to think about it?

A sheepish grin tugged at the corners of Raven's lips. "The sick and the maimed have certain privileges, although I know it's unfair of me to indulge in them. I mean, I'm not all *that* sick."

Harry was beginning to think that she had never met a more aggravating woman. And lovable. Yes, she might as well admit it to herself — lovable. "You're forgiven."

"That's a relief." She laughed. "You know, I'm worried about my apartment. It took me a long time to decorate it the way I wanted it, and with just cardboard over the window, someone could easily break in and steal everything. Or, worse yet, vandalize it."

"I can certainly take care of things, but I don't know exactly when I'm going to get out of here," responded Harry. "Maybe one of the others would be willing to do it. Do you want me to ask?"

"No, I will." Raven cleared her throat and asked, "Would you give me a drink of water?"

Harry got up, took the cup of water from the bedside table and held the straw up to Raven's mouth. "Are you in pain? Do you want me to ring for the nurse?"

Raven took a drink of water and shook her head. "No. I'm fine. I took a veritable tumblerfull of pills just before Richie came in. But I'm a bit tired now, so I'd like to sleep a little, if you don't mind."

Harry put the cup on the table and hugged her dressing gown around her. She bent and gave Raven another gentle kiss. "I'll drop by to see you later."

"That would be nice."

"Raven?"

Raven's eyelids fluttered.

"Can I stay with you?"

Raven's eyes stayed closed but she smiled. "Forever."

Harry tiptoed from the room, tired enough to take a nap herself. Momentous decisions always made her feel that way.

She had her hand on the doorknob to her room when Buck approached her.

"I was just coming to visit," he said, giving her a hug. He smelled strongly of cigarette smoke, although his clothes looked new. "Lord, I can't believe we almost lost you."

"I can hardly believe it myself," Harry admitted.

"Richie will never get over the fact that we left you behind when we rushed out of that burning building," Buck said, his voice troubled. "Neither will I, in fact."

"Buck, stop berating yourself," Harry urged. "Raven and I did the same thing, at my instigation. We banged on your door and then gave it up and got out as quickly as we could. Otherwise, I don't believe either of us would still be alive. So don't feel guilty — I saw how stiff and sore Richie was, so I can just imagine what a tough time the four of you had getting through the fire."

Buck looked perplexed, but he nodded and said nothing.

"The main thing is that we're all alive," Harry added.

"You're right, of course," Buck agreed. "Are you sure you should be on your feet? You look as if you're going to fall over."

"I am," Harry admitted, opening her door. "I'll feel better after I have a little nap. Why don't you and Richie drop by this evening?"

"We will," Buck said, giving her another hug.

Harry stepped into her room and closed the door.

"Where have you been, casing the joint, department by department? Hanging out with the x-ray gang? Consulting with ultrasound? Eating greasy pizza with the guys in the emergency ward? And where's your sense of style, not to mention modesty, traipsing around the hospital in a dressing gown like that?" Moira asked.

Harry opened her mouth to say something and grinned instead.

"Oh, never mind, it doesn't matter. I'm worried about you, child. You look like death warmed over." Moira was sitting on the bed and looked dishevelled and wild-eyed.

"I'll be fine after I get a little sleep," Harry said.

Moira jumped down from the bed and patted the covers. "Come over here and I'll tuck you in, then."

Harry hesitated. She could smell the acrid odour of smoke emanating from the older woman.

"What's the matter? Do you really think that I set the fire?" Moira asked with a slightly frenzied laugh. "I'm disappointed, niece-of-mine — I thought you were different from the rest of them. I thought you could see through the looking-glass and out the other side."

"It's just that I have such a sore throat and you smell so strongly of smoke," Harry stammered.

"All those ruined clothes," Moira moaned. "I never even had the chance to try on most of them. And the house, the *house*! I know I said I didn't want it, that I couldn't afford to own a mansion like that, but once I thought it was partly mine, I became accustomed to the idea of being a gentrified lady of leisure. Oh, I'm not entirely insane, so I would be the first to admit that I have no idea how long that particular state of grace would have lasted. I don't have two dimes to rub together, but it would have been heaven to have a warm, safe place to live in, at least for a while. And now it's all gone."

"The house can be repaired —"

"It's gone, I tell you," Moira interrupted, shaking her head. "And, what's more, everyone thinks I set the fire. I'm a convenient person to blame, of course — I've been hospitalized, I've been certified insane, and I've got a record."

"What for?" Harry asked, crossing the room to the window, intending to open it. The smell of smoke was stronger now, and it was mixed with the sour odour of Moira's sweat. She slid up the window as far as it would go and leaned against the sill, shivering in the damp, foggy air.

"Most of the time I was picked up for loitering," Moira said with a cynical laugh. "But I was charged with prostitution a couple of times when I was pretty desperate for something to eat. And then there was possession of dope — for personal use, you understand, not for trafficking. That was before I cleaned up my act, of course."

Of course, Harry thought. What else was new? "You need a shower," she said more sharply than she had intended. "And a change of clothes."

"I'd borrow your bathroom and take a shower if I had some clean clothes to put on, but, unfortunately I don't," Moira replied. "I went back to my room after the fire only to find that it had been trashed with a vengeance. That's a good name for a movie, don't you think? *Trashed with a Vengeance*: It could be about nearly anything, couldn't it? Some vicious cops tossing a room, the competitive fashion industry, a squabble between gangs, a nasty book review. But where was I? Oh yes, telling you about my room being vandalized. They broke the few dishes I had, threw all my food on the floor, slit my clothes with a knife, gutted my mattress and then spread excrement over what was left. As you can imagine, I went down to the janitor's and gave my notice. Then I went back upstairs to salvage what I could, but the only thing they hadn't destroyed was this," she added, pulling a pair of cotton panties from her pocket and waving them over her head.

"So you're homeless," said Harry.

"Effectively," Moira replied, her voice unemotional.

Celia chose that moment to enter Harry's room, her arms full of shopping bags.

"You," she said, giving Moira a distasteful look.

"The one and only." From Moira's voice, Harry easily deduced that she didn't much like Celia. At least the feeling was mutual, she thought.

"I brought you some clothes and I also took out some cash," Celia said, placing the bags on the chair and handing Harry a wad of bills.

"Thanks," Harry said.

Celia glanced distastefully at Moira. "I'll come back later, then. After dinner."

Harry nodded. As soon as Celia was gone, Harry handed the money to Moira.

"What's this?"

"I don't know — I didn't count it," Harry replied nonchalantly.

"Don't get smart, child," Moira said, her voice affectionate. She swiftly counted the bills. "There's five hundred dollars here."

"So go rent a room and spend the rest on a change of clothes and some food," Harry suggested.

"Oh, sure." Moira hooted. "And where's the money going to come from after you've gone home? Do you know what rooms go for in San Francisco, even those that come complete with flaking paint, broken light fixtures, leaky plumbing as well as lice, fleas, roaches and various other vermin? I walked out on Fran only after I'd spent weeks looking at dozens of rooms and found one I could afford. I can't go out and take the first one I look at — a good quarter of them have serial killers hanging around the front door, another quarter have roofs about to clatter into the street and kill every pedestrian in sight. And for this, poor people pay good money."

Harry wanted to apologize for the whole middle class, but Moira didn't give her the chance.

"And how, I ask you, am I supposed to pay the rent every month and still have enough spare change left over from my welfare cheque to eat?"

"I know you can't quite believe it yet, but I'm sure the insurance on the house will enable you to comfortably support yourself."

"Maybe." But there was more hope than doubt in Moira's voice.

"It's not just maybe," Harry insisted. "It's a certainty."

"You're as crazy as I am to give me this much money, do you know that?" Moira blustered, although Harry could tell that she was touched. "But what the hell — why shouldn't I have a little fun at your expense? It's your money, after all, and if there's anything I absolutely adore, it's spending other people's money."

"Money exists to be spent."

"Don't go existential on me," Moira scolded. She stuffed the wad of bills into her pocket and left moments later, claiming a prior appointment, although they both knew that she was fleeing because she didn't want Harry to see her cry.

Harry partially closed the window and got into bed, a self-satisfied smile on her face. Some time later, a resident woke her from a deep sleep, gave her a thorough going-over and told her she could leave in the morning. Harry was relieved, although she wasn't in the mood to be alone. Perhaps they would also let Raven go home tomorrow.

She had just finished dinner when the door burst open and Celia rushed in, a small, leather suitcase in her hand. "Is that awful woman gone? Good. How are you feeling?"

"Better," Harry replied, pushing her tray away. "But Moira's not awful." She debated telling Celia what she had done with the five hundred dollars she had given her, and then decided not to. Celia wasn't particularly understanding when it came to women she didn't like, and anyway, what had transpired was between her and Moira and not for public consumption.

"That's your problem, Harry — you're just too much of a pushover," Celia said, settling on the edge of the bed. "Haven't Buck and Richie arrived yet?"

"No, although they said they'd be by," Harry responded, wishing she had a comb to run through her hair. She had the feeling half of it was sticking up in the air. "How are you getting along?"

"I've been pretty busy, actually," Celia reported. "I dropped by Raven's room after I left you, and she asked me to see to the repairs in her apartment. I hung around there nearly all afternoon badgering the glazier to install new glass in the window and the security company to weld on iron bars. Anyway, it's done now, so she can stop worrying. Nobody can just walk in and take off with all her stuff, and her furniture won't get ruined if it rains."

"I know she was worried about it, so I'm glad you were able to help," Harry said.

"No *problema*," Celia replied. "I naturally assumed you would do it once you got out of the hospital, but it's one of those things that shouldn't be left hanging too long. Sooner or later someone would have discovered how easy it was to break in, and I'm positive her insurance company wouldn't have covered a damn thing once they realized that there'd only been a piece of cardboard tacked over the window frame. Raven also asked me to pick up some clothes for her. It was kind of fun going through a punk's closet, actually. Anyway, I'll just drop this suitcase in her room and then I'll be back."

Harry watched her go. She believed that the mugging, subsequent attack and fire had all been attempts to silence Raven. Whoever was set on murdering Raven had obviously been ruthless enough to risk killing everyone sleeping there that night. Unless the arsonist had wanted to clear the slate entirely by slaughtering them all. Now, there was a thought.

The door opened and Richie popped in. "Are you decent?"

"Yes, luckily for you," Harry responded.

"If you've seen one, you've seen them all," he quipped.

"I won't ask which one you've seen," retorted Harry.

Richie guffawed, slowly made his way to the wood chair beside Harry's bed and carefully lowered himself into it. "I don't know why these rooms only have one chair."

"Maybe they think people don't have many friends, or they want to discourage visitors," Celia said as she entered the room.

"So how are you feeling?" Richie asked Harry.

"Good. My throat's not so sore and my lungs don't hurt every time I take a breath. In fact, the doctor said that, barring any complications, I could check out in the morning."

"That's great. We can do some clothes shopping together after you get settled," Celia said enthusiastically. "I'm going to take you to some boutiques that you're going to love."

"Hey, don't forget she's got some recuperating to do," Richie pointed out.

"As do you," Harry said to him. "You still seem to be pretty stiff. I'm still not quite clear on how it happened. Did you fall on the stairs when you were leaving the house or something?"

"I don't know." He shrugged. "I just don't remember. I was scared shitless and trying hard not to show it, and it was only when I got out on the street and into the hands of the paramedics that I realized I was all banged up."

Buck came in and went over and stood behind Richie's chair. "I thought you got some of those bruises the night before," he commented casually, bending down and kissing the top of his lover's head.

"Oh, never mind," Celia said. "The main thing is that we're all alive. What a vacation this has been! I'll tell you, I just can't wait to get back to Vancouver!"

"When are you planning to leave?" Buck asked.

"I'm not sure," Celia said. "Before last night, I was intending to stay for the rest of the Film Festival and Pride celebrations. After all, that was what we came for, and it would be a shame to miss it all. But things have gone a bit too far, haven't they? I'm even starting to wonder whether this trip is jinxed. I've rather lost interest in going to movies and marches and all that, but I do want to attend Fran's funeral. After that, I think I'll book a flight and fly home. Richie, has a time been set for the funeral?"

"The coroner's office released the body yesterday," he answered. "I've arranged a service at a funeral home for the day after tomorrow. I want to be certain everyone is well enough to attend."

"I'll be there, of course," Celia said with a nod. "And what about the two of you? When are you planning to leave?"

"Right after the funeral," responded Buck.

"With everything that's happened, I don't imagine the police will be pleased if we leave before they find out who killed Fran and set fire to the house," Harry remarked.

Celia looked perturbed. "You don't think they'd make us stay in San Francisco indefinitely, do you? Richie, did that damn detective say anything to you?"

"Well, he did ask me to let him know if I planned to leave," Richie admitted. "Of course I told him I would, and that was that."

"So I'll tell you what, Harry. Let's do a little shopping, attend Fran's funeral and fly back to Vancouver the day after that," Celia suggested.

"Actually, I'm not sure when I'll go home," Harry said.

Her three friends stared at her.

Richie raised his hands in a gesture of protest. "But surely the police will get to the bottom of it."

"Yes, give it up," Celia exhorted her. "You've been through so much in the past year, and you certainly don't need this kind of aggravation."

Buck took a pack of cigarettes from his shirt pocket, tossed it in the air and caught it. "I don't think you're going to change her mind. However, you're welcome to keep trying. I'm going out for a cigarette. After that, I'm going to find a fancy restaurant and have a good meal, and then I'm going to find the noisiest bar on Castro Street and have a few drinks."

"That sounds like a great idea," Celia said. "Would you like company?"

"Of course," Buck answered, holding out his arm.

"Richie? Are you coming?" Celia asked.

"Why not?" Richie nodded. "Another drunken night on the town is just what I need right now."

"Nobody said anything about getting drunk," Celia scolded. "We are simply going to mix and mingle among our gay and lesbian peers."

"Have one for me," Harry said wistfully.

"We will," Celia assured her. "I'll come by and pick you up in the morning."

"See you later, alligator," Richie sang, giving Harry a wave.

"In a while, crocodile," Harry said, trying not to sound glum.

Celia's parting shot was, "Be good!"

As if she had a choice. After they left, Harry got up and went into the bathroom. She turned on the shower, removed her hospital-issue dressing gown and johnny gown and took a long shower, thoroughly scrubbing the last of the bitter smell of smoke from her hair and skin. The hot water soothed her strained muscles and loosened her stiff joints. She bundled her soiled clothes and left them in a neat pile on the floor.

When she left the bathroom, Harry found Moira sitting on the bed. "I know I should have knocked, although I don't suppose it really matters since we're so closely related," Moira said, giving Harry's nude body a thorough perusal. "Actually, you've got an elegant body, niece-of-mine."

Harry's first impulse was to cover herself with the bedspread or whatever else was close at hand, but she resisted the urge and wrapped a clean johnny gown around her. "Did you find somewhere to live?"

"Yes," Moira replied. She was dressed in an flowing, flowery, ankle-length dress and a matching shawl, both evidently new. Her hair looked shiny and clean and she no longer smelled of sweat and smoke. "I rented a furnished room in a rooming house. The walls have recently been painted, the place is regularly fumigated and the occupants aren't on drugs or booze. Or, if they are, they're very discreet about it."

"I'm going to Raven's when I get out of here tomorrow, so give me your address. It seems I'm going to be living in San Francisco for a while, although hardly anyone knows that yet. As soon as I get settled and Raven feels better, we'll all have lunch."

"That's the best offer I've had all day, if not all month. I appreciate it, although I don't know why you want to bother," Moira said, holding up her hand to stop Harry from replying. "I know, nieces should show respect for their aunts. But in return I did something for you. I just spent some time visiting with that near-infant Rachel Birdie Stone, better known to you as Raven, and I made sure she realized what a genuinely nice person you are."

"Thanks," Harry said, thinking that it was nice to end the evening on a positive note.

Harry fell into a drug-induced sleep, but around one in the morning, she was wide awake and stewing in her bed. The sheets under her were rumpled, most of the blanket was on the floor, and her pillow was half out of its case. Something was bothering her. She had missed the significance of something someone had said, and she couldn't remember who had said it or what it was.

She got up, went into the bathroom and poured herself a glass of water. It was late and the ward was quiet; she should be asleep. She went back into her room and paced the floor, her bare feet quietly slapping the cold tiles. And then it hit her. Buck had said something that had given the game away, although she was certain he hadn't known the significance of his casual remark. Harry returned to bed, her thoughts tumbling one after the other. Earlier in the day, Richie had said that he had pulled some muscles and acquired several bruises during his escape from the burning house last night. He hadn't gone to a doctor because he didn't have medical insurance. But when Harry had mentioned Richie's afflictions to Buck, he'd looked confused, although he hadn't said anything. And later, when Harry had asked Richie how he felt, Buck had questioned his lover's timing. What was it exactly that Buck had intimated? That Richie had acquired some of those bruises the night before the fire?

Harry sipped her water and thought about where Richie had been two nights earlier, when she had unsuccessfully matched wits against someone who had invaded Raven's apartment. That had also been when Moira met Richie in the hall, dressed to the nines in leather.

Buck obviously thought that Richie's sprains and bruises had been acquired during a night of unmitigated passion with one or more strangers. Was that true, or had Richie been Raven's mugger, the person who had been about to do something deadly to Raven when she was asleep in her bed, the person who broke the window to get to Raven's fire escape and elude both identification and capture?

If so, then Richie had doubtlessly killed his sister and set fire to the house. Perhaps he had become frustrated with Fran's revolving-door wills and had made up his mind to cash in while the going was good, not knowing that Fran had already changed her will in Raven and Moira's favour. And maybe once Fran was dead and he discovered that she had modified her will, he had sought revenge on the two women who would benefit from his sister's death, starting with Raven.

Was it possible that a man she had known for years, a man she liked and enjoyed being with, was a killer? So what if his sister had spent years manipulating him, dangling the promise of future rewards for who knows what kind of loyalty? Any number of people lived under someone else's thumb without resorting to murder. And there were certainly other ways to escape being dominated besides killing the person doing the tormenting.

It was nearly two, and Harry was growing sleepy, but she decided to call Detective Manley and tell him about her suspicions. She picked up the telephone and tried to get an outside line, only to encounter a recorded message informing her that patients were not permitted to call out after eleven. She sighed and dropped the phone into the receiver. Did they think that people who were hospitalized were going to spend all night yakking on the telephone? That seriously ill patients were going to tie up Ma Bell's lines conducting frivolous business? That people on their deathbeds were going to dial 900 numbers?

The only thing to do was use a pay phone. She got out of bed, went to the closet and put on her dressing gown, belting it around her waist. She returned to her bed and took her wallet from the drawer in her bedside table and slid it into her pocket. Then she opened the door to her room. The lights in the hall had been dimmed, and the hall itself was deserted. Except for the drone of the air conditioning and various machines vital to the survival of some of the patients on the floor, everything was quiet. She couldn't hear a single voice.

She stepped out, letting the door to her room slowly swing shut. She was about to move forward when she had the strong impression that something or someone had stirred. She had only noticed slight motion out of the corner of her eye, but it was coming from the direction of Raven's room. Harry flattened herself against the wall and wished it was painted the same colour as her dressing gown. She slid along the wall step by step until she was standing next to the door to Raven's room.

What should she do? Harry glanced toward the nurses' station, but no one was sitting there. There wasn't time to get to a pay phone. She was going to have to handle this by herself. She heard a muffled thump. Either Raven had fallen out of bed or there was someone in there with her. Harry took a deep breath, pushed the door open and hurried inside, darting away from the door to escape being trapped in the light from the hall. The room was in darkness and, once the door swung shut, she couldn't see a thing. Although her strongest impulse was to freeze, she forced herself to move forward.

Someone suddenly rushed past, ricochetting off her and knocking her against the wall. She righted herself, her hands scrambling along the wall until she found the light switch.

"Raven? Are you all right?"

"I'm fine," Raven croaked, pulling herself off the floor beside the bed. One of the bandages on her hands was coated with what looked like blood. "The bastard tried to strangle me, so I gave him a good slug in the jaw. It hurt like hell, but I've never felt better." Raven paused, and then said, "I recognized his voice when he cursed. It was Richie."

Already half way out of the room, Harry said, "I know. I'll be back."

"I'm going to find a phone and call the cops. For god's sake, be careful Harry!"

"Don't worry." Harry rushed from the room. She hadn't wanted it to be Richie. In fact, she hadn't wanted it to be anyone she knew. She had hoped it would be a stranger, not a friend.

She looked around frantically. Had she lost him? She couldn't see anyone, although she could hear footsteps, and then the slam of a heavy door. She wouldn't be able to catch him on the stairs, not in her weakened condition, and especially wearing slippers. She hurried to the elevators, pressed the "down" button and impatiently shifted from foot to foot while the elevator rose. She rushed into it as soon as the doors slid open and pressed the button for the ground floor. She was gambling that he was headed for the main door.

She was on the slowest elevator in the world and she had no way of knowing if she was going in the right direction. What if Richie had gone up to the roof? To the basement or to another floor? There were a million and one places to hide in such a large hospital complex. And if she did track him down, she had nothing to use as a weapon. She nervously ran the palms of her hands over the smooth, cold metallic walls of the elevator.

The doors slid open. Harry rushed from the elevator, wishing she had eyes in the back of her head. Where was everybody? She hurried toward the front door, but she didn't see anyone. Had Richie got away? She pushed through the revolving door and went outside. Although the cement walk in front of the hospital was littered with cigarette butts, she was the only person there, and Richie wasn't in sight. Where the hell was the security guard? Curled up on a sofa taking a nap or reading a book or watching TV in one of the waiting rooms? She decided to return to the lobby and find a pay phone. But the moment she turned her back, she heard a scuffing noise in the shadows. She spun around. "Richie?"

There was no reply. Perhaps it had been an animal, a cat out for a nocturnal prowl, a lost dog, a rat searching for the day's rotting pickings.

Suddenly Richie materialized from out of the bushes. The front of his tee-shirt was splattered with blood and one of his nostrils was still seeping.

"Come out, come out, wherever you are," he sang with an ugly laugh. "I thought I'd got away. I would have if I haven't stopped to catch my breath. You know, I think that bitch broke my nose," he remarked casually, wiping the back of hand across his mouth.

Harry tried to keep calm. "There's no point running away," she said. "Too many people know about what you did."

"All I wanted was what was rightfully mine," he said indignantly. "She broke her promise!"

If he took one more step forward, she was going to bolt and run, Harry decided.

"She lied to me. She never meant to give me anything. It was all a game and I was always the loser because that was the way she planned it," he continued, his voice growing louder. "Well, I showed her who the real loser was, didn't I?"

Harry took a step backwards.

"*Didn't I?*" he roared as only an actor with a trained voice could. He wasn't much taller than Harry was, but, in his fury, he seemed to tower over her.

"Yes, yes." Harry nodded. She clasped her hands together in front of her.

"It was payback time. Oh yes, long past payback time. She made a fool of me once too often, changing her will as frequently as people change their underwear. She took great pleasure in sending me copies of all her wills. She knew I would suffer, that I'd be on pins and needles every time she named me as beneficiary. After the first couple of flip-flops, it didn't take a genius to figure out that she must be doing the same things with some of her lovers, too. The bitch." He spat. "She started teasing me about her will, threatening to change it again. And then Celia started sucking up to her and, before I knew it, they were in bed together. I'm not dumb — I could see the writing on the wall. Fran was going to cut me out of her will yet another time with absolutely no guarantee that I'd ever get back in. But I'd been through that too many times before, and I had no intention of letting her cheat me yet again. You can understand that, can't you?"

"Yes, but —"

"She was a miserable excuse for a human being and she deserved what she got," Richie interrupted. He paused to wipe the steady trickle of blood from his chin and then continued. "She was always after me to move down here, promising that she'd arrange some screen tests in Los Angeles. It probably wasn't true, but I wasn't sure I could pass up her offer. What if I hit it big in Hollywood and made a pile of money? Then I could tell Fran to go to hell, something I've been wanting to do for years. What a bitch."

"Richie —"

"I was sitting next to her in the theatre that night, and you wouldn't believe how easy it was to give her a little nudge over the railing. She was tipsy from sucking up the vino with Celia, you see. So I simply stood up when she did, and when she leaned forward to say something to Celia, I put my hand in the small of her back and pushed. Then I sat down. She went over as smooth as Humpty Dumpty. I would have liked to see her hit the floor, but that wouldn't have been wise, would it? She probably didn't have a clue what happened to her, and Celia was looking down at the stairs, so she didn't see a thing."

Harry shivered at the vivid picture Richie was painting.

"But she'd already made her new will, and everybody began making a fool out of me. You all pretended that you didn't know everything should be mine. *Rightfully* mine. She left everything except a few useless pieces of furniture to those bitches of the west. I was her *brother*, after all. So I had to show them, didn't I? Especially that snotty punk lover of yours. She thought that she deserved to have my sister's house because she'd been her lover for a couple of years. But blood is thicker than water, you know. I decided to give her what she deserved, but the bitch has as many lives as a cat. I thought you were my friend, but you had to go and help her, didn't you? That was when I decided that you deserved to get it, too."

Richie lunged toward her, his hands outstretched. Harry had been waiting for him to attack her, so she side-stepped him and turned to run. But he was fast and, before she could escape, he was on her back. His hands closed around her throat, cutting off her scream. Suddenly they were surrounded with police officers, and Richie was pulled off her.

Detective Manley stepped forward. "A nasty piece of goods," he remarked. "I'm glad Ms. Stone called us when she did. He could have done you real harm."

Harry said nothing. Richie had been her friend, but her silence had nothing to do with loyalty and everything to do with the exhaustion and the disillusionment she was feeling. As she turned and watched several uniformed police officers lead a struggling Richie away from the hospital, a sudden breeze arose and ground fog swirled around her legs. She shivered and hugged herself. Enough of violent death and unethical friends. She would never understand how evil invaded a human being's soul, no matter how old she lived to be.

"I'm going back to my room," she said to the detective. "If you have questions you want to ask, come by in the morning."

Harry was awakened just before dawn when Raven slid into bed beside her.

"The doctor told me I could check out as long as there was someone around to look after me while I had these bandages on," Raven told her.

"That's great," replied Harry. "I wasn't relishing the idea of being by myself."

"Anyway, I want to give you a proper 'good morning,'" Raven whispered after they kissed.

"I'm not sure if I have the energy," Harry whispered back. "Or the stamina."

Raven laughed. "Just leave everything up to me."

That sufficed for a while, but as the sun rose in the sky, so did Harry. There was only so much Raven could do with bandages on her hands, after all. When they were both satiated, they lay side by side on their backs. Harry closed her eyes and let that distinctive, post-orgasmic relaxation propel her toward sleep.

"You shouldn't have gone after Richie by yourself," Raven said. "After I called the police, I was on my way to help you when one of the nurses stopped me."

Harry stirred enough to reply. "It was just as well she did. Richie was really angry with you."

"Because I inherited half of Fran's house."

"Yes."

"I can't imagine disliking anyone enough to commit murder," mused Raven. "Or even physically hurt them, actually."

Neither could Harry. Moira maintained that some people deserved what happened to them, and that she wasn't surprised Fran had been killed. But Harry still couldn't fathom resorting to murder.

"Real hatred is an evil thing. But we're safe now. It's over." Harry turned her head, kissed Raven on the shoulder and fell asleep.

Some time later the nurse came by and got them up without admitting that there was more than one person in Harry's bed and that they were both naked.

"Am I invisible?" Raven grumbled as Harry helped her slide her long tee-shirt over her head.

"Not to me," Harry assured her. She rummaged through the clothes Celia had purchased for her, cursing audibly when she saw that the lone bra and panty set was mostly constructed of crimson lace. What did Celia think, that she was planning to spend time in a bordello?

"Wow!" was all Raven said. "I never knew you were into lingerie."

"Never mind." Harry slid into a pair of jeans made of soft, faded denim. They fit perfectly, as did the black denim jacket Celia had bought to replace her old one. She sat on the bed, pulled on a pair of socks and buckled up the sandals Celia had chosen. Harry would have to shop for shoes soon or suffer from cold feet.

Raven was pawing with bandaged hands through the suitcase Celia had packed for her. "Help me get dressed," she said to Harry, pointing to a pair of plaid bikini panties.

Harry rather enjoyed helping her get into them. "Can we do this every day?"

"Stop fooling around." Raven chuckled, brushing Harry's hands away, although not too swiftly. "We can finish this at home. While I know that nurse thinks I'm invisible, I'm not so sure she could carry it off if she walked in when we were in a compromising position. And now I want those black tights and that paisley tunic."

Harry pulled the tunic over Raven's head. "As soon as I get you settled, I'll do a little grocery shopping. Is there anything I shouldn't buy?"

"No meat. And no soft drinks. They're too salty. I think I'm just about out of herbal tea — get the mixed pack. And fruit, lots of fruit. I'll make a list when we get home. You should pick up some things you like, too."

This was certainly going to be different, Harry reflected. Uncertainty made her heart beat faster. She turned and began to repack her suitcase.

"Are you regretting your decision to stay?"

Harry felt Raven's bandaged hand on her shoulder. "No. I am a little frightened, though."

"Don't be," Raven said, pressing her body against Harry's back.

Just then Celia breezed into the room. "Do you two never stop making out? Never mind, I don't really want to know. Envy is bad for the skin so early in the morning. Listen, I heard about Richie when I got up this morning. It was all over the radio and TV news, and on the front page of the newspapers. 'Man kills sister over inheritance,' and the like, not to mention a few more salacious stories in the tabloids."

"I can imagine," Harry said.

"So why didn't you think to get in touch with me?" Celia complained. "I worried all night long that we were in grave danger, and you could have relieved my concern by making a simple phone call."

"I was rather busy with the police and all," Harry fibbed, not wanting to hurt Celia's feelings by admitting, that once she had survived her confrontation with Richie, she hadn't given anybody else a single thought. Except for Raven. "Have you spoken to Buck?"

"I've just left the poor boy at his bed-and-breakfast," Celia told her. "He's simply distraught. I think he's in shock. And to make things worse, that damnable detective arrived just as I was leaving, and he was likely going to put Buck through the wringer again. Buck told me that he knew Richie despised his sister, but he had absolutely no idea Richie was capable of resorting to violence. Apparently Richie joked around about how Fran pissed him off, but he kept his anger under wraps most of the time. I suppose that's something an actor is quite capable of doing."

Harry wondered whether Buck knew more about Richie's activities than he was admitting. Wouldn't he have noticed the hatred festering inside Richie? Perhaps he had been distracted by his relationship with Joel.

"I'll give him a call later," she said.

"I'm sure he'd appreciate it," Celia said. "Anyway, I'll see you later, probably at Fran's funeral tomorrow. Then Mandy and I are flying back to Vancouver."

"Are the two of you getting back together?" Harry asked.

"Are you out of your mind?" Celia shrieked.

Raven gave Celia a look and went into the bathroom.

"I hope you'll teach her a few manners while you're at it," Celia said in a low voice.

Raven and Celia were never going to be close friends, that was certain, but Harry couldn't let the chance pass by. "If you don't want to be with Mandy, you should tell her that in no uncertain terms and set her free."

Celia made a face. "You're right. I will. Neither Mandy nor I needs to keep torturing the other. Life's too short for that."

Harry fervently agreed.

"And you, my old friend, what are you up to?"

"Ask me that again in six months," Harry said with a wry smile.

Celia perched on the hospital bed and began folding Raven's clothes. "I might as well pack for her. She can't do it herself with all those bandages on her hands. You know, I envy you, in a way. You're starting all over again, while I seem to be fated to repeat myself." She dropped a pair of jeans into Raven's suitcase and raised her hands. "I know, you don't have to tell me, it's my own damn fault. You reap what you sow, et cetera. But, damn it, I wouldn't dare put myself at the mercy of a woman half my age. I wouldn't even take my clothes off in front of her. I'm not as brave as you are."

This was supposed to make her feel better? Harry wished Raven would stop loitering in the bathroom. What was she doing in there, scouring every inch of her body with a toothbrush?

"Raven!"

The door opened and Raven's face appeared. "Yes?"

"It's time to leave," Harry said.

"I rented a car, so I'll drive you home," Celia said, tossing a tee-shirt in Raven's suitcase and closing it.

"I see you've packed for me," Raven remarked.

When Harry saw Celia steel herself, she realized that she was intimidated by Raven. "That's not a problem, is it?"

"Of course not." Raven grinned, holding up her bandaged hands. "I mean, I couldn't do it with these, could I?"

Celia nodded. "That's what I thought."

Harry lifted her suitcase from the bed. "Let's go. I'd rather get out of here before Detective Manley arrives. I'm sure he's got lots of questions, but he can reach me later. There's no rush now."

They went to the nursing station, signed several documents and took the elevator to the main floor. Harry and Raven waited for Celia to fetch the car from the parking lot, and then Harry tucked Raven in the back, fastened her seat belt and got in the front with Celia. Since Celia drove with her foot on the gas and her mouth in third, Harry's heart was in her throat all the way to Raven's apartment building.

Much to Harry's surprise, Raven asked Celia if she would like to come up, but Celia begged off, claiming another commitment, although she did help carry Raven's suitcase to the door.

"And here I leave you," Celia announced, ceremonially passing Raven's suitcase to Harry.

Harry kissed her on the cheek. "Thanks. We'll see you at the funeral."

Celia looked at the two of them and then said, "Well, who's going to carry whom across the threshold?"

Raven rolled her eyes and stalked into the apartment.

Celia smirked.

"You enjoy needling her, don't you?" Harry asked.

"It's a tough job, but somebody's got to do it," Celia agreed, giving Harry a wink. "Ta-ta, now."

Harry watched Celia hop down the stairs, and then followed Raven into the apartment and closed the door. "So who *is* going to carry whom across the threshold?"

"Don't *you* start," Raven said plaintively.

"Come here, you," Harry whispered.

Raven grinned and went.

More entertaining, fast-paced mysteries in the acclaimed Harriet Hubbley Mystery Series by Jackie Manthorne

Last Resort: A Harriet Hubbley Mystery

"*Last Resort* is a novel with all the twists and hidden corners one would expect." *Lesbian Review of Books*

"… delivers character, plot and setting." *Capital XTRA*

ISBN 0-921881-34-7 $10.95

Deadly Reunion: A Harriet Hubbley Mystery

"Manthorne has a clean, crisp style and a heroine likeable enough to create something of a following." *Bay Windows*, USA

ISBN 0-921881-32-0 $10.95

Ghost Motel: A Harriet Hubbley Mystery

"Manthorne knows how to keep the action moving and she never lets the dialogue sink to polemic." *The Globe and Mail*

ISBN 0-921881-31-2 $9.95

Jackie Manthorne is the author of two collections of short stories, *Fascination and Other Bar Stories* and *Without Wings*, as well as the Harriet Hubbley Mystery Series (all from gynergy books). Her writing has appeared in numerous magazines and anthologies, including *Lesbian Bedtime Stories II* (Tough Dove Books) and *By Word of Mouth: Lesbians Write the Erotic* (gynergy books). She is also the editor of *Canadian Women and AIDS: Beyond the Statistics* (Les Éditions Communiqu'Elles). She lives in Toronto, where she writes full time.

Best of gynergy books

Bordering, *Luanne Armstrong*. Louise is "bordering": on coming out as a lesbian, on imagining her future, on leaving the small town that keeps her pinned down. But before she can cross over to a new life, she must face up to the old.
ISBN 0-921881-35-5 $10.95

By Word of Mouth: Lesbians Write the Erotic, *Lee Fleming (ed.)*. "Contains plenty of sexy good writing and furthers the desperately needed honest discussion of what we mean by 'erotic' and by 'lesbian.'" *Sinister Wisdom*
ISBN 0-921881-06-1 $10.95/$12.95 U.S.

Hot Licks: Lesbian Musicians of Note, *Lee Fleming (ed.)*. From the beginning of women's music in the '60s to the centre stage of mainstream concert halls in the '90s, lesbian musicians are coming out. In *Hot Licks*, they proudly and eloquently reveal their passions, politics and musical influences. Beautiful design, large format and high quality photographs make this the ideal giftbook.
ISBN 0-921881-42-8 $24.95

Lesbian Parenting: Living with Pride & Prejudice, *Katherine Arnup (ed.)*. Here is the perfect primer for lesbian parents, and a helpful resource for their families and friends. "Thoughtful, provocative and passionate. A brave and necessary book." *Sandra Butler*
ISBN 0-921881-33-9 $19.95/$16.95 U.S.

To Sappho, My Sister: Lesbian Sisters Write About Their Lives, *Lee Fleming (ed.)*. This one-of-a-kind anthology includes the stories of both well-known and less famous siblings from three continents, in a compelling portrait of lesbian sisterhood.
ISBN 0-921881-36-3 $16.95

gynergy books titles are available at quality bookstores. Ask for our titles at your favourite local bookstore. Individual, prepaid orders may be sent to: **gynergy books**, P.O. Box 2023, Charlottetown, Prince Edward Island, Canada, C1A 7N7. Please add postage and handling ($3.00 for the first book and $1.00 for each additional book) to your order. Canadian residents add 7% GST to the total amount. GST registration number R104383120. Prices are subject to change without notice.